Rex's Release

HOWLERS MC SERIES BOOK 8

Rex's Release

Howlers MC Series Book 8

T.S. TAPPIN

Rex's Release
T.S. Tappin
Published by T.S. Tappin
Copyright © 2023 T.S. Tappin
All rights reserved. In accordance with the U.S. Copyright Act of 1976, the scanning, uploading, and electronic sharing of any part of this book without the permission of the publisher is unlawful piracy and theft of the author's intellectual property. Thank you for your support of the author's rights and work. This book is a work of fiction. Names, characters, places, and incidents are the product of the author's imagination or are used fictitiously. Any resemblance to actual events, locales, or persons, living or deceased, is coincidental.
Cover Design by: T.S. Tappin
Editing Services: Elisabeth Garner
ISBN: **9798388430052**

Dedication:

For science...

Other works by this author:

Under the name T.S. Tappin
Howlers MC Series:
Bk1: Axle's Ride
Bk2: Trip's B*tch
Bk3: Pike's Pixie
Bk4: Siren's Flame
Bk5: Bullet's Butterfly
Bk6: Dragon's Kiss
Bk7: Rebel's Fairytale
Bk8: Rex's Release
Bk9: Trick's Elite
Bk10: Top's Peace

Tiger's Claw MC Series:
Bk1: Crush's Fall
Bk2: Halo's Haven

HTC Related Anthology Story:
Bride's Bail Out
Through Newsletter
Catnip Shenanigans
Coming soon:
Joker's Second Chance: A Howlers MC Series Novella

Under the name Tara Tappin
On the Clock: A Spicy RomCom Novella Charity Project

Acknowledgements:

My PIC: For pushing the *publish* button for the first time for me. I Heart You.

My family: I appreciate your support and believe in me. You are my reasons why.

Elisabeth: None of this would have been possible without your support and knowledge of the grammar, O' Grammar Chosen One! And for restocking my Benadryl cream. You're a real one. HGS 4 Life!

Kim: I've given you a fellow sub… Try not to turn him into a brat, k? Thanks. You are the Howlers Wiki, and that deserves a certain level of respect. Hats off to you, Ma'am. Thank you for all your help and support! Seriously… THANK YOU! HGS 4 Ever!

Dawn "Doc" Dugle: I'm pretty sure I checked off everything in your list. You licked 'em… Licked 'em really good. And now he's yours! Thank you for designing a character and letting me run with it! Team Punny Forever… for science, of course.

The HypeGirlSquad Discord: For keeping up my spirits each and every day, I thank you.

My Beta team: If not for you, none of this would make sense. Thank you for wading through the mess to find the good stuff.

My ARC team: Thank you, thank you, thank you for taking a chance with my work! You are one of the most important parts of the publication of my books. Without you, none of this would be possible.

Content Warnings

Dear Reader,

There are themes in this book that may affect readers negatively.

The following are those themes:

Death
Violence
Weapons
Hostage Situation/Stalking
Torture
Possessiveness
Controlling behavior
Cussing/strong language
Explicit sex/BDSM elements

If you encounter something that isn't listed and feel it could negatively affect a reader, please email me at booksbytt@gmail.com

Thank you!
T.S. Tappin

T.S. Tappin

Chapter One

Rex

In Warden's Pass, Michigan, war had raged between motorcycle clubs. Literal war. Guns, knives, claws, and fangs had been used to cause death and destruction. The Howlers MC and the Tiger's Claw MC were the side that had come out on top, which wasn't exactly a surprise, since most of their members were shifters capable of turning into predatory animals in the blink of an eye. They hadn't come out unscathed, though. Eight people were lost, and several more were injured on their side.

Back at their compound, later that evening, Terrence Lee 'Rex' Piccolo was faced with a problem. Rex didn't think it was the best plan in the world, but it was the only one he could come up with at the moment. After getting the kids of the club settled in Ginger's room with her, Rex left to check on their injured.

He was one of the older members of the Howlers MC, and a wolf shifter, but they weren't all wolves. They also had tigers, bears, and lions among them.

Rex finally convinced Siren, his lion shifter club brother, to let someone check on his hand that had a knife wound through the center of it. The bastard had wrapped it in a dirty strip of fabric from someone's tee when they got back, saying he wouldn't worry about it until after he saw his mate, Sugar, which Rex understood. Siren was worried about how Sugar would take the news about Gigi, but damn, she wouldn't take him dying from infection any better.

Gigi, real name Georgia, was the sister-in-law to their president, Axle. Gigi had recently gotten married and wasn't even out of her teen years. Earlier that very day, she kissed her mate goodbye and climbed in her car. Emerson, her wolf shifter husband, watched as she turned the key in the ignition and the car blew up, killing her right in front of him. None of them would ever forget the howl of grief that came from Emerson as he hit the ground on his knees in that security footage. The sound was more heartbreaking than anything Rex had ever heard before. It was full of pain and the realization of one's hopes, dreams, and plans for the future going up in smoke. It would take some time for all of them to grieve for Gigi, but some more than most.

Sugar was one of the some, being one of Gigi's closest friends. She had seemed upset after they returned from the following battle, but she firmly sided with Rex and shoved Siren toward the room the doctors were using as a triage area.

Siren was only one of the many injured from the battle that took place outside of town in the field next to an old, abandoned farmhouse. Their side managed to decimate their opponents, but not before they sustained damage and the world learned of the existence of the shifters. The fallout of that was yet to be seen, since it had only been a matter of hours.

The Howlers MC, along with their ally club, the Tiger's Claw MC, and the assistance of the champions sent by actual fucking *gods*, they managed to stop the other side from their ultimate goal of ending the Howlers.

After finally convincing Siren to let a doctor examine his hand, Rex checked on two of the Claws members — Rita and Nails. Both already had their wounds wrapped up and were sleeping in their rooms at the compound.

Satisfied they were okay, he moved on to the next on the injured list — Axle's father, their former president, Joker. He walked in on Joker fighting with a doctor about how to patch him up. Rex left them to argue, knowing that his presence wasn't going to make it any easier on the doctor.

When he checked in on Bullet earlier, his tiger shifter club brother, he cursed and looked him over. Bullet was lying on his bed in tiger form and sleeping. Earlier in the night, when Rex had convinced Butterfly to let Bullet rest, Bullet had still been in human form and was knocked out on pain drugs. The surgeon had already cleaned up and stitched Bullet back together. He had not liked leaving Bullet in that bedroom instead of a hospital room, but Top had convinced him that they would keep a close eye on Bullet and showed the surgeon the door, knowing the surgeon wouldn't let up on it if he stuck around. They needed Bullet at the compound so that his shifter healing could take care of business and not raise brows at a hospital. The Howlers could also keep Bullet protected in their territory. With the world let in on the secret of the shifters, taking one of them to a hospital to recover was only asking for something worse to happen.

When he found that his brother had shifted to his tiger form and had ripped his stitches, Rex cursed and tried to figure out how to handle it. He couldn't call the same surgeon since Bullet was in tiger form, and the other doctor who knew of shifters, and had for a long time, was still busy working on Siren's hand. Bullet's wounds needed to be taken care of, but at least they weren't bleeding as profusely as earlier. After mulling all of that over, he made a decision that he would just find another doctor as quickly as possible.

In the meantime, he'd have Top watch for one of the doctors at the compound to become freed up. If that was the case, Top could show them back to Bullet's room.

That was when Rex remembered the veterinarian who had just moved into a house a few blocks down the road. Mama Hen had mentioned her when he stopped in to thank her for letting them use her hotel for a few days. It didn't surprise him that Mama Hen had already met the woman. She was the resident welcome committee, a kind soul, and a social butterfly, making new friends easier than most people breathed.

Supposedly, the vet was joining the local animal clinic. Maybe she'd be eager to make connections in the community and would be willing to help them out. He prayed to the gods that she was home as he hopped on his bike.

Rex knew it was a horrible idea, but it was the only one he could come up with, so it would have to do. He drove the three blocks and pulled into the driveway of a modest ranch-style house with navy siding, white trim, an attached garage, and a white picket fence around the front yard.

After killing the engine, he climbed off his bike and made his way up the walk to the front door. When he raised his hand and knocked, he noticed the blood and dirt on his hands. *Shit!* He hoped she assumed it was just from the hurt animal he was about to try to convince her to help.

He heard the locks twist and disengage before the door was pulled open. Standing in front of him was a woman in her late thirties or early forties with blond hair cut short around her perfect face. What got him, though, were the big blue eyes staring up at him, open and engaging. Rex felt like he could happily fall into them and live there forever. Mentally shaking off that ridiculous thought, he focused on what she was saying to him.

"Can I help you?" Her gaze dropped to his shirt, and he knew she was seeing the blood and dirt on his clothes. "Is there someone hurt?" Her brows drew together, no doubt assessing how that much blood and dirt ended up on a person who didn't seem to be injured.

"Uh… I'm a member of the Howlers MC. Our compound is down the road," he said and zipped closed his cut in an attempt to hide most of the blood and dirt.

She nodded and waved her hand in a circle in front of her that said *get on with it*. "Mama Hen told me about your club. Said you were good guys."

Rex made a mental note to bring Mama Hen a gift basket of all of her favorite things. "Yes. Well, we have a badly hurt tiger at the compound. I was wondering if you had a moment to come look at him. We didn't want to move him."

The second she heard the words *badly hurt tiger*, she visibly shifted into doctor mode. She slipped on a pair of shoes by her door and bent over to snatch a black bag off the floor that looked a lot like one of the medical bags you saw in television shows.

She looked ridiculous and sweet in her outfit. Her shoes were those clogs that all doctors and nurses seemed to own, but these were a bright yellow color, On her long legs, she wore a pair of ratty, cut-off jean shorts, and her shirt was a bright red, with the words *mutt squad* in white inverted script on the front. Fucking adorable.

When she saw where he was looking, she shrugged. "I make videos and post them online about how best to take care of your pets. The inverted words make it easier to film on my phone. It's most efficient."

Rex smirked at her. "I like it."

She raised a blond brow at him, putting her free hand to her hip. "Are we flirting, or are we helping your tiger?"

Rex bit back the growl that his wolf insisted on. His wolf wanted to do more than growl, though. It was obvious to him that his wolf liked the vet and wanted her closer. *Fuck!* He needed to pull his shit together.

"The tiger," he replied, and cleared his throat. He stepped back as she came out of the house and turned to face the door. "Do you know how to get to the compound?"

As she locked her front door with her key, she answered, "Just go straight down the road two blocks past the hotel. The road dead ends there, right?"

"Yes."

"Then yes, I know the way. Want to tell me why you have a tiger when it's against the law to have an endangered species without meeting certain criteria

I'm sure your club does not meet?" Her question was more of an order.

"Uh... no."

"Didn't think so," she mumbled, and turned to face him. "We'll revisit that later. See you at the compound."

"Meet you there," he replied and returned to his bike. As he mounted it and started the engine, he told his wolf they couldn't play until after she fixed up their brother. His wolf gave a whimper but laid down as he backed out of the driveway and headed for the compound.

Rex pretended not to notice the doctor's skeptical looks as he led her into the apartment building, up the stairs, and down the hall. He hoped she didn't raise any of the questions in her eyes.

He wasn't that lucky, he realized, when she asked, "You were so worried about moving the injured tiger that you carried it up a flight of stairs? Tigers are heavy."

Kicking himself in the ass for not thinking through what he would say when he went to ask her to help, Rex replied, "We found him up here in the hall."

"The injured tiger came into the building and climbed the stairs while injured? And you guys managed to move an injured tiger without the tiger fighting to protect itself?"

"I guess," he mumbled, and opened the door to Bullet's room. "He's in here." Rex looked around the door to make sure Bullet was still in tiger form. He was, so Rex stepped aside and let her in.

He tried to follow her in, but the doctor faced him and firmly stated, "Wait outside. If it wakes up, it can be aggressive. I can handle it. I have tranquilizers, but I don't need to be distracted by worrying over your safety. If you want to help, I could use some warm water and clean towels, white if you have them."

Rex nodded to the door to the bathroom. "There are clean towels in the bathroom."

"Great. Wait here." Then the doctor shut the door in his face.

Rex wouldn't call her demeanor rude, but it was abrupt, demanding, and confident. What he didn't understand is why he liked that so much.

Chapter Two

Axle

After holding his mate, Gorgeous, until she cried herself to sleep, grieving for her younger sister, Axle carefully laid her on their bed and covered her up. As quietly as possible, he took a shower and got dressed. His intention was to check on the injured and then spend some time holding Nugget, his baby daughter. He needed to look into those beautiful blue eyes of his baby girl and see hope. His soul needed some good, and Nugget was wholly good.

When he made it to Bullet's room, he found Rex sitting on the floor just outside the door. Stopping, he looked down at his brother. The man was a good ten years older than Axle and had the graying blond hair to prove it, currently pulled back in a ponytail at the nape of his neck, but Axle still looked at him as a brother.

"How's Bull?"

"Uh… well…" Rex scratched his bearded jaw and avoided looking up at Axle. He'd never heard Rex stammer before. That was interesting, but it also alerted him to something being wrong. "He's tiger right now."

"He shifted?"

Rex gave a nod and let out a humorless laugh. "And we didn't have a free doctor to take care of the ripped stitches."

"Okay. So, he needs to be stitched up?" Axle turned, ready to go find a doctor.

"No, not anymore."

Annoyed that Rex was dragging it out, Axle barked, "Fucking say it."

Rex cleared his throat. "I went and got the new vet from down the street."

Axle blinked, then he blinked again. "A vet?"

"Well… he's a tiger right now." Rex shrugged. "It was the best I could come up with on short notice without having to explain to someone what shifters are or that yes, we're real and why we're not evil be—"

The door flew open, and a blond woman Axle had never seen before stormed out, saying, "Nope. Nope. Nope," under her breath as she shoved stuff into a medical bag. She was shaking her head, making her short hair wave side to side slightly.

Rex jumped up to his feet and followed the woman. "Wait!"

Curious, Axle approached the open bedroom door and stepped inside. There was Bullet, lying on his bed in human form, his head flopping side to side, but he wasn't exactly conscious.

Well, shit.

Rex

After Axle ordered Rex to stop her, like he wouldn't have anyway, Axle headed down the hall in the other direction, while Rex went after Doc.

"Wait." Rex caught up with the doctor before she could step onto the stairs that would take her down to the first floor. He moved in front of her and looked into her eyes. "What's wrong? What happened?"

"I'm losing my mind. That's what happened." She looked calm, but Rex could see her chest heaving with her barely contained panic.

"Maybe... but why don't you tell me what you think happened, and I'll tell you if I think you're losing your mind?"

She narrowed her eyes on him, but answered, "That tiger just turned into a man. A man! Tell me I'm not losing touch with reality now."

He liked it when she looked at him like that. That challenging, assessing gaze and the demand in her tone made his juices flow and his cock twitch.

Rex shrugged and let his smile grow on his face. "What if I told you I could do that, too, but a wolf, not a tiger, and that you're not losing touch with reality?"

"I would tell you that *you're* losing touch with reality."

"What if I proved it?"

She set her bag down on the floor. When she straightened and crossed her arms over that ample chest, she gave him a questioning look and a nod before saying, "Prove it."

Rex chuckled. "Okay, but promise me you won't run. I'll explain everything once I'm done."

"Yeah. Yeah. Yeah." Like she did at her front door, the doc waved off his words and recrossed her arms, then she stared at him, expectantly. There was an order in that stance.

Gazing into her eyes, Rex allowed his wolf out. Once he was shifted, he looked up at her and waited.

She stared at him with wide eyes for a long moment, then breathed, "Holy motherfucking shit balls."

Rex leaned forward and dropped his head. He licked her knee and was shocked when she swatted his head.

"Bad dog!" She let out a humorless laugh. "Shit! Fuck! I just swatted a wolf." Taking a few steps back, she rubbed her face with her hands.

Rex shifted back and rubbed the back of his head where she had hit him. It didn't hurt, but he used it to his advantage. "There was no need for that," he grumbled.

"Sorry. Shit." She dropped her hands and glared at him. "Why am I apologizing? You shouldn't have licked me without my consent. Consent is a thing, ya know. It's also the fucking law." She began to pace in front of him. "Not to mention, you're the one who just did the impossible and changed forms in front of me. How is that possible? Science tells us that isn't possible, but yet, you did it and so did your... friend. Do your lungs and heart work the same? Internally, are your systems the same as humans or animals? There are so many questions."

When Rex took a step in her direction, she held out a hand and ordered, "Stay."

He cursed himself for listening to the order like a fucking golden retriever, but he didn't think disregarding her order would work in his favor. Once again, he was reminded how much he liked a demand coming from her beautiful mouth.

Settling in his spot on the landing, Rex crossed his arms and waited while she made pass after pass, pacing in front of him, until she finally stopped and faced him. That assessing, challenging gaze back.

"You're not losing touch with reality," he told her.

"I'm still not so sure about that."

She waved off the topic, causing Rex to chuckle. *Fuck.* He liked it when she did that, too.

"So, when you are in wolf form, are you a wolf or a human? Are you human in general? How can you shift back and forth? Does it hurt? What does it feel like? Were you bit and turned? Are your parents like you?"

Rex held up his hands in front of him to stop her barrage of questions. "Hold up. I'd be happy to talk to you about all of this, but that's a lot of questions all at once."

She shrugged. "It's science. I'm a doctor. Science is my jam."

"Fair." Rex smiled at her. "Did you finish sewing Bullet up?"

"Bullet?"

"My brother who can shift into a tiger."

"Oh, shit!" She snatched up her medical bag and headed back toward Bullet's room. "I think so, but I better check."

Following her, Rex chuckled and shook his head.

Hours had passed with Rex sitting in the corner of Bullet's room, watching Doc work on his brother. In his mind, he had taken to calling the vet *Doc* because he didn't know her name. He wasn't sure he wanted to know now. It wouldn't make a difference. She would always be Doc to him.

His wolf whined at the distance between them, even if it was only a few feet. Rex knew what it meant. He'd heard enough stories about how his brothers' animals had reacted to their mates to know that was why his wolf was behaving so oddly, but he wasn't ready to admit it out loud.

He didn't even know what she thought about shifters yet. Her reaction was so strange. It wasn't fear, but he wouldn't say it was happiness, either. It intrigued him. Everything about her intrigued him. He wanted to know all of her thoughts and her hobbies and her passions. He wanted to know how she sounded in every situation, how she tasted everywhere, and her boundaries. Rex wanted to know everything that made up Doc.

"Tell me why you keep looking at me like that, Fido."

Rex smiled, but his smile turned into a grin when he heard Bullet snort a laugh. He looked over at his brother and saw Bullet open his eyes.

"Think that's funny, do ya?"

Bullet nodded and coughed, wincing at the pain it caused in his abdomen. "She... She?" He looked at the doctor and the doctor nodded, confirming her pronouns. "She called you Fido. Of course, I think that's funny."

Doc smiled as she lifted the bandage and checked on Bullet's stitches. "Well, listen here, Tony, you shouldn't laugh. For one, you need to take it easy. Also, you flashed your stripes at me a couple times over the hours."

"What?" Bullet looked at her like he didn't understand English, then he turned his head to look at Rex.

"You shifted. You were human when you were first worked on, then you shifted and tore your stitches, so you were tiger when I brought in Doc. She stitched you back up, then you shifted… and shifted… and shifted."

"Yeah, so think you can stop doing that?" Doc looked at Bullet and raised a brow. "You keep ruining my good work."

"You… shifters? You… know?"

Doc gave a humorless laugh. "I didn't until you shifted while I was bandaging your wounds. I was going to leave, because I was positive I lost my mind, but Fido proved that I was still sane. Then I remembered that I took an oath, so… here I am. I'm full of questions, and Rex will answer them eventually, but you need to take it easy."

Bullet sputtered as he tried to process her words. Rex chuckled. "It's fine, Bull. Just try to stay human until your healing takes care of things. You had a rather large hole in your abdomen."

Still confused, Bullet nodded. "Where's Butterfly?"

Doc stopped in the middle of checking Bullet's vitals and turned to look at Rex. "Oh god… please don't tell me there are butterfly shifters, too." Her eyebrows shot up as her eyes widened.

Rex smiled at Doc. "Nah… just us predators. Butterfly is his mate. She was in here earlier. She introduced herself as Harlow."

"Oh." Doc let out a deep sigh. "I thought those news reports were just a quirky twilight zone-esque part of the town, but… well, I guess it is… depending on how you look at it. The physiological changes as you all shift boggles my scientific brain. How? Why? What happens to your muscle structure? And your bones… how do they lengthen and shorten to accommodate the form of an animal? And the fur… where does it come from, and where does it go?"

Rex bit back a laugh as she mulled that over and put her doctor stuff back in that medical bag. Having her around was going to be fun. Now, he just needed to figure out a way to convince her to be around.

"I need water," Bullet commented. "Yeah. I think that's why I can't think."

Rex stood and went for a glass of water from the bathroom as the doctor replied, "Water can only help. Well, I assume. I mean, I don't know much about shifters, but you seem to have the physiology of a human when human and that of a tiger when shifted, so yeah... water."

Smiling at her words, Rex brought the glass to Bullet, helped him sit up enough to drink it, and held the glass to Bullet's lips. When Bullet was done, Rex set the glass down on the table next to the bed.

Bullet looked up at him with a knowing smirk. "She's yours, isn't she?"

Rex rolled his eyes and gave a nod. "You're not having too much trouble with thinking, are ya?"

"Fair enough," Bullet replied, and grinned.

"Uh... if you're talking about me, the answer is Negative. I belong to no one."

"Sure, Doc," Bullet replied breezily, and closed his eyes.

Rex shifted his attention to the doctor and saw her looking at him with that assessing expression she always gave him. In response, he winked at her.

Her eyes narrowed more. "You boys are insane... and not just because you can be animals whenever you want."

"Yeah, but we can also be animals in bed," Bullet mumbled as he fell back to sleep.

Rex shrugged. "He speaks truth."

Doc raised a brow. "Not if I don't give you permission to be."

And that was the moment Rex knew his future had been decided, and it included the beautiful doctor across the room.

T.S. Tappin

Chapter Three

Jolene

Light streamed in through the open curtains of her bedroom window, falling on her face, and forced Jolene to consciousness. She groaned as she rolled over and slammed the pillow over her head to block out the light.

Why in the hell had she left the curtains open? It was part of her nightly routine to close them before she crawled into bed. Working in the medical field often meant long nights and endless days, and very little reprieve. Jolene learned to cherish the precious hours of sleep when she found them. She gave herself a routine, preparing the space around her and herself for the most effective slumber in order to recharge.

As she laid there under her pillow and comforter, Jolene tried to piece together how she managed to go to bed without closing the curtains. Searching her mind for the last thing she remembered from the night before, she started with what she knew. Her afternoon was spent filming videos about recall training. She remembered being interrupted by a knock on the door.

When she opened it, there was a strange man on the other side.

The tiger! Her mind flooded with memories of stitching up a tiger in a bedroom… and that tiger suddenly turning into a man. She remembered the man from her porch stopping her from leaving and turning into a wolf right in front of her eyes.

Was that real? Did that actually happen? Or was that just an extremely vivid dream? It had to be a dream, right? Things like that didn't really exist. Sure, she'd heard rumors, but that was just quirky stories from a small town, probably embellished tales meant to make things more interesting.

Shoving away the pillow and tossing off the comforter, Jolene climbed out of bed. When she stood up, she looked down and found that she was still wearing her jean shorts. "That's odd," she mumbled to herself. She never wore shorts to bed, let alone *jean* shorts.

Rex must have brought her home and put her to bed. That was the only possible explanation for why she didn't remember coming home or getting in bed. It also explained the fact that she was still wearing her jean shorts.

Annoyed with herself and the weirdness of the morning, Jolene yawned and headed out of the bedroom. She called out to her dog as she headed for her kitchen.

"Beast! Where are you?"

That was odd. Usually, her Yorkie was sitting at the side of her bed when she woke up, waiting to go out for his morning constitutional.

Jolene looked everywhere for Beast and eventually found him under the bed in the guest room. On her hands and knees, she peeked under the bed and tried to coax the dog out. "Come on. Everything's okay."

Her poor pup was shaking. What freaked the animal out that badly?

It took Jolene ten minutes to convince the pup that it was okay to come out. She rewarded Beast with a treat and let him outside.

As she watched the dog from the window in the back door, her phone began to ring. It sounded oddly muffled. Brow furrowed, she went in search of it and found it in her medical bag. Why it was in there, she wasn't exactly sure.

Thoughts of the whys and hows left her brain when she saw that the number of her mother's neighbor was on the screen. She pressed *answer* and put the phone to her ear.

"Hello?"

"Jo," the elderly woman said with a sigh of relief. "Dear, I'm so happy you answered! They just took your mother into the hospital. They said she'd be okay, but Jo, she was hurting. I don't know how lon—"

"Phyllis," Jolene interrupted. Her mother's neighbor could chatter for hours and give very little information. She knew the woman needed direct questions, or Jolene would never get what she needed out of her. "Who is *they*?"

"The paramedics. Or are they EMTs now?"

"Okay. Why was Mom hurting?"

"Oh! It was just awful, dear! She fell in the backyard while pulling weeds. Hit her hip on that stone flamingo statue Mr. Rogers gave her for her birthday last year. Mr. Hampton heard her shouting for help. It was just… just *awful*."

Jolene headed back to the bedroom and began gathering what she would need for at least a short trip home. "And she was brought to which hospital?"

"Sacred Heart," Phyllis replied. "I'm waiting for my son to get here. He's going to drive me up there."

"Thank you for calling me, Phyllis. I'll get on a plane and head out as soon as I find someone to take care of my dog."

"Take your time, dear. I'll take care of your mother until you can get here."

Jolene thanked her again and ended the call. After letting Beast back in the house, she packed her smallest suitcase and called Mama Hen. She knew Mama Hen would agree to dog sit. Her Yorkie, Maxie, would love a playmate.

Once she was packed and changed into a comfortable traveling outfit, she fed Beast and filled his water dish. Mama Hen agreed to stop by and pick Beast up after her shift at the Inn she owned, The Hen House. She had her spare key, so Jolene didn't have to drop the pup off. That was one less thing for her to worry about. Jolene grabbed her medical bag and went through it to prepare a to-go bag of essentials. Most things, she would be able to get in Pensacola, Florida, where her mother lived, so she wouldn't need much. As she was going through her bag, she came across something that made her stop in her tracks.

Stuck to the side of the bag, just inside the zipper, was a *tuft of tiger fur*. Staring at it, Jolene took a deep breath and let it out slowly. *Holy shitballs!* She had sewed up a tiger who changed into a man and back again. It was true. It really happened.

Shaking her head, she forced the freakout from her brain. She had to get to her mother. This was something she could deal with later.

After gathering everything she was taking with her and setting them by the front door, Jolene quickly brushed her teeth and hair, then headed out to her car.

Once she was parked at the airport and headed inside, she called the veterinarian clinic where she worked to inform them that she had a family emergency and wasn't sure how long she would be gone. Thankfully, she worked at a clinic in a small town where they seemed more understanding about these sorts of situations. Jolene breathed a sigh of relief when the owner told her not to worry about work and focus on her mother.

After buying her ticket at the counter and getting through security, she called the Sacred Heart on the way to the gate. She wasn't surprised when they told her they couldn't give out patient information over the phone and told them she would be there as soon as she could. Through very careful wording, the nurse she spoke with relayed that her mother was expected to be okay, but she should get there as soon as possible.

Rex

The next morning, Rex checked on their injured members before he hopped on his bike and headed over to see Doc. He wanted to thank her again for taking such great care of Bullet. And, yeah, he wanted to see her, too.

While watching over Bullet the night before, she fell asleep in the chair she had been occupying in the corner of the room. He didn't have the heart to wake her. Instead, he carefully carried her and her medical bag out to her vehicle. Once she was buckled in, he drove her home, brought her inside, and put her to bed. He felt bad at how freaked out her dog was when he stepped inside, but nothing he did convinced the dog that he was a friend. The poor pup hid under a bed and wouldn't come out.

Rex was astonished at Doc's ability to sleep through all of that, but he was happy she did, since she apparently needed the rest.

His wolf spent the rest of the night and the morning whining for him to go to her, but he managed to hold off until ten. Parking his bike at the curb, he headed for her front door and frowned when he saw that her driveway was empty. She must have left, but he knocked on her door to be sure.

After a few minutes without an answer, he let out a sigh and turned around to head back to his bike. Just as he reached it, Mama Hen pulled up next to him in her lime green Cutlass and rolled down her window.

"She had to leave town. Her mother had a medical issue."

Rex wasn't surprised when the urge to be with her increased. She was his mate, after all, even if she didn't know it yet. It was in his nature to want to be there for her through any difficulty.

"She gonna be okay? Where does her mom live?"

"Florida. Something happened with her hip. Jolene wasn't sure what injuries she had, but she flew out to be with her."

Florida? That wasn't within a reasonable distance to make a chance meeting believable. He was just going to have to wait for her return.

He gave Mama Hen his best smile. "Mind keeping me updated?"

Mama Hen's smirk told him she saw right through his shit, but she replied, "I'll call you when I know how long she'll be gone."

"You're a peach."

"And you're a bullshitter." Mama Hen rolled up the window and took off.

Jolene

The next morning, after another visit from her mother's doctor, Jolene told her mother she would be back and headed across the street from the hospital to the coffee shop. After grabbing a coffee, she sat down at a table in the corner and called Mama Hen on her cell.

"Hen House. The main chick speaking. How can I help?"

"Hey. It's Jo."

"Hey! How's Mom?"

Jolene sighed and answered, "They ended up having to do a hip replacement. She is doing much better today, and they will most likely send her home soon, but it's going to be a few weeks before I can head back. I need to be here to help her with recovery."

"Well, I'm sorry she went through all of that, but maybe she'll come out of this better than ever. New hip? She got an upgrade."

Smiling at Mama Hen's optimism, Jolene sipped her coffee. "We can hope. Anyway, I'll see what I can do about arranging care for Beast, but it might be a couple days before I find something."

"Nonsense. Beast has care. *Me.* Saves me from having to chase Maxie around the backyard. They're wearing each other out. Both of the pups slept like the dead last night. Didn't even wake me up to go outside until eight. It was nice."

"You really don't mind?"

She heard Mama Hen give a disapproving sigh on the other end of the line. "I'm just going to pretend you didn't ask me that ridiculous question. You're welcome, Jo, but you don't need to thank me. It's what friends do."

Then the amazing woman hung up on her.

Rex

It was going to be a long damn day, and Rex was transferring supplies from the club van to the clubhouse when Mama Hen pulled into the parking lot. She parked next to the van and rolled down the window.

He grabbed the towel from over his shoulder and wiped his hands on it as he approached her car. "Hey, Mama Hen."

"Hey. Just heard from your girlfriend."

Rex frowned. "She's not my girlfriend."

Mama Hen chuckled. "Yet."

After rolling his eyes, Rex smiled. "How's her mom?"

"Hip replacement. Jo's gonna be out of town for a few weeks, maybe longer. She has to help her mom through recovery and rehabilitation. I'm taking care of Beast for her."

"Beast?"

"Her pup."

"Ah… okay." He nodded. "I appreciate the update."

A sly grin grew on her face. "You're gonna go after it when she gets back. Right?"

Rex shook his head at her barely veiled order. "Yes. That's the plan."

"Good." She patted the side of her car. "Both of you deserve some fun, and isn't it about time you settled down?"

He raised an eyebrow and just stared at her. She was older than he was. He didn't know much about Mama Hen's life, but he knew she wasn't a saint. He highly doubted her private life was *settled*.

"You mind your business," she told him, still grinning, before she drove around the van and headed out of the parking lot.

T.S. Tappin

Chapter Four

Rex

Rex loved it when his daughter came home to visit. The fact that Nevaeh lived in a big city on her own at the age of nineteen drove him up the wall with worry. She was a pretty girl — a model and a singer represented by an up-and-coming talent agency. She was doing quite well for herself and had yet to touch the money he sent her every week. He sent it anyway, because that's what fathers who had the means did.

Yes, he loved it when she came home to visit, but what he didn't love was when she brought her trio of best friends with her. Two of the three were growing boys who would eat him out of house and home, and his daughter and her friend Kennedy required copious amounts of ice cream.

While it did a number on his bank account, it also made him breathe a little easier. A model in the big city could develop a number of issues with eating and weight. His girl had yet to show signs of any of that. She ate, and she enjoyed her food. He'd buy her as much ice cream as she wanted.

Okay, he didn't hate it, but his bank balance wasn't a fan.

He left the four young adults at his house while he made a run to the grocery store. Their visit had been a surprise, so he didn't have his pantry stocked the way it normally would be, but he always told his girl she didn't need to ask to come home. She could just show up, and that's what Nevaeh did.

As Rex parked his truck in a spot in the middle of the parking lot in front of their local grocery store, he reflected on some of the choices he made as a parent. One of the things he had always done was tell Nevaeh that her friends were always welcome at his home. It drove her mother crazy, because she didn't have the same rule.

When Nevaeh was in high school, he would come home to find eight or nine teenagers hanging out in his living room. Was his house always a disaster that he had to spend hours cleaning after they were there? Yes. Did he know what his daughter and her friends were up to? Also, yes, which made it all worth it.

Her friends trusted him and came to him for advice. They told him about their struggles and their successes. They told him about their heartbreaks and their first dates. He knew it all, but in return for that trust, he gave them the best advice he could and kept their secrets unless it was a safety issue.

When he got out of his truck, he snagged a row of carts from the corral and pushed them toward the front of the store, making a mental list of what he needed to get.

Nevaeh liked chocolate ice cream. Kennedy liked the salted caramel. Hunter and Devin requested beef jerky and peanuts. He also needed to get the ingredients for meals. He decided on hamburgers,

Chicken Chili, and Taco Lasagna for dinners. For lunches, he added lunch meat, bread, cheese, and the makings of salads to his mental list. French Toast and cereal would work for breakfast.

Stepping into the store, he took one of the carts and left the rest near the entrance and gave a nod to the older woman who was working the register. She was a sweet woman, but she didn't take any shit. He liked that. He also liked that when he came through the line, she was able to efficiently ring up the order and have a conversation without holding things up.

After getting the return nod and smile, he took a left and headed for the produce section. After grabbing lettuce, tomatoes, potatoes, avocado, onions, and green peppers, he grabbed lunch meat from the deli section and headed for the bread section in the back left corner of the store. Rex had just put two loaves of white bread and two packages of hamburger buns in his cart when he heard a familiar voice coming from his right.

"Ah." A loud, deep sigh came from beside him. "There's nothing like tender meat."

Rex snorted a laugh as he turned and saw Doc standing in front of the meat section with a package of high-priced steaks in one hand and a container of meat tenderizer in the other. Wearing a set of scrubs, light blue with cats and dogs all over them, she turned and put both in her cart. When she went to turn back to the meat section, her gaze lifted and met his own.

Rex headed in her direction, happy to see her again after two and a half months. Mama Hen had told him Doc would be returning sometime this week, and there she was, looking as beautiful as the last time he saw her. "You're a meat lover, are ya?"

Doc straightened and turned her body to face him. "Who can deny good sausage or a slab of beef? Not I."

Smiling, Rex stopped his cart next to hers. He grabbed two large packages of hamburger and a package containing four large chicken breasts.

"A breast man, I see."

Rex gave a nod. "But I also like a good rump... roast."

As he went to put them in his cart, she asked, "Are you one of those I-grill-all-my-meat types?"

Rex put the items in his cart, looked down at his crotch, and then looked over at Doc. "Well... not *all* my meat."

As Doc laughed, Rex reached around her and grabbed a container of chorizo and two packages of bacon. As he set the items down with the rest, he looked over at her cart. She had various meat products, veggies, and fruit.

"Are you a once-a-weeker, or a multiple times a week type?"

She raised an eyebrow. "If you're asking how often I like meat, I'm not sure that's appropriate grocery store conversation."

Grinning, Rex commented, "We could always have it over dinner. How about some tenderized meat and veggies?"

"Are you asking me out?"

Rex shrugged. "I'm asking you in."

She looked over at him with amusement in his eyes. "I am all for letting the dogs in the house."

"I'm a wolf, Doc."

"Okay, Fido." Doc pushed her cart forward toward the dairy section. "And if I agree to this date, does this mean I have to cook for you?"

Rex's Release

Walking next to her, pushing his own cart, Rex answered, "No. I'm very capable of cooking. I would just need to know if there are any no-gos in the culinary department."

Doc looked surprised that he knew how to cook, if her widened eyes and lifted brows told him anything.

"What?"

"You grocery shop and you cook?"

Rex stopped his cart and turned his body, so he was facing her. "I'm a single forty-one-year-old man with a grown daughter. It was either shop and cook or starve. I happen to like to eat, so I learned."

Her surprise turned back to amusement. "You may not know it, but your sex-quotient just went up, Fido."

"Does that mean you're going to come over for dinner?"

"It means I'll consider it."

"Okay. Well, let's do this." He pulled his wallet out of his back pocket and retrieved a business card. Handing it to her, he said, "This is my personal cell. Text me your no-go foods and what evening you're free. I'll respond with my address and a time, then I'll dazzle you with my cooking skills and my charming personality."

"You're awfully confident," she replied, but she took the card and slid it in her pocket.

As they made their way to the dairy section, Rex noticed her eyeing his cart. "My daughter came home for a visit and brought three of her friends with her. So, here I am, doing a grocery run to feed them. They are all nineteen, two of them young men, so they eat a lot."

"But I bet your daughter loves the fact that you're willing to take in her and her friends and feed them. Not all parents would be cool with that."

Rex shrugged and grabbed two dozen eggs. As he set them in the cart, he replied, "If they're at my house, I know what they are doing. If buying them food is the cost for my peace of mind, I'm cool with that."

The smile she gave him hit him in the gut and made his wolf stand up and take notice. She kept her eyes on him as she reached down and grabbed her own dozen eggs. Holding them up, she said, "That's egg-cellent."

Rex chuckled and grabbed the three kinds of cheese he needed — the super-sized bag of shredded Colby-jack, two packages of sliced Colby-jack, and a block of Pepperjack. As he dropped them in his cart, he uttered, "That's so cheesy."

The belly laugh that came from her was the cutest thing he'd ever heard. Fuck... he was in trouble. His wolf let out a whine and swished his tail, letting Rex know he agreed with that assessment.

While she laughed and grabbed what she needed, he grabbed sour cream and milk. Together, they moved to the next aisle of frozen items.

As he opened one door of the freezer and grabbed the ice cream the girls had requested, she said, "You scream. I scream. We all scream for ice cream."

Rex set the pints down in the cart and raised an eyebrow at her. "You give me the sign. You and I will be screaming, but it won't be over ice cream."

As she stared at him with her mouth open, he pushed his cart down the aisle and around to the next one. He was grabbing a variety of cereal when she joined him. He bit his lip to stop himself from laughing at her expression as he grabbed a bottle of syrup.

She reached up and grabbed a box of bran cereal, eyeing the syrup in his hand. "That's awfully saucy of you."

Chuckling, he followed her to the ethnic foods aisle. He grabbed two cans of refried beans, a package of soft flour tortilla shells, taco seasoning, salsa, and two jars of taco sauce. "Now, *this* is saucy."

She held up a bag of dried black beans. "Bean there, done that."

They were both laughing as they moved to the canned foods and pasta aisle. He grabbed mushrooms and lasagna noodles while she loaded her cart with different kinds of pasta.

"You can make lasagna?"

He shrugged. "Yes, but this is for taco lasagna. Nevaeh, my daughter, loves it. She requests it every time she's in town."

"Taco lasagna?"

"Yes. If you like American tacos, you'd like taco lasagna."

"My brain is having trouble computing it."

He smiled at her. "I'll prove it. Come over for dinner, and I'll make it."

"You'd eat it twice in a week?"

"I'd eat it every day," he replied as his gaze traveled down her body and back up.

"Heel, Fido," she said and pushed her cart down the aisle. "I'll text you… or not."

When they got to the end of the aisle, he had to stop and grab snacks. She smiled at him over her shoulder as she kept pushing her cart toward the front of the store.

He went down the paper products aisle to grab paper towels and more toilet paper, then he headed for the registers. When he reached the front of the store, he found her unloading her cart onto a belt and the older cashier ringing things up.

Rex moved to the next aisle and did the same. Grinning like a fool, he told his wolf he was sure they would be having dinner with Doc and to have patience.

Chapter Five

Jolene

The man was funny and handsome. Jolene already knew that from her interactions with him while tending to the tiger. Bullet. She had learned that he liked to be called Bullet, and Mr. Sense of Humor was named Rex. Mama Hen had informed her of quite a bit since that night.

Along with the names of the ridiculously handsome men of the Howlers MC, she also talked Jolene through the shifter thing after a particularly twisty spiral her brain had taken, trying to understand how it was possible they existed in the first place. It involved gods, shenanigans, and magic. Instantly, her clinical and methodical brain rejected the notion, but Jolene couldn't deny that there were things in the world that were unexplainable through scientific methods of study and explanation.

Knowing it was likely exactly what Mama Hen said it was didn't stop the millions of questions from running through her brain. Most of them revolved around the change, or what Mama Hen called *the shifting*. Jolene wanted to know about the change in bones and muscles. She was curious about how it felt and what it was like. Did they think like animals when in that form? And then there was the healing. The medical professional in her wanted to study how their bodies managed to heal gunshot wounds in a matter of days, and knife wounds in hours. What did their bodies do when faced with disease? Were they even capable of contracting disease?

Endless. The questions just swirled around, over and over, multiplying.

For the most part, he seemed like any other man. Her body sure as hell reacted to him in the way it would any other man she found attractive. And she absolutely was attracted to Rex. She liked the long blond and gray hair and beard, his solid body, and easy grin. Those ice-blue eyes were a definite plus. But grocery shopping and cooking? Sign her the fuck up.

If the man took orders as well as he took care of his friends, there was potential there for a *satisfying* arrangement.

Intrigued with the idea, Jolene put the last bag in her truck and climbed into her car before she sent him a text.

Jolene: Monday. 7pm.

She was halfway home when she heard her phone ring with a notification of his reply. Once she parked in her driveway, she checked it. It was his address, followed by another message.

Rex: I was supposed to tell you what time to be here.

With a grin, she sent a message back before she got out of the car and brought her groceries inside.

Rex

Jolene: It's best you learn now that you're not the one calling the shots. I'll be there at 7pm and will be ready to eat. If you're good, Fido, I just might give you a treat.

Fuck. Doc was bossy and sassy, but he fucking loved it. As a biker, people tended to be cautious around him, no matter where he went. He wasn't a small guy, and he had tattoos. When you throw a leather cut on top of that, it wasn't uncommon to see women clutch their purses closer or men cross the street to avoid getting too close. It was refreshing as hell to have someone go head-to-head with him. Not only did Doc push back, she often won, and to Rex, that was sexy as hell.

Grinning from ear to ear, Rex sent his reply and pulled out of the parking lot.

Rex: Yes, Ma'am

He couldn't wait for Monday, which was odd. Normally, he relished his rare weekends with Nevaeh. He would still enjoy it, but his attention would most definitely be divided.

When he pulled into his driveway, he turned off his truck and gave himself a bit of a lecture.

You will not spend the next three days thinking of nothing but Doc. You are a father, and a damn good one. You will act like it, or I swear to the gods, I will not even try for anything more than dinner.

He barked out a laugh. Okay. He wasn't lecturing himself as a whole. He was lecturing his cock.

When his wolf began to whine, he rolled his eyes and climbed out of his truck. He was losing it because a pretty woman ordered him around a bit. So much for that alpha male bullshit.

The front door of his house swung open, pulling his attention in that direction. "It's about time," Nevaeh yelled out to him with a giant grin on her face. "We're *starving*."

"You're always starving," he replied, and gave her a wink. "Send the boys out to help."

"Can't handle a few bags, old man?"

Chuckling, Rex grabbed a few bags from the back seat of his truck and headed for the door. "I paid. They can carry."

When he got to the door, the boys stepped past Nevaeh and jogged to his truck. They may eat for ten, but they were good boys.

Rex bent his head down and kissed his daughter's cheek. "Go preheat the oven. And I'll get your favorite going."

Nevaeh did a little shimmy as she threw her hands in the air. "Taco Lasagna!"

Jolene

When Jolene showed up at his front door on Monday evening, she was surprised at the look of the place. He was a biker with long hair, a long beard, and tattoos, but he lived in a nice two-story home that had a nice manicured lawn and actual porch decorations. Everything that screamed mild-mannered suburban dad.

Staring down at the elf statues that all had grumpy looks on their faces as they stacked small boxes around a four-foot-tall Christmas tree, Jolene tried to picture the rough man setting them up. Or was it his daughter who decorated? Either way, she didn't see him as the type to have novelty items like that on his porch.

Staring into the glass pane of his door, she inspected herself to make sure nothing was out of whack. Her hair was fine and so was her makeup. Her royal blue blouse and charcoal gray slacks fit her well and complimented her eyes and her figure. Taking a deep breath, she told herself to knock it off. She was too old for the first date nerves, or at least to the extent she was feeling them.

Jolene hadn't even knocked on his door yet, but it swung open, and he stood there staring at her through the screen door. The smile on his face was warm, and the look in his ice-blue eyes was inviting. He truly was a handsome specimen.

"Hey," he said low and swung the screen door open. Holding it with one large hand as she stepped through.

"Hey," she replied and started to pull off her jacket.
"Can I help?"

He lifted his hands up to her shoulders but didn't go any further until she gave a nod. With permission granted, he helped her remove her jacket and hung it on the coat rack near his front door.

She looked around at the interior and was less surprised by the inside than she had been by the porch. There was a dark gray sectional in the living area to the right. On the wall above one side, there was a large black and chrome art piece in the shape of a motorcycle. It looked to be made out of metal scraps. It was gorgeous.

There were various photos, many of which she suspected were his daughter, in chrome or silver frames on the wall above the other side of the sectional. The young woman was gorgeous and had her father's eyes.

Across from the couch was a large flat screen on the wall, with various electronics on a metal shelving unit underneath it. The coffee table and end tables were made of the same metal and style. Finishing off the space was a black and gray rug on the shiny wood floor.

The look was masculine and bold, but it was still stylish. She liked it, but it was obvious that a woman hadn't lived there in a long time, if ever.

The decor continued into the dining and kitchen area to her left. The countertops were black, and the cupboards were a dark gray to complement the black and stainless-steel appliances. Even the stools that lined one side of the island matched the stove and refrigerator, black and stainless steel.

"Not a fan of color, I see," she commented and turned to face him.

He shrugged. "This is just the first floor. Nevaeh's room is pink and purple *everything*. The guest room is green and tan. So is the bathroom."

She lifted a brow when he didn't go on. "And your room?"

His smile grew into a grin. "Maybe if I impress you with my cooking skills, I'll get the chance to show you."

Those words coming from his lips conjured a vision of him following her up the stairs she spotted across from the front door. Heat flooded her system, but she didn't let it show. Instead, she slowly scanned his body from head to toe.

Rex was wearing a plain white tee under his cut. The short sleeves hugged his biceps, making her want to reach up and give them each a squeeze herself. On his lower half, he had on a pair of dark blue jeans that weren't tight, but fit him just well enough to give her a good idea of what was underneath them. The kicker was his bare feet. What was it about a man walking around without socks or shoes on? Why did it conjure so many scandalous thoughts?

On her way back up his body, she let out a deep sigh. When she met his gaze with her own, she replied, "It better be some damn good food."

His quiet laugh settled in her lower stomach and told her just how much he had already earned from her. She would most definitely be seeing that bedroom before too long.

T.S. Tappin

Chapter Six

Rex

After dishing out the slices of taco lasagna, Rex carried the plates over to his dining table. He set one down in front of Doc and the other on the table in front of his chair before returning to the kitchen to grab the tray of toppings and drink choices.

He was man enough to admit he might have gone a bit overboard with the toppings. Usually, he only focused on tomatoes, lettuce, and sour cream because that was all he and Nevaeh used on it. He didn't ask Doc what she liked on her tacos, so he made another run to the grocery store to pick up onions, peppers, guacamole, salsa, and a variety of other things.

Rex hadn't told his daughter about his date, but he suspected Mama Hen or one of the Ol' Ladies had heard and filled her in. Nevaeh had chopped up the onions and peppers and had put the other toppings in small, easy to access containers before she left to head back to school.

As he looked down at the tray, he smiled. Damn, he loved that kid. She was good right down to her soul.

He set the tray on the table in the center and asked, "Would you like pop, wine, a beer, or something stronger?"

Doc smirked up at him. "Pop is fine. Maybe something stronger when we're done eating."

"Your wish, my command," he said and lifted two cans of pop from the tray. After handing one to her, he took his seat and set his can next to his plate.

They made small talk as they put their toppings on their lasagna, and Rex took note that Doc liked guacamole, sour cream, lettuce, tomatoes, and peppers. He filed that bit of information away for the next time he made it for her. Nevaeh had beat it into his head that he needed to manifest what he wanted, so that was what he was doing — manifesting more dinner dates with Doc.

He used to think that manifesting stuff was bullshit, but it made his daughter happy when he played along, so he did. In the process, he noticed that he was more optimistic and things seemed to go smoother for him. That was enough for Rex to make it a standard practice in his life.

After all the bullshit they went through a few months back, he was willing to do anything to bring good into his life and the lives of the people he cared about.

He watched as Doc used her fork to cut off a bite and lifted it to her full lips.

After she chewed the food, she let out a moan and swallowed. "That's... good." She looked over at him. "Seriously. It's simple but... really good."

Rex smiled around the bite he was chewing and nodded. After swallowing, he said, "Comfort food."

"Exactly."

For the next few minutes, they focused on eating their food and didn't say much. He didn't realize how much her opinion of their favorite food would mean to him until she let out that moan. That quiet sound sent his body in several different directions.

His cock took notice and imagined her making that noise while he was deep inside of her. His wolf started panting and pacing, excited that they had pleased their mate. His pride swelled at her acceptance. One small noise from Doc, and Rex was all over the place.

Jolene

After dinner, they carried all the dishes and leftover toppings into the kitchen and Rex went to work rinsing the dishes and putting them in the dishwasher. She offered to help, but he just prepared and handed her a short glass with a couple fingers of whiskey and ice, and gave her a kiss on the cheek before he went back to the dishes.

"I am capable of doing dishes."

Rex grinned and slid a plate into the dishwasher tray. "I think you're capable of a good number of things, but this is kind of a one-person job. How about this… you hit me with those questions swimming in your beautiful eyes while I take care of these?"

Jolene sipped her whiskey and watched the muscles in his arms flex and release with his ministrations. "Okay. So, you're a wolf shifter? Is that the right terminology?"

He nodded, his long blond and gray ponytail at his nape shifting with the movement. "Yes."

"When you're a wolf, are you… do you…" She cleared her throat. "Do you think like a wolf or a man?"

Rex finished rinsing out a pan and loaded it next to the plates. "I think like a man, for the most part. My instincts are heightened, but I'm still able to think logically. I know who people are and understand words. When I'm in human form, I can feel my wolf inside of me. Its desires and reactions are in my head, but they are more in the background."

"So... like it's part of you, but not?"

He nodded again. "The most important part is that you know that you are never in danger with me as a man or a wolf. Even injured or anxious, I would never hurt you." He shut the dishwasher and turned to face her, his ice-blue eyes staring into her soul. "You never have to worry about that with me or anyone in the Howlers or the Claws."

She gave him a nod, mostly because he seemed to need it. His shoulders visibly relaxed after she did. It was obviously important to him that she felt safe around him.

"What else do you want to ask?"

He poured himself a glass of whiskey, then he led her to the living room, bringing the bottle with him.

Settling on one side of the sectional with him, Jolene sipped her whiskey as she considered what to ask next. "Mama Hen mentioned that it has something about the origin of the shifters having to do with gods. She didn't have details, or at least, she didn't share them."

She watched as he settled and put the bottle down on the coffee table. Facing her with one leg up and bent on the cushion in front of him, he replied, "We didn't know the origin story until *very* recently." He paused and studied her, but she wasn't sure what he was contemplating until he spoke again. "If I tell you these things, I need you to promise that it stays with us. There are some people who believe shifters are monsters who need to be eradicated. Because of that, there are some things that we have to keep as quiet as possible. Not to mention, some of this is really the secret of the gods, and it kinda feels like sharing the business of others."

Jolene nodded. "I understand. I can keep it between us, but you don't have to tell me anything you don't feel comfortable sharing. It just fascinates me is all."

Rex smiled, and Jolene took a larger sip of her whiskey to coat her mouth that suddenly felt dry. "The story goes... the God of Chaos was causing too much trouble on the earth, causing the gods to make a decision to pull away from humanity to try to limit their involvement and influence. However, they have responsibilities, so they had to have champions living among the humans to do the deeds they used to. I guess the gods all had their favorite creatures, and through magic, they fused those creatures with humans, causing a number of different new creatures... like shifters. So, the original champions were created by the gods through magic."

Jolene's brain started spinning with the possibilities. "What other creatures are there? Does that make you a champion of the gods? Is this just a tale that you heard? Is there proof?"

His chuckle sounded in the air as he reached out and set his glass down on the table. "Whoa. Okay. One question at a time. My poor old brain can't keep up." He stopped laughing, but his smile stayed in place. "As for other creatures, there are the usual suspects — vampires, witches, dragon shifters, etc."

"Vampires? Dragons?" She knew her voice was rising, but *holy shit!*

He nodded. "I've met a few. The dragon shifters aren't so bad. Came in clutch during the battle we fought. The vampires, however..." He sighed. "They are arrogant."

She scoffed and took a drink of her whiskey. "Wouldn't you be? Fuck. I bet they never even have to try to get laid. Partners just fall into their beds, left and right. I'd bet on it."

He raised a brow, amusement in his eyes. "Yeah, those vampires must have it easy, unlike us poor measly wolf shifter bikers. Always have to be out here begging for a pity fuck."

She rolled her eyes. "You know what I mean."

"Yeah... I should've been a vampire. Probably wouldn't have had to cook."

She snorted a laugh. "Smartass."

"I try." He reached out and took hold of her free hand, just holding it on the cushion between them. "To answer the rest of your questions, no, I'm not a champion of the gods, but I guess you could consider me a descendent of the original champions. As for proof, I met some of the champions, myself, and Axle has met one of the gods, so... yeah, we've seen proof."

She shook her head in astonishment. "This is... I have a hard time wrapping my head around all of this."

He nodded. "I know. I imagine it's easier for me since I've been a shifter my whole life. Makes believing in all of this much easier."

"So, you were born this way."

"Yup. One of your parents has to be a shifter in order for you to be one. Like Nevaeh, for instance, she is a wolf shifter, too. Her mother is full-human."

"Obviously, there are more than just wolves around here, since I treated a tiger."

"Right. We have some lions and some bears, too. Not all of the members of the club are shifters. There are some humans."

"And Axle is your president?"

"Yeah." He ran his thumb along the back of her fingers. "He's the president of the Howlers. Crush is the president of the Claws. Both clubs work very closely together, so we're a big family."

"It's really awesome you have that. I'm sure it was great for Nevaeh… to have a big family to watch out for her."

His smile widened again. "She loved it when she was a kid. For a few of her teen years, she might have traded them in. It's hard to date when you have eighteen uncles who wear leather, have tattoos, and ride motorcycles."

Jolene laughed. "Oh no. Did you all ruin her dates?"

He shrugged. "*I* didn't, but I won't comment on whether my club brothers did."

Shaking her head at him, she tsked. "That poor girl."

They both laughed for a few moments, before it faded and Rex uttered, "Can we address the elephant in the room?"

"Is that another kind of shifter?"

He rolled his eyes, but they were still sparkling with the proof of his enjoyment of their conversation. "You have a way of giving orders, instead of making requests. And a time or two, you've said things that have alluded to… the fact that you like to be in control. How far does that reach?"

Jolene took another drink of her whiskey and set the glass on the coffee table. She wasn't sure if they were going to broach that subject on their first date, but there it was, right out in the open. She wasn't about to hide who she was or what her needs and boundaries were. If they were going to do this, he needed to know what he was getting from the very beginning, and it would be the perfect opportunity for her to find out what he was comfortable with and what he was not.

Turning so she was facing him on the couch, mirroring his position, she met his gaze and answered, "I am most comfortable in a position of control in most areas of my life. It doesn't need to be a constant thing, but I desire it more often than not."

Rex gave a nod. His amusement slid away and was replaced by a look of contemplation, his brows pulled together slightly, and his attention solely focused on her. "Is there something… that… incited this?"

She shrugged. "If you asked a therapist, I'm sure they would say it had to do with my childhood being somewhat transient, along with not having much control with most of my young adulthood. Until my thirties, I was subject to the whims of bosses and professors… and others. Even now, the clinic where I work is owned by someone who micromanages everything." She sighed and added, "So, yeah, I guess there's a lot that goes into it."

Rex gave her hand a squeeze of support. "Do you ever feel comfortable in a moment of… submission?"

"Comfortable? Sure." She smirked. "Satisfied? Not yet."

After giving her a wink, he ran his tongue along his bottom lip and chuckled. "You like being in control in the bedroom." It was said as a statement, but Jolene could tell he was waiting for her to respond.

"Yes." She let her eyes run over his body, taking in his strong body, rugged exterior, and handsome face. "Is that something you want?"

Rex leaned forward a bit. "Doc, I would let you do a great number of things to me if it meant I got to taste you for only a moment."

T.S. Tappin

Chapter Seven

Rex

Rex ignored the sudden tightness of his jeans. The conversation was too important. Fearing moving to adjust himself would steer the conversation to something else, he pretended he wasn't in pain and kept focused on Doc.

His wolf was going apeshit inside of him, pacing and letting out short, low howls, demanding he claim her.

"This isn't a phase, Rex," she stated calmly.

"I'm aware."

"That means, more often than not, I would be the one calling the shots in the bedroom."

He gave a nod. "Again… I'm aware."

Doc reached over and picked up her glass. After taking a sip, she said, "We're talking mostly sensation play and light bondage."

A vision of being tied to his bed while a naked Doc straddled him and poured candle wax onto his skin had his cock twitching in the confines of his jeans. Allowing a slow grin to grow on his face, Rex replied in a low voice, "You want to tie me up and make me feel?" His tone turned sarcastic. "Oh. No. Please, don't."

Doc rolled her eyes but smiled. "I'm being serious."

"Seriously, I'm liking what I'm hearing."

Her eyes narrowed on him. "How familiar are you with BDSM?"

He retrieved his glass from the table and took a sip before he shrugged. "Besides some light play of my own? Not much, personally. I mean… one of my club brothers is most definitely a Dom. His woman is very much not a submissive in public, though, so that gets… interesting."

Doc chuckled. "Snagged himself a brat, did he?"

"He seems to enjoy that about her, even when she's doing his head in."

"That's often the case." She took another sip and returned her glass to the coffee table. "As for outside the bedroom, I'm not looking for a full Domme/sub relationship. I won't be telling you how to run your life or anything… if this goes anywhere."

Rex raised a brow and slid a bit closer to her. "Doc, let's not pretend we aren't going to head upstairs at some point this evening."

"Awfully sure of yourself," she returned, but he watched her attention shift from his eyes to his lips.

"Or just calling things the way they are."

Her gaze lifted to his again. "We need to talk about more before we can go there. Establish boundaries. Safe words. Be clear about what is expected from each other."

"Okay." Rex lifted her hand to his mouth and kissed the back of her knuckles. Gently rubbing his lips against her skin, he said, "I'm not really into deep pain or humiliation. You want to tie me up? Blindfold me? Use toys? Try new things? Candles? Ice? Feathers?

Stuff like that? Hell motherfucking yes." He lowered their hands to his thigh.

There was amusement in her bright blue eyes as she asked, "Ass play?"

"You or me?" Rex was enjoying the back and forth between them. The topic of conversation was definitely stimulating, but he was sure that it didn't matter much what they talked about. He would hang from her every word, no matter what.

"Me? Probably, but I was asking about you."

Rex swallowed hard and considered her question. He could honestly say he'd never had an urge to do that, but before he answered, he waited to see if any anxiety grew in him at the thought. When it didn't, he admitted, "I've never thought about it, honestly, but now that I am, I'm not against it."

The corners of her lips twitched. "I was kidding." She cleared her throat. "If we're going to do this, I need you to pick a safe word."

He lifted a brow and his glass. "Whiskey?"

She shrugged. "Works for me."

"Is that yours, too?"

A nod. "We can use whiskey. Keeps things simple and easy to remember. And I'm assuming you know you can always use it... no matter what we're doing."

"Yes." He winked at her. "If one of us says it, everything stops. No resentment. No anger or frustration. It's for safety and emotional health during what could be very deep situations. I may not have delved too deep, but I'm a curious man, Doc. I might have done some research."

"Now you're just talking dirty."

Chuckling, Rex leaned forward and pressed his lips to her cheek, before he whispered, "I can't wait to feel you."

"Then go upstairs. Strip naked. Lay on your back in the middle of your bed. Arms above your head and spread." She turned her head and nipped at his bottom lip. "You have five minutes."

Rex wasn't an idiot. He stood and headed up the stairs, grabbing their glasses and the bottle, bringing them with him.

Laying there on his navy sheets, staring up at the textured, stone-colored ceiling, Rex took slow breaths to keep himself calm. His wolf was pacing inside of him, whining and demanding they claim their mate. He didn't know much about her, but he had full faith they were perfect for each other. The pull he felt toward her was stronger than anything he had ever felt before. For once in his life, he was seriously considering a full-on relationship with another person.

Rex was forty-one and had never been in an actual romantic relationship. He'd had more than his fair share of one-night stands and flings. His daughter was the result of one of his weekends of fun. Her mother wasn't anyone special to him before he got her pregnant. After he found out she was pregnant, she became one of the most important people in his life. He made an attempt to be her friend and offer her as much support as he was able, but she didn't want that. Nevaeh's mother, Samantha Wiles, made it clear that he was just Nevaeh's father and nothing more. He let it be and focused on giving Nevaeh the best life he could.

Rex wasn't a relationship guy, but he was fully ready to commit to Doc. Sure, that could have a lot to do with his wolf identifying her as his mate, but he had trust in that. After watching his club brothers finding their mates, one right after another, Rex had seen the magic work. He'd seen how wonderful those matchups could be.

He wanted that for himself, which was a surprise, but a welcomed one. The thought of coming home to her being there in his space was tempting. Having her come home from a shift at the clinic to him making her dinner and running her a hot bath was even more tempting. He wanted to provide for her, take care of her, *worship* her. Then, when they stepped foot into their bedroom, he wanted to submit to her every whim.

His heart started pounding faster as visions of what she might do to him flashed into his brain again. That was when he heard the telltale click of high heels on the wood floor of his hallway, slowly getting louder, closer. He could almost picture her slow-walking toward him. His heart started pounding hard enough that he heard the swishing in his ears.

Not wanting to miss a moment, he lifted his head and looked toward the open bedroom door. One beat. Two beats. On the third beat of his heart, she stepped through the doorway, wearing only black lace underclothes and her heels, and Rex swore that his heart stopped beating all together.

His wolf even stopped pacing, instead letting out a howl. And just like that, the word *mine* shot to the front of his mind, confirming what he already knew. Doc was his, he was hers, and he would do whatever it took to complete that bond.

Jolene

After undressing down to her panties, bra, and heels, Jolene grabbed a couple of things from her purse and headed up the stairs. As she ascended, Jolene considered how to handle the evening. The one thing she knew was she was going to ride that man until both of them were breathless and sated. How she got them to that point was still up in the air.

She heard him, and even believed him, when he said he was down for her taking charge, but people said a lot of things when they were faced with possibilities. She would give him a heavy dose of what she needed and see how he reacted. If he was truly down for it, they would be on the right path.

At the top of the stairs, she turned and headed down the upstairs hallway. She passed the first door. It was closed and had a sign hanging from it that said *The princess is out* in purple script. Taking a guess that it was Nevaeh's room, she moved on to the next door. It was open, and she saw that it was a bathroom. Stepping in, she looked around to see what she could use to make their night even more enjoyable. Her eyes landed on the navy loofah mesh hanging from a hook in the shower, next to a pink one. Grabbing the navy one, she left the bathroom and moved on. Passing the next open door, she saw it was the guest room, decorated like he said in green and tan.

The last door in the hallway was toward the end and across the hall from the first three doors. It was open, and there was a faint glow coming from the doorway. Setting the objects she had gathered on a table in the hallway a few feet from the door, she approached the entrance and looked inside.

His head was lifted, and he was staring at the doorway as he laid exactly how she instructed on the bed. He was quite the sight with his hard muscles, tattoos, and impressive cock on display. Rex was a sexual playground for a woman like her. All that body and all the possibilities had her core clenching with anticipation.

As she stood there, taking him in, she heard a low, deep growl right before a blue light shined out from his eyes. She stilled and waited for the fear to build inside her, but it didn't. Instead, she only felt more intrigued by the man.

"I'm taking that as a good sign," she commented as she took three slow steps into the room and put her hands to her bare hips.

"It is," he replied in a voice that was more wolf than man, based on the growl factor.

She gave him a wink before she took the time to look around his room, knowing the anticipation was building for him. The look on his face told her that he wasn't sure what she was going to do. Rex seemed eager to get to the good part, but he wasn't in charge. She was. This was her domain.

His walls and ceiling were textured and a light gray that looked like stone or concrete. Above his headboard was a round painting that looked like the moon. Fitting for a wolf shifter. His bed was covered in navy sheets and pillowcases, and the light gray blankets had been shoved down to the footboard. The black metal frame of the bed was perfect for tying his hands and feet to, causing her to smile.

Yes, this was going to be an enjoyable evening. If nothing else, at least they'd get a night of fun out of it. But she was woman enough to admit that she was hoping for more. The thrill of new partners had worn off years ago. She was ready for steady and was hoping Rex was the right one. From everything she knew about him, he was a good man and a good father. If that extended to her and Beast, she could see them together.

Jolene took a few more steps toward the bed, the sound of her footsteps ceasing as she reached the navy rug that was on the floor under the bed and trunk near the footboard.

All the while, Rex's blue glowing gaze followed her every movement. She could see the tension in his muscles from a man who was fighting his instincts to move and reach out to her. Her smile grew as she noticed that he hadn't moved an inch.

Reaching out, she ran a fingertip softly up his thigh. "You're being so good, laying there, not moving." Her finger slid up and over to his abdomen before following his happy trail down to the tuft of hair above his cock.

Another growl sounded in the air.

"Such a good listener."

"You look... perfect," he practically breathed, his chest heaving with the effort it took to keep himself in place.

Jolene was impressed.

"If we were at my place, I have ties to use for your hands, but we'll have to improvise."

A grin appeared on his face as the blue glow dimmed. "Top drawer," he said and nodded at his dresser to her right.

Turning, she pulled open the drawer and found four navy strips of silky material. Raising a brow, she picked them up and faced him again. "Done some tying of your own?"

"I like to keep things spicy."

Dropping two of the ties back in the drawer and closing it, she moved further up the bed and took hold of the wrist that was closest to her. Lifting it, she ran the back of his knuckles down the valley between her breasts and watched as that blue glow brightened again.

As she lowered his wrist to the bed near the headboard and began to tie him up. "Tell me about the light."

"When a shifter feels extreme emotion, it happens. Like anger, pain, love, lust, etc. Usually, we can keep it in check. It usually only happens when we allow it to or we are pushed beyond our limits."

She nodded and rounded the bed. As she tied the other hand up, she asked, "And what is it now?"

"Lust," he answered, and stared at her. "And I want you to know it."

After he was secured, she reached down and fisted the erection that was lying against his lower abdomen. Giving it a stroke, she replied, "It was already evident, but thanks for that." With a grin, she released him and wasn't surprised at all when his hips lifted off the bed as if to follow her hand and a groan came from his mouth.

Returning to the drawer, she removed another of the ties. They were just wide enough to suit her other purpose, but she would need to buy supplies if they were going to continue this. Compiling a list in her head, she climbed onto the bed, straddled his chest, and wrapped that tie around his head, covering his eyes.

"You're doing really well. You'll be rewarded, but first, we're going to play."

He groaned again. "Fuck. Doc, play all you want."

"Oh, I will."

Doc kissed her way down his chest and abdomen as she climbed off of the bed. His head lifted as if he was trying to see where she was going before it flopped back down. She wasn't gone long, though, only long enough to grab her supplies from the table in the hallway. Setting them on the nightstand next to their glasses of whiskey, she got back on the bed and straddled his hips.

"For a second, I thought you were going to leave me here," he said with a chuckle.

"I wouldn't do that. I make it a point not to let a good erection go to waste."

He snorted a laugh. "Wouldn't want that."

"It would be a shame." Grabbing the loofah, she bent down and put her lips near his ear. "Someone has spent the last hour staring at a handsome biker and wondering what his beard would feel like rubbing against the skin of her thighs. I wonder if it would feel like this." She straightened and reached back, softly dragging the loofah against his inner thigh.

Rex's legs instinctively spread a little, giving her better access, and his breathing picked up. "If you want to know, come up here and sit on my face, Doc. I'd be happy to give you a demonstration."

She tsked and moved the loofah to his other thigh and did the same thing. "You don't get to give orders, Rex."

"Can I make requests? Because if I can, that's a standing request for the rest of forever."

"Patience." She bent down and placed a soft kiss on his lips. "We'll get there."

Chapter Eight

Jolene

Switching out the loofah for the tingling nip and lip balm, Jolene twisted the top off and used her fingertip to apply it to each of his nipples.

When the air hit his nipples, he pulled in a swift breath and breathed out with a quiet chuckle. "That feels… nice."

After removing her bra and doing the same to her own nipples, she put the top back on and returned it to his nightstand.

Grinning, she bent down and blew a steady stream of air on one of them, causing the tingle to intensify and a moan to come from him. She stopped blowing long enough for him to settle, then she switched to the other nipple and sucked on it.

"Fuck yes," he said as his arms pulled on the restraints for the first time.

After releasing his nipple, she blew on it a bit, watching as his jaw tightened and his biceps bulged with the force with which he was fighting his instincts to ravage her. She could see it in every ridge and bulge of his body. He was holding himself so still that he was probably going to feel some aches in the morning from that act alone.

"I feel like it's time to give you a reward," she commented as she slid up further.

"Yes," he panted. She knew from experience that his nipples were still tingling, sending jolts of pleasure through his body. It was one of her favorite bedroom products.

"Open up," she ordered. When his lips parted, she cupped her breast in her hand and ran her nipple along his bottom lip.

As soon as he felt it, his tongue snaked out and began to circle the bud, giving her much the same sensations that he was feeling.

"Suck on it."

He growled again, right before he sucked her nipple into his mouth.

She moaned softly as pleasure shot to her clit, making it ache for his attention. "Release," she whispered, and it took a moment, but he did as she ordered. Moving over a bit, she gave him her other nipple. "Suck."

Rex, being the good little wolf shifter that he was, did as she instructed. As pleasure once again coursed through her, she mentally chided herself for the comment. There was nothing about Rex that was small.

"Release," she told him, even though she wanted him to keep doing that for the rest of their lives.

When he stopped sucking, she pulled away, her gaze landing on his right hand, clutching the tie tightly. He was doing really well at stopping himself from doing what his body was telling him to do, and she felt the need to reward him even more. Luckily, any reward she gave him was pleasure for her, too, so, *bonus*.

As she slid down his hard body, she kissed and licked, stopping briefly at his nipples to reactivate the balm. When she reached the tuft of hair she had ruffled with her fingertip, Rex's breathing had picked up considerably. Smiling, she shifted until she was on her knees between his spread thighs.

"Whatever I do, your hips are not to move unless I give you permission. Do you understand?"

"Yes… Ma'am."

The added honorific had her core clenching. She wasn't someone who would demand one, but the fact that he felt the need to give it to her did the same thing to her body that his lips around her nipple did.

Jolene wrapped her hand around his erection and gave it a stroke before she held it in her open palm and licked up the underside from base to tip. As his breath hissed out of him, she wrapped her lips around the head of his cock and sucked.

"Fuck!" His barked word was followed by the clenching of his hands.

She pulled off and licked around it, teasing him. "You have a choice to make, Rex."

"Wh-what?"

"You can have my mouth or my pussy."

"Fuck," he repeated under his breath. "Uh… whatever you want to give me."

She grinned and replied, "Smart man." She sucked him in, before she pulled off, then repeated the process. Taking him all the way in until the head of his erection was hitting her throat, she moaned, loving how he whimpered from the vibration.

After a few moments, she released his cock and returned to straddling his hips. Reaching up, she pulled the blindfold from his eyes and waited. His gaze shifted to her, and that blue glow was once again shining out at her.

"Doc," he breathed, his chest still heaving.

Retrieving a piece of ice from her glass of whiskey, she held it to his lips. "Suck on that until it's melted." When he opened his mouth to take it in, he ran his tongue along the tips of her finger, once again sending pleasure through her body that settled in her lower abdomen. With a slight smile on her face, she retrieved the condom package from the nightstand and opened it before she put it on him.

Grabbing a pillow from where he had pushed them off to the side, she shoved it under his head, propping him up a bit. She gave him a moment of gentle caresses to his chest and shoulders to calm a bit. When the glow faded and his ice-blue eyes were roaming all over her body, she lifted a bit and took hold of his erection with one hand. Pulling the gusset of her panties aside, she lined him up to her entrance. Staring into his eyes, she slowly lowered onto him.

"Ah fuck, Doc, yes," he moaned as his eyes dropped to where they were joined. "Fuck, you feel amazing."

Cupping her breasts, she lifted and then slid back down, taking him in, and allowing him to fill her. His cock felt beyond good inside of her, bringing her to the edge already. After lifting and dropping a few more times, she settled and retrieved another ice cube from their glass. Again, she held it to his lips and had him take it from her.

As she circled her nipples with her fingertips, she met his gaze. Raw desire filled his eyes, letting her know he was right there with her. He wanted more of her, just as she really wanted to ride him until she couldn't move.

"I want you to suck on these while I ride you," she told him.

Rex bit his bottom lip and moaned. After releasing it, he asked, "Can I move my hips?"

She bent down and brushed her lips against his. "Only because you've listened so well."

Putting her hands to the bed and carefully leaning forward enough so he had access to her nipples, she lifted her hips. When she started to drop back down, his hips lifted. She gasped when the new position and twist of his hips had his erection hitting her in new places. Her clit was twitching with need and rubbing against that tuft of hair just above his cock.

"Rex," she moaned as she quickened her pace, his hips keeping up.

He lifted his head and sucked her nipple into his mouth, the coolness of his mouth tightening the nub, causing her pleasure to build. After biting down slightly on her nipple, he released it and moved to the other.

The throbbing of her clit intensified until it was almost painful. She needed to come, and she needed it now. When he released her nipple, she lifted her upper body and put her hands to his chest for leverage.

As she lifted and dropped, harder and faster each time, Rex was moaning words, encouraging her. "Yes, Doc! Fuck, that feels amazing! *You* feel amazing. So damn sexy."

With every word he gave her, her orgasm grew closer. It built and built until she was tossing her head back as pleasure exploded in her core and radiated out through her limbs. Her muscles tensed, along with her core, as she moaned his name and let her climax wash over her.

Rex

Doc was breathtaking as she embraced her pleasure. Watching her take it from him was something he wanted to do over and over again. Pride filled him as he realized it was him that was giving her that pleasure. Talk about a stroke to his ego.

He liked it when she ordered him to do this or that, telling him what she wanted, but he was surprised at how well she was able to identify what would intensify his pleasure. The sensory play was something he hadn't ever put much thought into. If he would have known what it would do for him, he would have probably spent a hell of a lot more time on that with his previous partners.

As he watched her come back down from her orgasm, he realized that things happened for a reason, and this beautiful, forceful woman was meant to show him that. He grinned as her gaze landed on him. The pink in her cheeks and the slightly glassy look to her eyes had his ego inflating even more, even if he had very little to do with it.

"Your turn," she said as she widened her thighs a bit and started riding him again.

Hell, he had totally forgotten about his own release as he had watched her. Never before in his life had he been so taken by a woman that he didn't even think of his climax in the middle of the act.

"Tell me what you need, Rex," she panted as her pace quickened.

"Your lips," he replied as he pulled his knees up and thrust up against her.

A moan escaped her, and she bent down and drank him in like iced tea on a hot summer day. He groaned as her tongue licked against his bottom lip. Sucking it in, he wrapped his hands around the ties and pulled in an attempt to hold off his orgasm. He wasn't ready for the jolts of sensations and pleasure to stop yet. He wanted to prolong it as much as he could, terrified that it would all disappear as soon as he shot his load, that *she* would disappear, because his brain couldn't quite comprehend how he found the perfect woman.

As they kissed and moved their hips against each other, Rex lost himself in her, in her taste and in her body. His heart was pounding out of his chest, and he lost all control of his hips. They were doing what they wanted. Luckily, they wanted to meet her thrust for thrust.

When the pressure built in his lower back and balls, he broke the kiss and locked eyes with her. His climax shot down his shift and up his spine just as her head fell back and his name left her lips.

Fuck, she was so damn beautiful. He was keeping her, and he would let her tie him up every night, if it meant he got to watch that look cross her face every time.

After she untied his hands and let him take care of the condom, he returned to the bed, and Doc cuddled up to his side. They laid there for a while, caressing each other's skin and trying to get their bearings.

When his heart rate had returned to normal, along with his breathing, he turned his head and left a kiss on her forehead. "I never realized how amazing sensation play could be," he commented, and pulled her tighter against his side. "Then again, I've never given over control so completely before."

"And… did you like it?" She lifted her head from his shoulder and looked into his eyes.

Rex grinned and replied, "I fucking loved it."

"Guess you *can* teach an old dog new tricks."

He snorted a laugh. "Leave it to a veterinarian to figure out how."

As they laughed together, Rex rolled over on top of her and settled between her thighs. He took her lips in a deep, wet kiss. When he pulled back, he asked, "You want to tie me up again this time?" As he spoke, he reached over to grab another condom from the nightstand, this time from his stash in the drawer.

She smirked. "As long as you do what I tell you to, I don't think that will be necessary."

Chapter Nine

Jolene

As Jolene opened her eyes, she felt uncomfortably hot. Groaning, she tried to shove the blankets off of her, but something was holding them in place. Glancing down her body, she saw a blanket covered lump along her waist. Confused, she pulled the blanket away and saw a hairy tattooed arm.

There was a sleepy moan behind her before that arm tightened on her waist, pulling her back against a hard, hot body. *Rex.*

"Can I give you a proper good morning?"

"Gotta potty," Jolene replied, and gave his arm a little shove.

His beard rubbed against her bare shoulder before his lips pressed against her skin. "Hurry back... please."

Jolene smiled at that. He was carefully choosing his words in an effort to please her. He didn't need to do that as a general rule, but they were still in bed, so he was acting accordingly. The thought in the gesture made Jolene want to give Rex a treat. She'd have to think about what to do for him.

Turning her head, she gave a quick kiss on his lips before she climbed out of bed and hightailed it to the restroom.

After doing her business, she returned to the bedroom and stopped just inside the door. Propped up on a mountain of pillows, Rex was lounging on his back with one of his arms bent with his hand behind his head and his other hand resting on his bare abdomen between his belly button and the sheet. One of his legs was stretched out down the bed, and the other was bent and cocked to the side with the sheet covering his fun bits, but he still looked hot as sin. His long hair was loose, spread around him, and those ice-blue eyes were sparking desire as they slowly scanned her still naked body.

When he bit down on his bottom lip as that hand at his abdomen slid down under the sheet and began moving, Jolene pressed her thighs together. He was the biggest temptation she had ever been faced with.

She crossed to the bed and climbed on, his eyes never leaving her. On her knees, between his legs, she reached forward and pulled the sheet down. His actions stopped, but his hand didn't leave his erection.

"Don't stop," she said.

Rex let out a growl and started moving his hand again, up and down. Jolene wrapped her hand around his erection just above his, moving with him. Her gaze trailed up his forearm, following the protruding veins and muscles up to his shoulder and over to her face.

His attention darted between their hands and her breasts. His chest was heaving with his quickened breathing and his teeth were biting down hard enough on his lip to almost break the skin. Letting go of his shaft, she crawled up his body and straddled his abdomen.

As he continued to stroke himself, she leaned forward and gently pulled his lip from his teeth, before pressing her mouth to his. Rex quickly took the lead, and she let him, recognizing his need. She slid her hands into his hair and rolled her hips, using his happy trail to stimulate her clit. Combined with the kissing and the knowledge of what he was doing behind her ass, it was just the right amount of friction to have her riding the edge of climax.

Against her lips, he growled, "I like the way you use me. Just feeling your hot pussy rubbing against me makes me ready to come."

Jolene felt the pressure gathering in her lower abdomen and heat radiating out through her body. She gazed into his eyes, their faces almost touching, and ordered, "Come."

Rex's breath caught as his brows pulled together, and a moment later, she felt the proof of his pleasure hit her ass. That was all it took to send her careening over that edge.

Rex

After their fun in bed, Rex wrapped her up in his arms and carried her to the bathroom. They showered, where he spent a ridiculous amount of time using that navy loofah on her body. Nevaeh bought it for him a year ago, but he had never used it, thinking it to be a waste of money. After what Doc did with it, his mind was thoroughly changed on that.

Once he had her clean and made out with her until the water had gone cold, he dried her off and wrapped her in a towel. While Doc brushed her teeth with one of the new toothbrushes they kept in the cupboard, Rex gathered her clothes and brought them to her.

"Thanks," she said as she dropped her towel and began dressing.

Rex forced himself out of that bathroom, when he really wanted to lift her up onto the counter and have his way with her. He couldn't do that, though, because they both had work to get to. Sure, his brothers would totally understand Rex being late because he was screwing his mate, but he doubted the owner of the veterinarian clinic would feel the same way.

He quickly got dressed, brushed through his hair, and pulled it back into a ponytail at the nape of his neck. He was just sliding his cut onto his shoulders when she stepped into his room and bent down to grab her shoes from the floor.

Because he was a dirty old bastard, he shifted closer and pressed his hips against her backside as his hands settled on her lower back. *Fuck*. Would he always want her like that?

Doc stepped forward and straightened, smirking at him over her shoulder. "Later," she said, and it sounded so much like a promise that Rex let out a little whimper. She began giggling as she strutted out of the room, with him following closely behind her.

After watching Doc drive away in her dark gray Toyota RAV4, Rex checked the weather app on his phone. It looked like it was going to be a clear day, so he decided to take his bike. While the weather in Michigan could turn at the drop of a hat, especially in the fall and winter months, he felt confident he would be fine. He was only going a handful of blocks from his home. If need be, he could borrow the club's van to get home if rain or snow made a sudden appearance.

A smile grew on his face. Or he could have Doc swing by and pick him up.

Decision made, he opened his garage door and went inside. After mounting his bike and walking it out, he started it up and rode it around his truck, down his drive, and onto the street.

His place was one of only a few houses on his block, and he was pretty familiar with all the vehicles that would have a reason to be around there. It was why he noticed the Pathfinder, black with dark tinted windows. It didn't belong. Taking note of the license plate number as he passed it, he kept riding. It was probably nothing, but so much had happened in the previous eighteen months that he felt better erring on the side of caution.

Even with that mindset, when the Pathfinder started up as he reached the stop sign, Rex told himself they probably just happened to be leaving at the same time he was and that it wasn't anything to worry about. He repeated that to himself again and again, but he also noted the hair standing up on the back of his neck and the way his wolf instantly went on alert.

No, fuck that. Something was wrong. He just didn't know what it was.

T.S. Tappin

Chapter Ten

Rex

When Rex walked into the clubhouse, he knew he was scowling. He probably looked like he was ready to murder someone, but he was too focused on thinking about that Pathfinder to care. After crossing the main room, he stepped into the hallway and almost ran into Top.

"Whoa." His club brother and closest friend held up his hand in front of him to stop the collision and gave Rex an odd look. "You good, brother?"

Rex huffed out a sigh and nodded his head. "Yeah, I just…"

"What?" Top put his hands to his hips and waited for Rex to answer.

"I think I was followed here from my house."

"Followed?"

Rex nodded. "A Pathfinder." He gave Top a rundown of what happened. "Probably nothing, but…"

Top cocked a brow. "If your wolf is telling you something's wrong, then there's something wrong. You and I both know that."

Sighing and nodding, Rex crossed his arms over his chest. "We should mention it to Axle and see what he says."

Top gave a nod and turned around. Together, they made their way down to Axle's office.

His door was open when they reached the office. Rex glanced in and saw Axle cradling his baby daughter to his chest. Nugget was the light of his life, but his mate, Gorgeous, was his soul.

Axle looked over and saw them. He waved them in and gave Nugget a kiss on her forehead. "I have a meeting with Crush in twenty minutes, but what's up?"

After he and Top took seats in the chairs across the desk from Axle, Rex ran through what happened when he left his house. Almost instantly, Axle's expression darkened. The contentment of a new father was washed away and replaced with the look of an alpha president, determined to keep the people he cared about safe.

"Did you get the plate?"

Rex nodded.

Axle nodded to the pen and paper sitting on his desk. "Write it down. I'll have Keys look into it." He kissed Nugget's forehead again, before he turned in his chair and laid her down gently in the travel bassinet set up behind his desk. When she didn't wake up, he turned to face them again. "I want you to keep vigilant. Talk to Pike about this. He needs to be ready to make arrangements in case of a bigger issue."

"Will do."

"Did you see anything else?"

After shaking his head, Rex said, "The windows were too darkly tinted for even my shifter sight to see through. When I got to the road to the compound, they slowed but didn't turn. Then they drove off."

Top uttered, "They're either watching or—"

"Looking for opportunity," Axle said darkly. "I won't let them take another one of our family, if I have any say in it. Not. A. Fucking. Gain."

Top calmly said, "None of that was your fault, Axle."

Their president's angry swirling silver gaze shifted from Rex to Top. "Whether it's my fault or not, I will carry the guilt of our losses, *their sacrifices*, for the rest of my life."

Rex hated that Axle felt that so deep, but honestly, they all did. Every member of the Howlers MC and the Tiger's Claw MC felt responsible in some way for every death connected to them. They were supposed to be the protectors, yet they couldn't protect their own. The guilt and the grief were constant companions for them, and probably would be for a good long while.

Messer

Sitting in the backseat of the Pathfinder, Stella Messer listened as the other Elites from Black Forest Academy, a training academy for civilian soldiers and hunters joining the war on shifters, talked about their plans. The academy had been started just four months before, but the owner was a billionaire and money could buy you any resources you needed, except for information. Sometimes, that was a bit trickier to get.

While the other Elites chatted, Messer remained silent. She was stripped of any authority when she returned to BFA a couple months before without any new information on shifters and their abilities to assist the academy in their mission to eradicate them. She had been able to tell them where certain members of the Howlers MC and the Tiger's Claw MC lived, as well as some basic information about names, but that was all. Even with the help of some townspeople, and a man named Matthew, the details she was able to uncover were sparse. The clubs had been really good about not letting outsiders close.

After weeks of investigating, she was called back to the academy to answer for her inability to get the job done. Even with the help of Matthew, they were unable to gather new intel or to confirm or deny the information they were given by other townsfolk.

"I still say we should have more than one vehicle," Elite O'Halleron grumbled as she shifted in her seat to Messer's left as they shared the backseat of the Pathfinder.

"For the fifth time," Elite Perez bit out, "we don't know what they are capable of, since *someone* was unable to do her damn job, so we aren't splitting up."

Messer's anger rose inside of her as she stared at the back of Elite Perez's head while he drove. "I may not be great at gathering intel, but I could kill you without breaking a sweat."

The Pathfinder swung over to the side of the road and came to a stop. Elite Perez's gaze met hers in the rearview mirror, fury blazing in his dark brown eyes, peeking out from under perfectly tweezed brows, and he replied, "You're welcome to try, *subordinate*."

She would bide her time, Messer decided. At one point, the fucker would let his guard down, and she would make sure he regretted every jab he had thrown at her on that trip. She was taking note, keeping a tally. *You will pay, Perez, and it will feel so good.*

"That's what I thought," the fucker said smugly and pulled back into traffic.

Staring at the back of his head with narrowed eyes, Messer swallowed down all the words she wanted to say. *Let him think he had the upper hand.* It was the best course of action at the time. *Then make him pay.*

Jolene

Jolene told herself it would not be appropriate or professional to flip off Dr. Thatcher. It was the third time in ten minutes she had to give herself that reminder. She arrived at the clinic five minutes late, because she had to go home to change into her scrubs and take care of Beast. She was rarely late, but you wouldn't know that with the way he was going on.

"You're supposed to be professional," Dr. Thatcher grumbled as they both stood at the desk, looking over the patient paperwork.

One. Two. Three. Four. Five. Six. Seven. Eight. Nine. Ten. After completing her ten-count and feeling a bit calmer, Jolene replied, "Yes, and I'm sorry for being late. I will do my best not to be in the future."

"You do that," he stated, and stomped away.

Jolene rolled her eyes. When they landed on the receptionist, Marcie, the younger woman gave her a sympathetic smile and handed her a fresh coffee in an insulated mug with a lid.

"You are an angel," Jolene told her and took the mug. "I'm going to apologize now for his bad mood."

It was Marcie's turn to roll her eyes. "When *isn't* he in a bad mood?"

"Fair enough," Jolene said with a smile, before she took a deep breath and headed back to get started on seeing her patients.

Chapter Eleven

Jolene

By the time lunch rolled around, Jolene had lost all patience with Dr. Thatcher. She wanted to punt his five-foot-five-inch body out the plate-glass window in the lobby, but then she would most definitely lose her job. Then how would she pay for Beast's daily dose of *you're such a good boy* treats?

No, she couldn't punch her boss… no matter how much the balding asshole deserved it.

Every time she brought up new ways to improve the flow of the clinic or better ways to treat patients, he instantly shot her ideas down and went on a rant about his *years of experience* and how she *couldn't possibly understand his reasons for doing things.*

Usually, she just ignored him and did what she thought was right. He never knew, and it kept the other staff members from having to make excuses for long wait times.

That day, he blamed every issue on her being late. How her arriving five minutes after her normal start time, but fifteen minutes before the door opened, caused them to have more patients than a typical

Tuesday, she didn't know. Jolene was just sick of being his punching bag.

She was about to tell him where he could shove the job, but he announced he was taking the afternoon off. The second he walked out of the office, the rest of the staff cheered. She loved every single staff member they had. Jolene had wanted to start a clinic of her own, but she would buy the place if the old coot ever decided to retire and sell.

It was too bad he didn't realize the treasure he had when it came to the vet techs and reception staff who kept the place running.

She shook off her irritation with her boss and her thoughts about buying the place and focused at the task at hand. They *were* busier than a normal Tuesday, and now it was all resting on her shoulders. Glancing at the clock on the wall, she noticed that it was her typical lunch time.

With Dr. Thatcher gone, she wouldn't be able to leave to let Beast out or to grab food. She needed to make arrangements.

Rex

Rex was sitting at one of the tables in the cafeteria, hanging with Axle's family, Gorgeous and Nugget, while Axle had a meeting with the president of the Tiger's Claw MC, Crush, about club business. Since the two clubs were closely allied, shared the compound, and owned numerous businesses together, they often needed to meet to go over details of one sort or another.

Gorgeous had been trying to eat, but Nugget had thrown a stink every time Gorgeous lifted her fork to her mouth. Feeling bad for the new mom, Rex had sat down in a chair next to the seven-month-old's highchair and tried to distract her. He was attempting to play patty cake with Nugget when his phone vibrated in the pocket of his cut.

"Are you gonna start yelling if I answer my phone?" he asked the blond beauty who was showing off her new tooth as she laughed with her mouth wide open. "I know how jealous you can be when I give other people my attention."

The baby cooed and giggled in response.

Rex smiled at her as he pulled his phone from his pocket and answered it. "Yeah."

"Hey. You got a minute?"

Hearing Doc's voice on the other end of the line, Rex focused on the phone call. "Yeah. What's up? You good?"

"Just busy. Dr. Thatcher left for the day on a huff, and we're busy. I have Mama Hen going to let Beast out, but I don't have time to go grab lunch. Is there any way you could bring me something? If you're too busy, I understand."

"Doc, if you need something, you can always call me. What do you want me to grab?"

"Is this appropriate conversation for my baby girl to hear?" Gorgeous asked him with a grin on her face.

He gave her a wink and listened as Doc answered him, "I'm not picky. Just something I can nibble on while I do paperwork and check over lab results and such."

"Will a chicken bacon ranch wrap from TC's Diner work?"

He heard her quietly groan and the memory of her making that sound while riding his cock came to mind, making Rex have to discreetly adjust himself in his jeans. "Yes, that sounds wonderful. And a pop. Not picky about what kind. Just not diet."

"Be there in twenty," he informed her as Nugget yanked his finger to her mouth and began to gnaw on it.

"Thank you," Doc said.

"No need to thank me for taking care of you," he told her. "See you soon." After ending the call, he looked over at Nugget and raised a brow. "That can't taste good."

Gorgeous laughed and handed him Nugget's teething ring. "So... you and the vet who treated Bullet?"

He narrowed his eyes on the beautiful blond woman Axle had claimed, mated, and married. Her real name was Ashlyn, but everyone who had any connection to the club called her Gorgeous. It was her Ol' Lady name, and calling her that was considered a sign of respect in their culture.

"Who told you about Doc?"

Gorgeous rolled her eyes. "You Howlers are the most gossipy gossips I ever met in my life. Bullet told Butterfly who told all of the Ol' Ladies, so when Axle brought it up, I already knew."

"We aren't gossips," Rex protested, but when the woman he loved like a sister just stared back at him, he nodded. "Okay. Yeah, we are."

"Might as well be a bunch of new hosts of one of those morning talk shows where they talk about the latest fashions and which celebrity is dating which reality star and which athlete is getting divorced."

Rex snorted a laugh as he stood. He bent down and left a smacking kiss on Nugget's chubby cheek, making the baby break out in belly laughs. "Wanna get lunch next week, Nugget? How about same time, same place?" He winked at Gorgeous before he headed out of the clubhouse and across the street to get his woman some food.

Jolene

Sitting at her desk in the back area of the clinic, Jolene was typing notes for a patient into the computer system when a couple of the vet tech's came down the hall, whispering. It wasn't until they stopped next to her desk that she lifted her head and looked over at them. They were both standing there, staring at her with grins on their faces.

"What?"

The two techs looked at each other then back at her. Julie, the brunette, hiked a thumb over her shoulder, gesturing toward the front of the clinic. "There's a sexy biker out there with a lunch delivery for you. We thought he was a delivery guy or something, but he won't let us take the bag of food."

Helen, the redhead, shook her head and somehow managed to grin bigger. "Said he needed to see you. And when we asked what his name was, he said, *Tell her that her man's here*. His vest says, *Rex*."

"Cut," Doc immediately corrected, distracted by his use of the words *her man*. She didn't remember them having that discussion.

"What do you want us to do?" Julie asked.

"You can send him back," Jolene answered and returned to her notes, intent on finishing the current chart before she ate.

The girls walked away, giggling. Two minutes later, Jolene felt lips and a beard brush up against the side of her neck, then a bag of food was set on her desk next to her keyboard.

"Chicken bacon ranch wrap, an order of onion rings, and a piece of chocolate cream pie." He set a to-go cup next to the bag. "And a non-diet cherry cola."

"Thank you." She turned in her chair and looked up at him.

Rex took that opportunity to give her a proper kiss.

When he pulled away, she asked, "My man?"

He shrugged, looking hot as hell. He was wearing the same thing he'd been wearing the night before, jeans and a white tee under his cut, even though it was fucking December, but it was a great look on him. "I am."

"You are?"

His eyes narrowed, but they were amused. "Am I not?"

"We didn't have that conversation," she said.

Rex bent down, putting a hand on each side of her on the desk, boxing her in. With his face only inches from her, he countered, "When we talked, and you told me what you needed and I picked a safe word, I became your man."

"We've had one night together," she said quietly.

"Doc, if I'm being honest, I was yours the second you swatted me on the head and called me a bad dog months ago." The grin that grew on his face made her want to drag him into the nearest exam room and have a repeat of their activities from the night before.

"We barely know each other."

"I know enough, and I could explain why, but you don't have time for that conversation. So how about I meet you at your place at seven, and we talk about it over the pizza I'm going to bring with me?"

"You have a way with assuming things and expecting me to go along with them."

Rex nipped at her bottom lip. "You telling me not to come over? After all, you're the one in charge between us. Give the order, Doc."

She narrowed her eyes on him, but she didn't say anything. The truth was she wanted the sexy wolf shifter biker to play with her in her bedroom where she kept all her supplies, so there was no way she was telling him to stay away.

He quietly chuckled. "Yeah. See you at seven." He took her lips in a scorching hot, but way too brief kiss, before he backed off and turned to head to the front.

That was when they both noticed Julie and Helen peeking around the corner at the other end of the hall, watching them.

Louder than necessary, Rex said, "I'll plan on staying at your place when I come over, Doc. Have a great afternoon." Then his sexy ass casually strolled down the hall, like he wasn't just fueling office gossip.

T.S. Tappin

Chapter Twelve

Rex

When he walked out of the clinic and mounted his bike, Rex slipped his sunglasses on his face. As he pulled his hair back into a manbun, he glanced around and saw that Pathfinder parked a block down the road, facing him. Doing his best to pretend he didn't notice anything, he started his bike and checked for traffic, before he pulled away from the curb and did a U-turn. When he saw in his mirror that the Pathfinder began to follow, he barked out a curse and put on the speed. It was not a coincidence. He was being followed. He needed to have that talk with Pike.

Rex attempted to make turns to try to lose them, but it was almost as if they knew where he was going. Scrapping the decision to go to Pike's house, Rex headed for the compound. He needed to speak with their tech genius and have Keys check his bike for tracking devices.

Giving up trying to lose them, almost hoping the Pathfinder would follow him into the compound, but knowing they probably wouldn't, Rex turned right on the street that ran along the side of the Hen House.

Three blocks down, he turned onto the street that held the compound and watched in his mirror. The Pathfinder slowed to a stop at the entrance, and the window came down halfway.

Rex pulled off to the side and got off his bike quickly. Turning, he reached for his gun, not sure what they planned to do. He had just pulled his gun from the holster in his cut when the lens of a camera poked out. A few moments later, the window rolled up, and the Pathfinder took off.

As he returned his gun to his holster, Rex was still staring at the entrance to the compound when he heard Keys ask, "What the fuck was that?"

Rex swung his gaze to Keys and saw Ranger and Top standing with him. He made eye contact with Top. "That's the Pathfinder that was following me this morning."

"Wait." Keys held up a hand and asked, "What? You're being followed?"

After giving a nod, Rex explained what had happened that morning as well as the recent events, once he left the clinic. Keys listened intently, then he asked Rex to move his bike to the parking lot and said he'd be right back.

Rex moved his bike, and while they waited for Keys to return, members from both the Howlers and the Claws began to gather in the lot around him.

When Keys came out of the clubhouse, he had a small handheld device with a small antenna, a red light, and a small digital screen on it. They silently watched as Keys approached Rex's bike and slowly ran the device along it, keeping a few inches of distance. Nothing happened.

Keys glanced over at Rex and shook his head. "No tracking device. Let me see your phone."

Rex handed over his phone, Keys began to do his thing. "Did you run that plate I gave to Axle yesterday?"

Keys nodded. "It was reported stolen, so no luck there." As he hunched over the phone, his longish hair falling forward to shield his face from view, the members around him began discussing the situation.

"I noticed the same vehicle behind me twice yesterday," Shortcake said.

"Me too," Rock added with a nod.

"I might have, too," Pumps admitted. "I thought it was just two vehicles that looked alike."

Axle sighed. "We're going to have to be more vigilant."

Crush nodded and crossed her arms over her chest. "Maybe we need to stay in pairs until—"

"There is no way in hell I'm bringing one of you bastards to Doc's house with me tonight," Rex blurted and winced when he realized he said it louder than was necessary.

It felt like every eye in the crowd landed on him, but it was Score who opened his damn mouth and had something to say. "Doc, huh?" He stepped closer and took a sniff before he nodded and chuckled. "Feeling ill, Rex?"

"Fuck off," Rex grumbled.

"Did she run your insurance? Check your shot record to make sure you're up to date on your—"

Top's hand covered Score's mouth, cutting off his bullshit. Too bad Top didn't have twelve more hands, because Score wasn't the only one who had something to say.

"Flea bath?" Ranger grinned and quickly stepped away because he wasn't a stupid man.

"Don't let her near your balls," Trip uttered.

"Do you get a biscuit if you're a good boy?" Rex was shocked when those words came out of Dragon's mouth as a knowing grin appeared on his face.

"If he shows up with a cone," Skull began but he couldn't finish because he was cackling too loudly.

"Your phone is good. No tracking apps besides ours," Keys told him through a grin.

After snatching his phone from Keys's outstretched hand, Rex mounted his bike and started it, drowning out the rest of the dumbasses. He ignored the laughing assholes and the Claws as he rode out of the parking lot.

He didn't know how the Pathfinder was keeping track of him, but listening to the shit from his club brothers wasn't going to help him figure it out. He'd just keep his eyes open and be on alert.

Jolene

When Jolene finished helping her last patient, she quickly notated the chart and said goodbye to the rest of the staff. She was exhausted and wanted to get in a hot shower before Rex showed up at her place.

The drive to her house was a blur. Her body was on autopilot. When she pulled into her driveway and noticed Rex's truck parked at the curb, Jolene worried she'd be too exhausted to make their night anything but laid back. She'd see where the night took them.

Their relationship was so new that she didn't want to already be at the point of a movie and crashing out, but they were both near forty, and life was what it was. Energy was a hot commodity, but it was also fleeting.

After making her way into the house, she dropped her stuff on the table next to her front door and bent down to greet Beast. He was happy to see her, his body shaking with his excitement.

Scratching behind his ears, she softly uttered, "How was my little beast today? Did you have a good time with Mama Hen and Maxie? I bet you did."

"What I would give to have you touch me like that," Rex said in his sultry, deep voice from across the room.

She glanced up and found him leaning against the doorjamb to her kitchen with both his arms and ankles crossed. His long gray and blond hair was pulled up in a manbun, making him look ten years younger than he was. Instead of a tee like he had been wearing earlier in the day, he was wearing a charcoal gray, long-sleeved Henley under his cut, along with a pair of dark blue jeans that fit the man too damn well. Once again, his feet were bare, topping off the sexy package he presented.

"If you're a good boy," she said and gave him a smile as she straightened and kicked off her shoes.

He winked at her. "I tried to feed Beast, but he won't come in the kitchen."

"I think he's scared of you," she replied. "The night you brought me home and put me to bed, I found him hiding under a bed the next morning."

"Why? I've never hurt him. I wouldn't." His brows pulled together in concern.

She snorted a laugh. "Because you're the bigger dog."

His eyes narrowed for a moment, then he smiled and mumbled, "Ruff."

As she crossed the room and approached him, she asked, "Did you bring the pizza, Fido? I'm hungry."

Rex unfolded his arms and wrapped them around her, pulling her close. "So am I," he replied, his tone making it clear what he wanted to eat. "And yes, the pizza is on the counter. It should still be hot. Sit down and get comfortable. I'll bring it to you."

"I'm supposed to be giving the orders."

Staring down at her with his ice-blue eyes sparking fire, he replied, "If you want to forgo dinner and head right to the bedroom, you can give all the orders you want."

Her stomach took that moment to growl, telling her his suggestion was not an option.

After he took her empty plate from her hand and brought their dishes to the kitchen, Rex returned to the room right as she lifted a hand to rub at her right shoulder. His brows pulled together, and he moved behind her couch in the center of the room. Pushing her hands away, his large, strong hands massaged out the knots in her upper back and shoulders. Jolene closed her eyes and let out a moan as he worked his magic.

When his fingers moved up to her neck, she dropped her head forward, took deep breaths, and released them slowly. All of her stress and tension eased out of her.

He worked his way over her scalp and back down her neck before taking hold of both of her shoulders. As his massage gentled, his lips and tongue caressed the side of her neck, making a different type of tension work its way through her body.

"Can't have you stressed, Doc," he whispered near her ear. "Is that better?"

"Mmhmm," she mumbled before she turned her head and kissed his lips. When she pulled back and looked into his eyes, the sexual desires in her warred with the part of her that just wanted to cuddle up with him and do nothing. "You okay with watching a movie or something for a while? I just want to relish this relaxation."

He smiled and winked at her, before he rounded the couch and sat down as close as he could get, while also grabbing her television remote from the coffee table. Sliding his arm around her shoulders, he pulled her against him.

Jolene cuddled into his side and sighed. For the next few hours, they didn't say much to each other. It was nice that they could just *be* without anyone feeling awkward. Every once in a while, his fingers would distractedly play with her hair or he would turn his head and kiss her temple, but that was it. It was *easy*.

Every moment she spent with him, she learned more about the gruff, rough biker and liked it all.

Not only was he a good father and a good friend, but he was also thoughtful and kind. He worried about her dog not taking to him right away. He ran her lunch, dropping everything to do so. He was open-minded and gave over his complete trust in the bedroom. Rex was exactly the type of man she would have picked for herself if she had made a checklist.

For fuck's sake, he could cook and made grocery store runs. If he made a decent cup of coffee, she'd be hard pressed not to propose to the man on the spot.

"What's going on in that gorgeous head of yours?" He kissed her temple again. "Your hand just fisted in my shirt."

As she forced her hand to loosen, Jolene looked at him and gave a slight smile. She wasn't about to tell him what she had been thinking. "You up for some playtime?"

Rex chuckled as he took her hand from where it was lying on his abdomen and shifted it down to the bulge in his jeans. "Doc, that's a question you never need to ask. The answer is always yes."

She leaned toward him and nipped his jaw before she stood up and ordered, "Stay."

Chapter Thirteen

Rex

When Doc came up behind him while he sat on the couch and slipped the blindfold over his eyes, Rex smiled and let her lead him wherever she wanted him to go. He had a moment of sadness when she shoved him down on her bed that he didn't get to see what her bedroom looked like at night, but that passed when he felt her hands run up under the front of his shirt to caress his abdomen and pecs.

"What's your safe word?"

Her question was said softly, but he heard her clearly. "I won't need it."

"That wasn't my question," she said more firmly.

Rex chuckled but answered, "Whiskey."

"And when do you use it?"

"If something is too much or I want the situation to stop."

Her lips pressed to the skin just above the waistband of his jeans. "Good boy."

He couldn't help but let out a moan. Just that touch of her lips alone would have had him ready if he hadn't been already.

The deep, sensual chuckle had his blood racing. He would do anything to please his woman, even if it was just letting her do what she wanted to him. He would gladly play pawn in her sexual games for the rest of his life.

"How attached to this shirt are you?"

"It's yours to use as you see fit." It was true. Rex had a drawer full of Henleys, and he would happily buy more just to let her destroy them.

A pleased hum filled his ears as her hands caressed his sides and over his abdomen again. "Excellent answer. I'll have to reward you, but what. Shall. I. Do?"

"Whatever pleases you the most." The words popped out automatically, but they were an honest accounting of his position. He'd always enjoyed pleasing a woman, but with Doc, it was a whole new level of enjoyment. It was all-consuming. With her, it was a give and take. He'd been rewarded by her before for being agreeable, and it had been nothing short of mind-blowing. She could choose anything she wanted, and he'd love every second of it.

"Being a teacher's pet will get you everywhere."

Her lips met his, and he opened up, letting her slide her tongue inside. He moaned into her mouth as it tangled with his, and the kiss turned scorching. Between the kiss and not being able to see her, he was consumed with the sensations pouring through his body, making his toes curl. About the time he was debating whether or not air was really necessary, Doc broke off the kiss and slipped away from him. Immediately, he missed and craved more of her touch.

Doc pulled his shirt up ever so slightly, kissing along the waistband of his jeans. It was one of the few times Rex regretted wearing denim as he wanted her mouth closer to his dick, not blocked by thick fabric. Distracted by his internal self-lecture, when something thin, cold, and metallic was pressed against his skin, he inhaled sharply through his teeth.

It was too thin and heavy to be an eating utensil, but that only made his mind race with all the possibilities of what it *could* be. The only things coming to mind were edge weapons, and Rex didn't think she would use those without specifically asking him.

All was made clear when there was pressure and the very recognizable sound of fabric being cut by sharp scissors. With each snip, the cool metal slowly moved up his chest. Each movement sent goosebumps racing over his skin and made him a little harder. About the time the tip of the scissors approached where he knew his beard ended, he tensed. He couldn't see them with the blindfold covering his eyes, but he could feel the sliding of the metal along his skin and could envision where his beard was laying. He liked his beard. It had taken a while to grow, and he didn't want to sacrifice it, but for her, he admitted to himself he probably would.

The scissors left his skin, and Doc's soft lips were nibbling along his neck as her hand took the same path that the scissors had. "I wouldn't dream of touching your beard with anything other than my hands or my pussy," she whispered into his ear, sending shivers through his body.

The thought of her riding his beard had him moaning the words, "Yes, Ma'am."

Her breath hitched slightly at his response, and his wolf was also satisfied that Doc was pleased, solidifying what he already knew — Doc was their mate.

"Now, where were we?"

Rex swallowed hard and cleared his throat. "I believe you were about to remove my shirt."

"That I was."

The next thing Rex knew, a tearing sound filled the air, the result of finishing off his Henley, and then it was no longer covering him.

Immediately, Doc's lips and tongue were licking and biting his nipples, pulling groans from him as bolts of pleasure went straight to his cock. "I decided I didn't want to risk a single hair on that sexy head of yours."

As suddenly as her lips were all over his chest, they were gone, and an involuntary whimper came out. He needed to feel her touch. It had become his reason for breathing, or that might have been his erection talking.

Doc gently swatted his nose. "You know damn well I'm not done yet."

The scratch and hiss of a match caught his attention, followed by the smell of sulfur. *Was she lighting candles?*

Moments later, something hot splashed on his chest and the scent of lemon filled his nose. It surprised him and while it was alarming, causing his body to jolt, it wasn't too painful. Before he could overthink it, more of the hot liquid was poured lower on his stomach. Rex bit his lip at the sensation.

He thought the heat would have been too much, but it cooled off quickly enough, lulling him into an odd sense of security.

And then his phone rang.

Axle's ringtone. Shit.

Rex groaned, knowing he had to answer it, especially after what they had talked about earlier in the day, but he *really* didn't want to.

Doc chuckled and slid away, the bed shifting as if she left it. His suspicion was confirmed when she next spoke, since she had taken his phone from him when they first stepped into the bedroom, and he had heard it hit a wood surface. She sounded as if she was across the room when she said, "The screen says *Prez*. Should I answer it? Make you talk to him while I whip the wax off you?" Her voice held a smirk as if she liked the idea of someone listening as she worked on him.

For as much as he didn't want to talk to Axle right then, the thought of telling Doc *no* and disappointing her felt like a worse fate. Resigning himself to the fact that he was going to be hearing about the call for the foreseeable future, Rex choked out, "Yes, please."

"Excellent. Let's see how many strikes I can get in. You will sound completely calm, as if nothing is happening. Understand?"

He nodded, taking a deep breath and nearly choking when her hand cupped his balls through his pants and gave them a gentle squeeze.

"Use your words."

"Yes, Ma'am," he groaned.

"I'm answering the call now."

Rex braced himself for everything that was about to happen as he called out, "What's up, Prez?"

Crack.

Whatever Doc was using to whip Rex hit the cooled and hardened wax, and he barely swallowed back the moan that threatened to come out. The mixture of the sting from the whip and the wax peeling away from his skin had his cock throbbing even more.

"Everything okay over there?" Axle asked, sounding sincerely concerned.

If you only knew. Rex cleared his throat. "Just fine."

"Doc's okay?"

Crack.

The strike hit on the edge of the wax and caught some of the more sensitive flesh near his nipple. Half a moan came out before he could cough over it. "Yup. She's great." *And too damn good at this. Shit.* He didn't realize how much he liked pleasure pain.

"Nothing out of the ordinary?"

Other than me being tied up to bed, blindfolded, covered in wax, and being whipped? No, nothing out of the ordinary here. "Everything's qu… quiet here," Rex stuttered through the word as another strike hit, and she stroked his cock through the fabric of his jeans before she unzipped them. Next thing he knew, her hand was slick and was around his cock. This woman was going to be the death of him. Death by sex. He could live with that.

Was that heated lube? And when did she lube up her hand?

There was a snicker on the other end of the call. "What are your plans for tomorrow?"

This fucker. "I was planning on swinging by…" Rex grunted as the whip licked his skin again. "Swinging by the clubhouse in the morning after I—" Rex gasped as Doc deepthroated his very erect and leaking cock. "I drop Doc off at work." He was barely able to get the words out of his mouth as pleasure coursed through him.

"Are you sure you're okay? You don't sound like yourself."

Fucker!

Doc chuckled, and the vibrations on my dick nearly sent him over the edge. Rex desperately needed this call to end so he didn't have to control himself anymore.

"Axle, with all the respect I have, if you don't fucking hang up right now, I'm going to, and then I'll call Gorgeous."

He growled. "I hear you, Rex. Have a good night." He half-sang the last word, then began to chuckle.

Rex knew the call had ended when Axle's chuckle was cut off.

"Good boy. Now, I want to hear every moan while I clean off the rest of the wax, and then the *real* fun can start."

What else does she have planned?

"Now, no more listening." Headphones landed on his ears, and everything went silent.

As she yanked off his jeans, he examined what he was feeling. His wolf was content but still excited, and so was Rex. For him, it was odd being completely cut off from visual and auditory clues, but he was again surprised by the rush of arousal that washed over him. If he had to guess, it had more to do with the person he was experiencing it with and less to do with the actions. Because of that, he didn't fight it one bit when she lifted his hands above his head and secured them together with a soft strap of some sort.

His wolf was pacing inside of him, but not from anxiety. No, his wolf was anxious to see how their mate was going to make them feel good, and also maybe a bit impatient to get inside of her.

The next thing he knew, she was straddling his hips and her naked core was rubbing down his throbbing length, pulling a moan from him. His focus was narrowed on the slide of her wet pussy along his erection, which is why he jumped when something new was added to the equation, something soft that lightly caressed his skin as it followed the ridges formed by his tensed abdomen.

T.S. Tappin

The rhythm of her hips slowed a bit as the soft caresses worked their way up his abdomen and onto his chest. Rex's cock was so hard it was almost painful. In an effort to ease some of the ache, he bent his knees slightly and began to rock his hips opposite the motion of hers, increasing the pressure and friction. The feather-light caresses around one of his nipples, then the other, had his breath catching in his throat. *Fuck.* His woman knew exactly how to slowly build his pleasure. She knew better than he did how to satisfy him. Damn, if that in itself wasn't sexy as fucking hell.

When he felt her thighs tighten around him as her hips rolled, Rex sucked in a breath and held it as he bit his bottom lip and waited. Three seconds later, he was rewarded when his woman climaxed, and a rush of wetness coated his cock and slid down to his balls. He released the breath he had been holding on a moan. Even though he had a very small role in that masterpiece, a surge of pride filled him, and his wolf let out a satisfied howl.

After her thigh muscles relaxed, he was curious about what she would do next, but he was still surprised when another object was pressed against his skin. He suspected it was made of plastic and was a wheel of some sort. He knew that by the way it rolled along, but it must have been topped with spikes or something, if the small stings that accompanied its path were anything to go by. Every prick of his skin, every small bite of pain had him rolling his hips against her core and moaning.

Rex was on the edge. He didn't know how much longer he could hold out. He wanted to be inside of her and fucking her for everything he was worth. The urge to make her scream his name was strong, and it was amplified by the panting and pacing of his wolf.

It seemed like forever that she ran that wheel along the skin of his chest and abdomen, his calves and thighs, and his sides, but it was probably only a few minutes. All he knew was that his every nerve ending was on full alert for her touch.

Suddenly, one side of the headphones was pushed aside, and Doc's voice was silky smooth with arousal as she said, "I'm going to release your hands. You are going to roll us over and fuck me the way you obviously want to. Understood."

"Yes. Fucking. Ma'am," Rex growled out, his chest moving up and down at a rate that would normally have him thinking about heart attacks and such, but he pushed that thought aside. His mate was a doctor, and she didn't seem concerned.

The sound of Velcro being pulled apart ripped through the air, then his hands were free. He didn't waste time. She wanted him to fuck her, and that was exactly what he was going to do. After wrapping his arms around her, he rolled them, adjusted his hips, and slammed inside of her.

Fuuuuuck! The feel of her tight wet heat around him was like breath to his lungs — It was everything he needed.

The pace he set wasn't slow, but it was steady. He fucked her hard and fast, soaking up every moan or catch of breath or gasp he was causing. They were beautiful sounds that he cherished, but she wasn't screaming his name, and he wouldn't stop until he got it.

One of his hands slid up her side and cupped her breast. He twirled her nipple between his thumb and forefinger, grinning when she barked out a curse. He wanted to see her face, but he wouldn't take the blindfold off until she told him to, so he would have to be satisfied with the sounds and the feelings from their lovemaking.

"Yes," she moaned and pressed her heels into his ass when he curled his hips just right. "Just like that."

"What else do you need, Ma'am?" The way her core clenched on him when he used the honorific had him vowing to use it more often.

"Stimulate my clit," she ordered, causing Rex to growl. He liked when she used her Domme voice on him.

"Yes, Ma'am." He slid the hand that had been around her tit down her abdomen and to her slit. After taking a moment to caress where they were joined, he moved his finger to her clit and circled it as he kept fucking her and curling his hips on every thrust.

After yanking out the hair tie holding it back, Doc dug her hands into his hair and pulled his face to hers. As she held him to her with a double grip, he took her mouth in a deep, wet kiss. The position had him rubbing against her at multiple spots and also increased the pressure he was applying to her clit.

As the first telltale clenches of her pussy told him she was close to orgasm, Doc shoved the blindfold up. His eyes had just refocused on her as her head shot back into the pillow and his name came from her lips in a long, drawn-out moan. The sound went straight to his dick, causing his balls to pull up tight, and blue light to shine from his eyes, bathing her face.

"Fuck, Doc," he growled as he lost his rhythm, slammed inside of her, and let himself fly off the edge of that cliff into the sweet ecstasy that was his mate.

His wolf howled inside of him as he emptied himself inside of her, and they rode out their pleasure together. His gums tingled as he fought the urge to let his fangs slide down and bite into her shoulder. He wanted to claim her, the desire increasing tenfold every time he was in her presence, but he told his wolf and the urge to shut the hell up. He knew Doc wasn't ready for that.

Finally able to take in another breath, Rex did so and looked down at the woman that had thoroughly rocked his world and had him re-evaluating his life from a different perspective. She was the most beautiful creature he had ever met.

Bright blue eyes looked up at him, sated and half-closed. Her lips tipped up in a smile. "You have no idea how hot you are when you're restrained and naked."

Rex grinned down at her. "I'm glad you think so." He dropped his head down a couple inches and pressed his lips to hers. When he pulled back a bit, he whispered against her lips, "I love everything you do to me."

"Well, that's good, because I have no intention of stopping."

Rex kissed her lips again as he withdrew from her. When he reached down to take hold of the base of the condom, he realized he never put one on. *Fuck!*

"Uh…"

She let out a sigh, then she chuckled. "So… we should know better at our age, but alas, we do not."

"Shifters don't contract human STDs, and before you ask, no, I don't know how that is medically possible, and no, I'm not going to be your guinea pig while you try to figure out why."

"We'll discuss that again another time," she said, letting him know he hadn't talked himself out of her *research.* "Pregnancy is another matter, obviously, since you said Nevaeh's mother is full-human."

He nodded and opened his mouth to confirm, but she started speaking again.

"Luckily, I've been on the pill for as long as I can remember. I have no desire to have children. Beast is enough for me."

"So… we're probably good."

She nodded.

He nipped her bottom lip. "That's good… because I liked feeling just you."

"And the warming lube."

He chuckled. "And that." He kissed his way down her neck as he shifted off of her. "I'll be back to clean you up."

Chapter Fourteen

Jolene

As Jolene watched him prepare coffee the next morning, she had a hard time not dragging him back to her bedroom. He was wearing nothing but his jeans, which were unbuttoned, and his hair was loose and wild. It made her think about how much fun they had making it that way.

After cleaning her up the night before, he started at her ankles and kissed his way up her body, not missing an inch. It was lazy and playful, but it also had a sensual edge that had her desperately wanting him by the time he made it to her lips. Without saying a word, she had wrapped her legs around his waist.

The man was good with clues, because he arched a brow and grinned a moment before he slid inside of her. That time it was all about soft caresses and a slow, steady pace, nothing urgent or creative.

When she woke up in his arms, loose and relaxed, and not remembering the last time she had been that way, she decided the man had earned a reward. Between the massage, the cuddling on the couch, and the sex, she felt refreshed. It wasn't something she was used to.

He moaned into her neck and tightened his arm around her waist. "I don't want to get up."

"Okay. Well… you just lay here," she had told him and pulled his arm away from her. "I'll shelf that shower BJ for another morning, then."

She had never seen a grown man move that fast.

Laughing, she followed him into her bathroom. She wasn't at all surprised to find him standing under the spray that had to be still too cold, but there he was, soaping up his body as he shivered. Jolene appreciated the fact that he wanted to be freshly clean before she got her mouth close to him. She had also been amused to find that the cold water did nothing to shrink the erection he had been sporting.

"Is it cold still?"

He nodded, but after a few moments, he said, "It's getting warmer now."

She grabbed a couple towels out of the linen closet in the corner, along with the foam mat she used when she had to scrub the floor. After dropping the towels on the edge of the counter next to the sink, she headed for the shower. When his eyes dropped down to the mat in her hand, she shrugged. "My knees aren't what they used to be, and that stone is hell on them."

Rex's expression said, *impressed,* as he nodded and pushed open the glass shower door to let her in. "Can I borrow that when it's my turn?"

"My mat is your mat," she replied as she dropped it to the ground between them.

After gracing him with the no-fuss, all-fun morning blow job, they cleaned each other up. His hands had found her fun places enough times to have her bending over in front of him with her palms to the wall and demanding he fuck her. By the time he was done, there was just enough hot water for them to clean up again and to wash their hair.

As he dried his hair with his towel, he mumbled something about his hair being hell to brush when he didn't use conditioner, but it was worth it. She had made a mental note to grab some the next time she went shopping.

While she got ready for work, he had pulled on his jeans and disappeared. She found him in the kitchen and had leaned against the doorjamb to watch him work at her coffee pot.

He was hot as sin, but he was also mature. Thank fuck for that, because she had no patience for immaturity. Sure, it was hilarious to watch someone else deal with it, but she couldn't handle it when she was on the receiving end. While Rex pushed her limits and drove her crazy at times, he wasn't immature or irresponsible. No, he wasn't those things. He was just stubborn.

"If you keep staring at me like that," he began as he turned a bit to look back at her, "I'm going to need that mat so I can take my turn servicing you on my knees."

"Is that supposed to stop me?"

He chuckled. "No, but you're supposed to be to work in thirty minutes… and I'm going to need longer than that."

She grinned. "Fair. Rain check?"

"Done." He winked. "No blackout dates."

She tsked and crossed the kitchen to stand at his side. "You, Mr. Piccolo, are too much temptation."

"Mmm," he hummed as he dropped his head down and nibbled at her neck. "I would dial it back, but I don't think you want that."

She pulled her hand back before she swung and made contact with his jean-covered ass. "You better not."

He growled against her skin. "Never."

While they waited for the pot to brew, Jolene went in search of Beast and found him under the bed in the guest room. She coaxed him out and had to carry him out to the backyard because the poor dog wouldn't go in the kitchen while Rex was there.

After he was done with his business, she brought him back inside and set him down in the living room, before she went to the kitchen and retrieved his food and water. She figured she'd let him eat in the living room, since he was having such a traumatic morning with the much larger canine setting off his nerves.

Giggling to herself, she returned to the kitchen and took the offered to-go cup from Rex.

He kissed her lips and cocked a brow. "What's so funny?"

"Just another dog joke."

Rex rolled his eyes. "I'll lock up after I finish getting dressed."

"Thank you." She lifted up on her toes and gave him another kiss. "Text me later, and we'll decide when we'll see each other next."

"You'll see me tonight, but I'll text to find out where."

She gave him a glare at his presumption, but the display on the microwave was next to his head and the time distracted her. "Shit. Gotta go. Text me, and we'll argue about this later." Then she turned and walked away.

"Yes, Ma'am," he said, making her steps falter for a second before she walked out of the kitchen to the front door.

As Jolene headed for her little SUV, she took a sip of the coffee and moaned. Yup, she was pretty sure Rex Piccolo was the man for her... and she wasn't even mad about it.

Rex

Well, he tried. That was all he could say when he wasn't able to get Beast to come out from under the end table. All he was trying to do was to prove to the little Yorkie that he wouldn't hurt him, but Beast wasn't ready, and Rex decided to respect that. Eventually, the pup would see that he was just another cuddler who liked getting petted by the pretty veterinarian.

Giving up on trying to win the dog over for the day, Rex got dressed and made sure Doc's house was locked up before he made his way to his truck. He needed to at least go use some conditioner, or he'd never be able to brush through his hair. He liked it long, but it did come with some extra maintenance.

When Nevaeh was a little girl and had complained every time he tried to brush her hair, he had gone to Ginger to ask what to do. Ginger told him he needed to make sure he was using the right products on her hair and sent him to the spa and salon the clubs owned. One of the members, now retired, Sass introduced him to the world of hair care for long hair.

Rex had made it his mission to try to understand as much as he could of what Nevaeh would go through, so while staring at the wall of bottles and tubes, he had decided to grow out his hair. If he knew what she was going through, he would have more patience and understanding of any struggles it caused her.

Sure, to some, it was a ridiculous reason, and he could see that now that he was much older, but at the time, he was just a single dad trying his hardest to do the best he could for his daughter. Over time, he grew to like his long hair and kept it, even after Nevaeh had suggested he cut it short again.

Through all of that, he realized just how important conditioner was and made sure they never ran out of the good stuff. Knowing he would be spending a lot of time at Doc's, or at least hoping like hell he would, he made a mental note to grab another couple bottles of his hair care products and bring them with him the next time he went over there.

Climbing into his truck, he glanced around and cursed when he saw the Pathfinder parked a block down the road. Pissed, he started the engine and took off like a bat out of hell. The Pathfinder immediately pulled away from the curb and followed.

Seeing a stop sign ahead, Rex pulled his gun from the locked compartment hidden next to his seat and thumbed the safety. He stopped just before the corner and threw his truck into park, before he hopped out and headed for the Pathfinder. His wolf growled and snarled, hackles raised, with every step he made toward the approaching SUV.

He'd barely reached the ass end of his vehicle before the other automobile flew past him, ran the stop sign, and took off. He didn't know who the fuck was in the Pathfinder, but he was getting damn sick of being followed.

After securing his weapon in the hidden compartment, Rex put on his hazard lights and pulled his phone from his pocket. Dialing up his president, he told his wolf to calm the fuck down because hunting down the assholes without a plan was just asking for an orange fucking jumpsuit, and he doubted the prison guards would let him leave to have playtime with Doc. And they *needed* their playtime with their mate.

"Heard you were being neutered," Gorgeous said on the other end of the line. "Need an after-procedure pickup?"

Even through his anger, Rex could appreciate her humor and snorted a laugh. "Where's the boss man?"

"He's rocking Nugget. She was fussy this morning and needed Dad time. This important?"

"It is. Can you fill in for him for a few minutes? I'll make it as quick as I can."

"You got it," she replied, then he heard her telling Axle she needed to switch with him. Ashlyn 'Gorgeous' Weber really was the best thing that had ever happened to Axle. She was pushy when he needed it, but she always seemed to know when it was important for her to just take Axle's lead. She was strong, but she was also soft and sweet. It was what made her the perfect unofficial leader of the Ol' Ladies, the mates of the Howlers. She was to them what Axle was to the men, and she was damn good at it.

"What's up, Rex?" Axle's no-nonsense tone told Rex that Gorgeous had at least said it was important.

"Hey. Sorry to break up cuddle time with Nugget, but I was followed again this morning. When I left Doc's, the Pathfinder was a block away and followed when I pulled away from the curb. I stopped at a stop sign and got out with my gun, but they took off around me and ran through the intersection."

"Fuck," Axle barked out, which was followed by a, "Orlan Weber, I know you aren't cussing in front of my daughter," from Gorgeous.

"Uh oh," Rex uttered.

"Fuck you," Axle said low, before his voice raised again. "Sorry, Gorgeous, it just slipped out."

"That's what he said."

"Rex," Axle growled, "meet me at the clubhouse in twenty." Then the call disconnected.

Chapter Fifteen

Jolene

After a particularly bitter conversation with Dr. Thatcher, Jolene took a break and stormed out to her SUV. She took a few deep breaths and called her mother. If she didn't get her mind off of choking the life out of her boss, she just might give into the urge.

It took three rings, then her mother answered, "Jo, how are you?"

The cheerful sound of her mother's voice brought her a sliver of peace. "Hey Ma. I'm good. Just wanted to check in and see how you were doing."

"Well… I've been doing my small walks. My physical therapist and nurses are still coming to help me, but I'm making progress. Tell me what's going on in your life. I've been stuck at the house for *days*. I need gossip."

Jolene chuckled. "I went on a date. Okay… I'm still on a date, since every moment outside of work has been spent with him."

"Ooooo… And who is this man?"

"His name is Rex. He cooks, Ma, and grocery shops."

Knowing how important that was to Jolene, her mother's voice was full of awe when she asked, "When is the wedding?"

After laughing with her mother, she sighed, feeling less stressed. "I love you, Ma."

"Love you, too, Jo. I want a picture of this Rex, preferably with his shirt off."

"Goodbye," Jolene uttered, still laughing.

"Call me in a few days. And I wasn't kidding about that picture."

"Yeah. Yeah." Jolene ended the call, took another deep breath, and headed back inside.

Rex

Rex joined Axle, Pike, Dragon, Keys, and Skull in the room they used for church, which is what they called their club meetings. Being vice president of the Howlers, it made sense that Axle wanted Skull to be included. Keys was their tech guru, so it was important for him to have the information he needed in order to do anything tech-y. Pike was the sergeant at arms, and Dragon was an enforcer. They were the ones responsible for club security. All in all, the five of them in that room with him were the dream team.

After running through the story again and answering all the questions they had for him, Rex watched his president. Axle seemed stressed, scratching at his beard, jaw tight. His gray eyes were swirling, and it was obvious by the way he was twitching that his wolf was pissed off.

"We'll figure this out," Keys said, low. He may be human, but he was picking up on Axle discomfort and anger.

Axle gave a nod. "I'll contact Ordys and Lira to see if they have any insight. They might have news about Black Forest Academy, because I can't help but think this is connected to that fucking hunter academy."

"Logical assumption," Skull commented with a nod.

"What do you want me to do?" Pike leaned a bit forward in his seat across from Skull.

"Organize search parties to scour the town. I want that fucking Pathfinder found. *Now*."

Pike gave a nod. "Are we pulling in both clubs for church?"

"Yes. Tell them to close businesses down for the day if they fucking have to and be here in an hour. We'll do it in the cafeteria. Rex, organize with Top and Ginger a place for the Ol' Ladies and kids to be, but I want them on the compound."

"Until this is over?" Dragon asked.

"For the time being," Axle replied, which meant that it was going to at least be for the night. They had done this enough times to know Axle would err on the side of caution when it came to the women and children. He didn't fuck around with their safety.

"I'll get started on seeing what I can find on cameras around town," Keys said and looked over to Skull. "I might need help. You up for it?"

Recently, Skull had taken an interest in technology and learning what he could from Keys. As odd as it was for the vice president to be playing assistant to a member of the club who wasn't Axle, that's exactly what he had been doing.

"Yup, unless Axle needs me to do something else?"

Axle shook his head. "I'll contact Crush and have her call in her members. We can handle church. I want answers."

While Skull and Keys set up the computer equipment in their church room, the rest of them parted ways. Pike and Dragon went to gather members and contact their mates. Axle, no doubt, was calling Gorgeous to have her come to the compound with Nugget.

When he stepped out of the clubhouse, Rex headed across the street to the tattoo parlor, where he knew he'd find Ginger, and probably Top. Once upon a time, Top and Ginger had been married and had three children together. It wasn't a love match, really, even though Rex didn't doubt there had been love there. It was more about neither of them having faith in finding their mates, but they both wanted to be parents. They made a deal and gave that to each other. The marriage didn't last long after their third child was born, but they had remained close friends. Rex even suspected they still spent nights together on occasion, or at least they did before Top met Connie Taylor, Gorgeous's mother.

Connie had been a true mate to Top, but she had been a widow and was battling cancer. She refused to mate Top because she didn't want to saddle him with dealing with her illness. That had been what she had confided in Rex once, when he asked her why she didn't let Top claim her. He didn't have a heart to tell her that mating didn't work that way. Top was going to feel her suffering just as strongly without her carrying his mating mark, and that was exactly what happened. When she passed away, Top was just as torn up as he would have been had he mated her.

Rex didn't know if Top returned to Ginger's bed after losing Connie. He respected Top enough not to invade his privacy like that, but he would understand if Top had. He'd spent his own time in Ginger's bed when they had been young and still prospecting for their respective clubs. She had always been a beautiful woman. Once things progressed with them toward marriage, Rex backed off and had put his relationship with Ginger firmly in the friendzone.

They were close friends and that wouldn't change, but it wouldn't be anything more than that ever again. He held his friendship with both Top and Ginger very close to his heart. The two of them had always been his go-to friends when he needed anything. They often gravitated toward each other. Rex suspected it had to do with the fact that they were so close in age. Sure, he had other friends, and so did they, but he trusted no one more than he did them, not even Score, who he also considered a close friend.

Rex shoved aside his mental trip down memory lane as he yanked open the door to the tattoo parlor and headed inside. After nodding at Vixen, who was doing something on the computer at the front desk, Rex headed down the hall and found Ginger and Top sitting together on the couch in the breakroom in the back.

"Interrupting something?" Rex asked as he stepped into the room and shut the door behind him.

Cuddled into Top's side, Ginger shot him a smile. "Would it stop you if you were?"

Rex chuckled and sat down in the armchair at the end of the couch, turned toward them. He shrugged. "Probably not. I'm not against voyeurism. Recently, I've learned I'm not against a lot of things."

Giggling, Ginger wiggled her brows at him. "I heard you found yourself a woman who was... *bossy*."

"I did." Rex grinned back at her. "Seriously... I'm not trying to cockblock."

Top snorted a laugh. "Rex, as much as I love and respect you, if you walked in while I was trying to get in Ginger's pants, your presence wouldn't stop me. We were just talking about the kids."

"Oh." Rex sighed, all humor gone. "I was followed again this morning. Axle is pulling everyone in, including the Ol' Ladies and children. He wants us to watch over them while the clubs have church."

Ginger and Top both sat up, concerned. "What in hell is going on?" Ginger asked as her brows pulled together. "Why are they following our clubs? *Who* is following us?"

"Axle suspects it has something to do with the hunter academy, but he doesn't have confirmation," Rex answered.

Top let out a sigh and ran his hand through his curly brown hair. It wasn't long, but the curl game was strong with that one. "You gonna call your doctor in?"

Rex just stared at him for a long moment. They hadn't even talked about mating, and Rex hadn't yet claimed her at the table, but she was his Ol' Lady nonetheless. Would she listen if he asked her to stay with him at the compound? He didn't know.

"Guess I'll try," he finally answered.

Chapter Sixteen

Jolene

After giving the Basenji in room four its shots and cuddles, Jolene headed out of the examination room and went to her desk. She checked her phone and saw that she had a text from Rex.

REX: When you get a minute, I need it.

Confused and concerned, Jolene sent a text back.

JOLENE: Emergency? Otherwise, I have one more patient before lunch. Can call you at twelve.

She sat at her computer and set the phone down on the desk next to her mouse. As she notated the Basenji's chart, she kept glancing at her phone. A few minutes later, it finally pinged with a new message.

REX: Call at lunch. Between now and then, just keep your eyes out for suspicious people. I'll explain more later.

Warning bells went off as she read his words. Something was wrong… *really* wrong. Checking the time, she saw that her patient should already be in the waiting room, so she couldn't cancel the appointment or delay it. Whatever was going on would have to wait until after.

JOLENE: Will call as soon as next appt done

She was distracted from her concern when the only thing sent back was a red heart emoji. Her mind began to spin about what that heart meant. Was he just trying to tell her that he cared? Was he just acknowledging her message? Was he trying to tell her something bigger? He couldn't be trying to tell her that. They'd only had two dates! Sure, they'd met months ago, and the man could make a mean cup of coffee, but—

Jolene shook her head and forced herself not to go down that rabbit hole. She had a job to do. The rest could wait until later.

Rex

"What in the hell are you doing on my phone?" Rex snatched his phone from Ginger's hand and set it back on the side table that butted up against both the couch and the armchair.

Ginger grinned. "Just giving your relationship a little nudge. You got up to use the bathroom and got a message while you were gone. She'll call you after her next appointment, by the way."

Rex narrowed his eyes and picked up his phone. After opening up his text string with Doc, he sighed. No doubt his pretty mate was going to have a million questions about that one red heart.

Shrugging, he set his phone back down. Doc's questions would give him the perfect opening to the mate conversation. He needed to talk to her about it, in order to give her time to think it through, because she *would* insist on weighing the pros and cons.

Figuring Ginger did him a favor, he didn't bother arguing with her about it.

"Wow. No scowl? No whining? No tantrums?"

Rex flipped her off.

"If you haven't already, and I doubt you have, because you've lived your life like an eternal bachelor, tell the woman how you feel. It's not just your wolf, and we both know it."

"I hear you," he said quietly. After an awkward moment, he cleared his throat. "What are we going to do about the Ol' Ladies and kids?"

Top sat forward and rested his elbows on his knees. "Well, I figure we can take them to the diner and have them make their own pizzas for lunch, or we can hang in the main room of the clubhouse during church."

"I don't think Axle will want them sitting around the large windows of the diner."

After a nod, Top replied, "Clubhouse it is. I'll order pizza. Are we pulling kids from school?"

"Axle didn't mention that. I figure they're safe there for now. If we need to, we'll grab the passenger van and round 'em up."

Ginger nodded her agreement. "When schools start letting out for the day, I'll go pick them up. I'll send texts to the kids to let them know not to get on buses." She stood and headed out of the room, pulling her phone from her pocket as she went.

When Ginger was out of sight, Top tossed a throw pillow at Rex. "What's going on with you and the doc?"

"A lot, but she's… she's a woman of science, Top. She doesn't just jump. She wants to know all the whys and hows. She weighs everything out. I highly doubt I'll get her to agree to a mating for a while."

Top tilted his head from side to side as if to say, *Maybe, maybe not.* "Our animals are rarely wrong. Never, actually. Sometimes we're mated to bad people, but that doesn't mean they aren't a good match to us."

"She doesn't know anything about mates. I have to explain it. Then she'll have a ton of questions. After that, she'll want to marinate in the information for a while before she agrees to anything."

After a shrug, Top said, "So tell her about mates and answer her questions. Get that out of the way so you can get to the good part." He stared at Rex for a long moment. "Besides the fact that she's your mate, you like her, don't ya?"

Rex dropped his head back to the chair and chuckled. "I love everything about her. She tests me, pushes me, orders me around… and I fucking love it. Yeah, sexually, we fit, but she's… smart and compassionate and funny."

Top grinned. "She's it, even without the mate connection."

"She's it," Rex confirmed with a nod.

After reaching over, Top patted Rex on the knee. "Happy for ya, brother."

Chapter Seventeen

Jolene

As soon as Jolene was done with her next patient, which just happened to be Mama Hen and her Yorkie, Maxie, Jolene snatched her phone and keys from her desk and headed out the back door of the clinic. Her schedule had just said it was a last-minute appointment. When she mentioned to Mama Hen that she received a concerning text from Rex, she told Jolene she'd wait in the parking lot because she wanted to know what was going on. Jolene wasn't sure she'd be able to share, but whatever. Mama Hen did what Mama Hen wanted to do at all times.

Not sure where the conversation was going to take them, Jolene slid into the driver's seat of her SUV and dialed his number.

He answered immediately. "Doc."

"What's wrong?"

She heard his brief chuckle, then he said, "A few of our members, including myself, have been followed. We're trying to find out who it is and what they want, but until then, Pres is calling in all the Ol' Ladies and children. I need you to come stay at the compound with me for a night or two."

"Wait." She shook her head, hoping to shake the random pieces of information he gave her into some logical order. "What does that have to do with me? And... Ol' Ladies?"

Rex sighed. "I will explain all of it, but the fact of the matter is you are my woman, and that means you might be in danger."

"I can take care of myself, Rex." Jolene thought about all the times in her life that she had been in life-threatening circumstances and had to fight her way out. She couldn't tell Rex about all of that, though, because the kind of NDAs that she signed were for life. Little did he know, he was in just as much danger from her enemies if they ever found her.

"Doc, listen, I know you are capable of taking care of yourself, but it would eat me up inside if you were put in danger because someone was trying to get to me."

She sighed and glanced around the lot. There weren't any suspicious vehicles or people, just Mama Hen and Maxie watching from her car. "What about Beast?"

"You can bring him. There will be some kids around. Maybe the kids will make him more comfortable."

She thought about how Beast would react to a large group of strangers. Considering a large number of them were shifters, she suspected that it wouldn't go over well. Her eyes moved back to Mama Hen. "I could probably see if Mama Hen would take him for a couple days."

"That's a good idea," he agreed. "So, you'll come to the compound after you get off work?"

"I'll have to stop by the house first."

"Okay. What time do you think you'll be done for the day?"

"Maybe five. Four if my appointments don't drag on."

He sighed again, this time it sounded relieved. "Will you text me when you know what time?"

She frowned. "I suppose."

"Thanks, Doc."

The line was silent for a long moment, then Jolene stated, "When I get there, you will answer all of my questions. Do you understand?"

"Yes, Ma'am."

Jolene ended the call and took a deep breath. As she let it out, she thought about the locked room in her basement. If necessary, she was prepared. She may have left that part of her life behind in the general sense, but the skills she had learned would always be a part of her, and the tools she acquired were still in her possession.

Mentally clicking that part of her brain back into place from the box she had shoved it into years ago, Jolene climbed out of her SUV and headed across the lot to Mama Hen's car.

Axle

After hanging up the phone with Lira, Axle let out a long sigh. Lira, the lead champion of the God of Balance, didn't have any information about the people following his family. While some of them weren't blood, every member of both the Howlers and the Claws were his family, and he'd do anything to make sure they were safe. But that was hard to do when he didn't know what they were up against.

Ordys, lead champion for the God of Wisdom, said he'd look into it the best he could, but he couldn't promise he'd have anything quick enough to help them. Axle understood that. Ordys had his own responsibilities. He considered them allies, but he didn't expect them to take on the problems of the clubs.

He checked in on Keys and Skull, but they didn't have anything useful... yet. If there was something to find electronically, Keys would find it. Of that, Axle had all the confidence in the world.

Their problems never came at a *good* time. Axle didn't believe any time was a good time for problems, but it just seemed as if their troubles always came when they were in the middle of so many other things.

Both clubs were working on rebuilding the club that the Hell's Dogs MC had blown up. They were also making plans to patch over the UpRiders MC, located in the Upper Peninsula of Michigan. Axle was going to have to send a group up there to help with that. Not to mention, they recently bought a property they planned to use as a safe house, but it needed work before it would be habitable. To take on that project, he was calling in the retired members, including his father, Joker, the former president of the Howlers.

Add in the fact that he had a baby at home and a mate who was grieving the loss of her sister, and yeah, Axle was stretched as tight as possible.

Whatever their intentions, the assholes in the Pathfinder needed to be dealt with and out of the way, so Axle and Crush, the president of the Claws, could direct their members toward healing.

Determination renewed, Axle made his way down to the cafeteria, stopping briefly in the main room to give Nugget a kiss on her rosy cheek. Then, he shut the doors and turned to face the members of the Howlers and the Claws.

"Are you ready to hunt these bastards down and end this shit before they do something stupid?"

Crush let out a humorless chuckle. "They already did. Fucking with us is the stupidest thing someone could do."

That was when the room erupted in cheers, roars, and howls.

Rex

They had been driving around Warden's Pass, Michigan, and the surrounding area for a few hours and nothing. Two Pathfinders had been found, but neither of them had tinted windows like the one that had been following him. They checked with the Claws who had followed, and they said the same thing — The tint wasn't dark enough.

Frustrated, Rex barked out a curse as he sat on his bike at the town line. In front of him, Smoke and Score were just as pissed as he was. They were sick of this shit. All the Howlers wanted was to live their lives in peace, to love their women and children, and to ride. It wasn't too much to ask. The fact that many of them could shift into predatory animals was irrelevant. When they shifted, they spent most of their time running through the woods together, having fun. It was the rare occasion that one of them used their shifting abilities to harm, and it was always when provoked. If people would leave them alone and treat each other with respect, there wouldn't be a problem.

"Now what?" Smoke glanced back at him.

Rex was shaking his head as he tried to think of where else to look. The majority of the Howlers had broken up into groups of three or four and were scouring the area, but he hadn't heard news that they'd found anything.

His phone chimed with a new text.

"Not Axle," Score commented, pointing out the obvious since Axle's number had its own tone for text or calls on all of their phones. It used to be something a few of the members did, but recently, it had become a club rule.

DOC: Leaving the clinic now.

Rex's gut filled with anxiety. He didn't like the idea of her being unprotected. In most situations, he knew his woman could handle her own, but this wasn't a typical situation. He needed to get to his woman.

Looking up to his club brothers, Rex locked gazes with Smoke, who knew Rex well enough to guess what was going through his mind. They had been close friends for damn near twenty years.

"Go to her," Smoke said. "She's okay, right?"

Rex gave a nod. "I just… she's unprotected."

"We get it," Score replied. "There's nowhere else for us to look right now, anyway. Go get your woman and bring her to the clubhouse… and I'll be expecting a club vote soon."

Rex rolled his eyes, but smiled when his brothers chuckled. Claiming her at the table was something he needed to talk to Doc about and soon.

REX: Keep your eyes open.

He hesitated for a moment, then he sent another message that contained only a red heart. Ginger was right. They were meant to be, and he should just tell Doc how he felt.

After starting his bike and checking the road for traffic, he pulled off the shoulder and headed back into town. It wasn't even five minutes later that he was pulling his bike up in front of her house.

T.S. Tappin

Chapter Eighteen

Jolene

When Beast bolted for the guest room, Doc was confused, then she heard the pipes of Rex's bike. A bit annoyed, she approached the front door and yanked it open. Glaring at him with her hands on her hips, she watched his sexy ass walk toward her.

"I said I would come to the compound," she grumbled.

The annoying man had the nerve to chuckle. He climbed the few steps in front of her house and pressed a kiss to her lips. "I know. I'm here to help you pack."

"Pack? It's just work clothes for tomorrow. I could carry them in one hand."

Rex's hands landed on her hips as he walked her back in the house. Turning her and pressing her against the wall next to the door, he lowered his head and kissed her lips again. "You don't want to have playtime? How disappointing."

Doc fought the smile that threatened to form and scowled at him. "Who said you've earned it?"

"Earn it? How do you want me to do that, Doc?" His hands slid up her sides and cupped her breasts through her scrub top. "I'll do anything," he said against her lips.

Staring into his eyes, Doc reached over and shut the door. She used the same hand to grip his shoulder and shove him down to his knees.

When those ice-blue eyes began to glow up at her, she slid her hand into the hair on the side of his head and dislodged the tie holding it back. The growl he gave her went straight to her clit. He dragged his hands back down her sides to grip the waistband of her scrub pants and panties, and pulled them down her legs. When they reached her ankles, she slipped her shoes off her feet and stepped out of them.

Rex didn't waste any time. Once she was bared to him, he leaned forward and went to work on her. Using his tongue, fingers, and teeth, he had her on the edge of orgasm in a few minutes. Her hand tightened in his hair as she held him where she wanted him. The entire time, his eyes glowed up at her, and he continually growled against her clit.

"I'm going to come on your face. Then you're going to fuck me against this wall. Understand?"

"Yes, Ma'am," he rumbled, mouth still at her clit. The vibration sent her over the edge. Lights flashed in front of her as her head fell back to the wall, and her body tensed.

She called out his name as Rex moaned against her and lapped up the proof of her completion.

"Fuck, you taste good." As soon as he had her cleaned up, he was on his feet and was unzipping his jeans.

Rex's Release

Doc turned and put her hands to the wall. Tilting her ass out to him, she smiled when he groaned and took hold of her hips. "Fuck me, Fido."

"Ruff," he said through a chuckle a moment before he slammed inside of her.

Instantly, pleasure reverberated through her system, and she let out a moan. The man was good at what he did to her body. Letting go, she let him fuck her the way he wanted. Part of her wondered how she managed to be so satisfied in those moments, when she never before had been able to find it without being in control, but she figured it was the man. She knew he would submit to her every demand, without hesitation, if she chose to take control. It was a heady feeling, which allowed her to loosen those reins from time to time.

His thrusts were hard and steady. He didn't speed up in some off-the-mark idea of increasing her pleasure. Sometimes it wasn't about speed, but rather about a steady rhythm and good aim.

When his grip tightened on her hips, she groaned. He was on edge, feeling everything as deeply as she was.

"Fuck," he growled and slammed inside of her. "I can't get enough of you. You feel so good." As he continued his steady pace, he slid one of his hands up under her shirt and cupped her lace-covered breast, pinching her nipple between two fingers.

Ecstasy raced from her nipple to her clit, making it throb and causing her pussy to clench around him.

"Fuck yes." She felt his lips against her neck as his graveled words filled the room. He opened his mouth and sucked on the spot where her neck met her left shoulder.

That was what she needed. Moaning his name, bliss filled her. Tossing her head back against his shoulder, she rode the waves of pleasure that carried her away.

Blue light shined past her head and lit the wall in front of her as he slammed inside. "Mine," he growled and sucked on that spot again.

She was too satiated to argue with him about that at that moment, but she made note of it with every intention of bringing it up later. Lucky for him, he fucked her so well she was giving him a reprieve.

Rex

With his head resting on her shoulder, Rex tried to catch his breath, while his wolf whined and urged him to mate her. He didn't know if it was the fact that she was his mate or that he loved a woman for the first time in his life, but everything felt like *more* with her. Besides the effect she had on his wolf, when no other woman managed that, the sensations were always heightened. The anticipation gnawed at him when he wasn't with her. He loved talking to her and answering her never-ending questions. Hell, Rex even liked it when she called him *Fido*.

No, he didn't know exactly why, but he didn't really care about the reason. He just didn't want it to end. Even as he was recovering from his mind-blowing orgasm, he was ready to take her again.

Rex kissed the skin of her shoulder, right where he would eventually leave his mark, because he wanted to, but also to satisfy his wolf and the incessant urge to claim her. "Did I earn playtime?"

Her response of, "I better pack the big bag," had him chuckling.

After another kiss to her shoulder, he slid out of her. Not wanting to be away from her for even a second more than he had to, he bent down and scooped her up in his arms before he turned and headed for her bedroom.

"Poor Beast bolted for the guest room when he heard your bike," she told him.

Rex let out a sigh, remembering how he tried to coax the little guy out from under the table that morning. "Are you bringing him to the compound?"

"I think it will be too much for him," she told him. "Mama Hen said she'd take him. I have to drop him off at the hotel on the way."

"Yeah, that's probably a good idea. He and Maxie can hang."

She smiled. "He loves hanging with Maxie and Mama Hen."

"I'll have to tell my boy, Maxie, to put in a good word for me."

He went to set Doc on her feet in her bedroom as she started laughing at his joke. Then she stopped laughing and looked at him with what he was beginning to think of as her *I have questions* expression.

"No," he answered, "I can't talk to domestic dogs just because we're both considered canines."

She shrugged. "It was just a question." Then the orders began. She pointed at her closet door. "There's a large duffel on the top shelf. Grab it."

Rex pressed his lips to hers and whispered against them, "Yes, Ma'am."

T.S. Tappin

Jolene

After dropping Beast off at The Hen House with Mama Hen, she followed Rex as he rode to the compound and into the lock between an auto shop and another building. As he backed his bike into a spot, he pointed to an empty spot next to the auto shop. Figuring he was telling her to park there, she did.

By the time she put her SUV in park, he was standing at her door and pulling it open. He held his hand out to her, and she took it and climbed out. As she shut the door, he opened the back one and grabbed her duffel.

"I can carry that," she grumbled, feeling a bit adrift, being in a new place she knew very little about and having him do things for her. She wasn't used to it, and it was making her cranky... mostly because she liked it.

Rex's chuckle was quiet. "I know. I'm pretty sure you could lift my bike over your head with one hand if you were determined enough." He lifted the hand he was still holding to his lips and kissed the back of it. "I like doing things for you, so just let me."

"I'm the one who gives the orders, remember?"

"In the bedroom, yes, but if it makes you feel better to order me to carry your bag, then do it."

She glared up at him for a moment before she glanced at the other building. "What's that?"

"The clubhouse. It's for members and family only."

"Then where are we going?"

His brows pulled together for a moment in confusion. "Into the clubhouse. I mean... later, we'll go to the room I have in the apartment building over there." He nodded to a long, rectangular building at the end of the cul-de-sac. "But for now, we'll go in and have dinner… maybe some drinks. There's a kitchen and a bar in there."

"You said members and family."

Realization lit his eyes, along with his smile. "Doc, everyone in there considers you my Ol' Lady, which I will explain later, so that makes you family."

She eyed him for a while, trying to find a kinder way to say what was on her mind, but she couldn't. "Bikers are weird."

He snorted a laugh and started walking them toward the brick building. "We aren't known for being normal. That's for sure."

When they stepped inside the building, they entered a small foyer, before they made a left and walked into a room that looked like any biker bar in America. Wood-paneled walls were covered with neon lights and beer signs. The tables were worn, and the chairs were well used. Even the stools at the bar looked to be from decades ago, but they were still in decent shape.

"This is where we congregate," he explained. "Pretty much every party, family function, and meeting happen in this building."

She nodded to a few people she recognized around the room, but there were many she didn't.

"Doc!" A male voice bellowed from across the large space. Then she saw Bullet headed in her direction.

Jolene looked over and shook her head. It still amazed her how completely and quickly they were able to heal. Sure, it had been months, but there wasn't even a hitch in his step. She smiled back at him. "You look like that gut wound didn't slow you down a bit."

Bullet shrugged. "I'm tougher than that." He looked between Jolene and Rex, then his eyes landed on their clasped hands. "So, I was right, huh?"

The smug smile on his face had Jolene rolling her eyes. "I still don't belong to anyone."

Bullet chuckled, and his gaze shifted to Rex. "Uphill climb."

"Marathon, not a sprint," Rex replied.

Jolene looked between the two of them. "What in the hell are you two talking about?"

Rex looked down at her. "Later, I promise."

She really wanted to push him on it, but she was willing to push it aside for that moment, especially when she was still learning the lay of the land. The second they were alone, though, she was going to get answers. She wasn't completely ignorant of MC culture, so she could guess what the Ol' Lady term meant, but she also realized that every club varied on certain things. Jolene wanted to hear it from his mouth.

Bullet patted Rex on the back as he laughed. As Jolene watched them, she was engulfed in a hug from a woman with dark brown hair.

"Thank you! Thank you! Thank you!" The woman squeezed. "I owe you." When the woman pulled back and looked at Jolene with appreciation in her deep green eyes, then her gaze swung over to Bullet. "He's my... everything."

Jolene realized who she was and gave a smile. "Just doing my job."

The woman — *Butterfly, was it?* — shifted over into Bullet, who wrapped his arms tightly around her. "Still... thank you."

Jolene inclined her head in acknowledgment. "You're welcome."

"So… you're Rex's?" Butterfly asked with a grin.

That was the third time she'd heard something like that, and they had yet to talk about it. Jolene turned and glared at Rex. "No."

He just smiled down at her.

"Oh," Butterfly said, as if she said something she shouldn't have.

"Come on, Butterfly," Bullet said through yet another chuckle. "Let's leave these two to work that out."

When they were a few yards away, Rex uttered, "After dinner."

She shook her head. "*Now*."

T.S. Tappin

Chapter Nineteen

Messer

Killing them won't solve my problems. Killing them won't solve my problems. Killing them won't solve…

Messer continued the mantra over and over, the same way she had been for days. Every time she had a suggestion, they shot it down without letting her finish a sentence. This wasn't about following orders anymore. For the Elites she was forced on a team with, it was about killing. They were thirsty for the blood of shifters, with very little need for confirmation that their victims were actually the monsters they were hunting.

Their plan was ridiculous, and she wanted no part in it, but she didn't have a choice. She had no authority. She could leave, could walk out, but they would track her down and drag her in to face off with her superiors. How that would play out, she wasn't sure. They weren't a government sanctioned academy. Messer doubted it would just be a debrief and a firing. It was the unknown that kept her in that fucking Pathfinder.

Until she could devise a plan, she'd have to go along with whatever the blood-thirsty bastards wanted.

Rex

Once they were in his room at the compound, Rex set Doc's duffel on top of his dresser and busied himself by unpacking it. The majority of what she brought was for playtime, but he yanked open the top drawer and put the items in there before he put her clothes in the second drawer.

"Rex."

He wanted to have *the conversation* with her. He wanted to explain about mates and Ol' Ladies. He wanted to explain mating marks and property patches. His wolf was demanding him to get to it, but the fear of rejection had him procrastinating. Rex worried that her independent and scientific nature would balk at it.

"Rex." This time his name was said with more impatience.

Get your shit together! You are a grown-ass man! Rex took a deep breath in through his nose and let it slowly out through his mouth, ignoring his whining wolf.

"Your breathing technique is not filling me with comfort and joy," she bit out as she approached his side and grabbed his arm. Forcing him to face her, she looked up at him. "What is going on? What happened to all that arrogance you normally carry around?"

He frowned. "Arrogance?" He didn't think he was arrogant.

Her beautiful blue eyes rolled. "Fine. *Confidence.* Where did it go?"

Rex couldn't hold back the smile from forcing on his lips. "Once I tell you what I have to tell you, you'll realize this is probably the most important conversation I've ever had to have in my life, aside from the conversation where I explained to Nevaeh how to incapacitate a man with only her thumb."

Doc snorted. "That's a pretty important conversation for a father to have with his daughter."

Rex nodded and sighed. "Right?"

His heart started to race a bit as the seriousness of the situation finally sunk in. He was about to tell Doc that she was his mate. *Holy shit*. He found his mate, and she was there with him. They were amazing together, in his opinion, but what if she didn't feel the same way? They were always told that human mates felt a pull, but what if his scientific-brained mate didn't give in to it? *Fuck*. Rex could have the conversation and end up alone.

Suddenly, his face was in Doc's hands, and she was forcing him to look up at her. *Up? When did I sit down on the bed?*

"Hey," she said calmly but firmly. "Breathe with me. Come on, Fido. In." She sucked in a breath through her nose, and he followed suit. They exhaled together slowly and repeated the process a few times. "Feel better?"

Staring into her eyes, he gave a nod and swallowed hard. "Yes. Thank you."

"Good." She straightened and put her hands to her hips. Glaring at him, she said, "Explain."

Rex tried to figure out where to start. *Mates? Ol' Ladies? Which one?* He looked to his wolf, like he could help him, but of course, his wolf just panted in reply.

"Rex," she bit out.

"Okay! Okay. Fine. Uh... What do you want to know first? The MC culture version or the shifter version?"

"Well... start with the MC culture. I think I have a basic understanding, so prove or disprove it for me, then we can move on to the rest."

Not for the first time, Rex was grateful for his mate and her *just the facts* approach to life. "Do you know what the term Ol' Lady means?"

"I think so. It means they are the spouse of a member of the club, right?"

"Yes," he confirmed but sighed, "but it's more than that. You can be a spouse, girlfriend or wife, and not be an Ol' Lady. To bikers, the title of Ol' Lady means that they were claimed at the table by their biker and the club approved it. It means you aren't just my spouse, but you're also their family. It means you would get a property patch from my club, from me. It means that to the rest of the MC world, you are taken and protected, off-limits." He watched her spine snap straight and rushed on in order to hopefully fend off the lecture that was brewing in her eyes. He held up his hands in front of him. "Before you get mad about the language, it's just part of the culture. With the Howlers, it's a little different. Yes, we use the same terminology, but basically, it's so that other clubs understand that our women are off-limits. In other clubs, the women and children are property, but the men aren't. With the Howlers, you're my property, but I'm also yours."

He paused and let his words sink in. She was still scowling at him, but he could also see that the wheels were turning in her head.

"We do the claiming at the table and the vote, but that's more ceremonial than anything. Then the Howlers would give you a property patch, a cut that says *Property of Rex* and *Rex's OL*. I would get a patch for my cut that says *Property of Doc*. With that, you would officially be a part of the Howlers family, and my brothers would do anything to keep you safe or help you."

He stopped and waited for her to respond. It took longer than he expected, which did nothing but make his heart start to pound out of control again and made his wolf begin to pace.

"Okay. So… it's like a biker marriage… but more?"

Rex nodded. "We can still get married if you wanted to."

"And… you want that… with me? We barely… know each other."

Seeing his assertive mate stumble through her words made Rex even more on edge, but it was too late to turn back. His wolf let out a short, sharp growl, encouraging him, and Rex decided it was best to just say it. "Yes, because you are my mate."

Jolene

Stunned. For the first time in her life, Jolene had no words. Nothing. Not a noun. Not a verb. Hell, not even an adjective. Wordless. It took too long for her to even come up with, "Wait. What?"

She watched as Rex slowly stood up from where he sat on the bed, then he explained, "Shifters have fated mates. My wolf recognized you the last time we were in this building together."

The last time? "But… that was months ago."

He nodded. "Yes."

"What do you mean by *recognized*?"

"I dunno… He just… identified you as our mate." Rex yanked the hair tie from his hair and began running his fingers through the long blond and gray locks. "It basically means that we are compatible and *right* for each other. It means we were meant to be."

"We... You... We barely know each other, Rex."

Rex's ice blue gaze landed on her, and his voice was sure when he said, "I know enough. I want you. For the rest of my life, I want *you*."

"But... how?" Jolene was having a really hard time believing that something like fated mates was real. Sure, men shouldn't be able to turn into predatory animals, but still...

"I know you don't like it when I say this, but... *magic*." He chuckled. "Doc, I don't know how, but I just know it's true."

As her brain tried to process what he said to her, she felt his body press up against the back of her. She knew he must have walked around her, but she didn't clock it. Jolene pushed that aside and refocused on the fact that he was telling her she was his magic soul mate.

Rex slid his arms around her waist and pulled her back against him. Against the side of her neck, he whispered, "Don't you feel it, Doc?"

"You can't fuck your way out of this conversation."

"Can *you* fuck my way out of this conversation?"

Jolene snorted a laugh. The man was ridiculous. As she shook her head at his nonsense, his use of the words *our mate* came to mind. "Wait. You said *our mate*."

He kissed and licked along her neck. "My mate and my wolf's mate."

"I'm not into beastiality, Rex."

He chuckled against her skin before he nipped her earlobe. "My wolf is a part of me. We've been over that. The only one you'll be fucking is me... as a man."

"But your wolf is a part of you… and besides those brief moments a few months ago, I haven't spent any time with your wolf." She tried really hard to ignore the effect his soft breath had on her as it caressed her wet neck.

"Doc, every moment you've spent with me, you've spent with my wolf. He has reactions to every move you make, everything you say, every breath that you pull. I feel them inside, along with my very male reactions."

She turned her head and looked up at him, curious. "Really? What reaction is he having right now?"

Rex pressed a kiss to her lips. Pulling back barely an inch, he answered, "He's demanding I mark you and claim you as ours. He's anxious. Pacing. Panting. Scared you're going to turn us away."

While her brain was spinning with neurological theories and possible hormonal causes, the very female part of her that cared for the man pressed against her wanted nothing more than to just accept everything he was saying. Knowing she wasn't going to be able to find a balance right then, she admitted, "I'm going to need some time."

Rex pressed his forehead to hers and tightened his arms around her. "I expected that. Just know, Doc, that my feelings won't change. I want you. I know we are meant to be. And I can wait for you to realize that on your own."

She snorted another laugh. "*There's* the confidence."

"Miss it?" He grinned.

She turned in his arms and wrapped hers around his neck. "Yeah."

His large hands palmed her ass and lifted her a bit as he pressed her more firmly against him. "I'm hungry." His eyes flashed blue light. "Can I eat?"

"You better eat it all," she said with a smirk.

He gripped the waistband of her leggings and shoved them down past her ass. "Yes, Ma'am."

Chapter Twenty

Rex

After using his mouth and hands to bring Doc to completion twice, Rex took a chance and worked his way up her body on the bed. She didn't protest when he gripped the back of her thigh and lifted, wrapping her leg around his hips, before he slid inside of her sweet, tight core.

Once fully seated, he gave her a moment to adjust and give him a sign that she wanted something different, but all he got was her rolling her hips and her heel pressing into his ass, urging him to fuck her.

So, he did.

And he didn't stop until both of them were thoroughly sated.

After carrying her to the shower and giving her a kiss, he set her on her feet under the hot spray and told her he would be right back. Leaving her to clean up and get ready for bed, Rex headed for the clubhouse. He needed to get them dinner and to check in with the men to see if there were any updates.

His wolf was appeased for the moment, and Rex was exhausted. Not just from the sex, but from the stress of the situation with the Pathfinder and the anxiety their conversation caused. His wolf wasn't doing much better. He was laying down, but the worry was vibrating off of the beast. While it might be a *slim* possibility, it was still a *terrifying* possibility that their mate would reject them, and Rex didn't know if they'd make it through that.

Leave it to him to have one real relationship in his life, and it would be the one that could literally break him. He should have had some experience under his belt, especially with a woman like Doc. He was just winging the relationship stuff. The sex stuff was easy. He had experience in spades in that department, but that was where his knowledge ended. Fuck, he was such an idiot.

Did he handle it right? Did he say the correct things? Was he supposed to be that nervous about it? Or was it normal to feel that way? He needed to talk to one of his brothers who was mated and find out.

When he stepped into the main room of the clubhouse, his eyes landed on Trip. Nope. It would travel through the clubhouse like wildfire if he talked to Trip about his insecurities.

Bullet? Might as well tell Trip, because eventually, Bullet would.

Siren? Rex was pretty sure the only thing Siren was ever worried about was saving his woman, Sugar, from the crazy ex that kidnapped her.

Dragon? He couldn't imagine Dragon admitting to something as vulnerable as anxiety.

Top. He needed to talk to Top. He glanced around, but didn't see his closest friend anywhere. Spotting Ginger sitting at the bar with a beer in front of her, he headed that way. Slipping onto the stool next to her, he asked, "Where's Top?"

Ginger took a sip and chuckled. "Avery has a date this Saturday. She wanted a new dress, so we were looking at ones online to try to decide what kind of dress she wanted. Top saw some of Avery's choices and decided *he* was taking her dress shopping."

"A little too short?" Rex guessed.

After a nod, Ginger added, "And not enough fabric."

Rex sighed. "Is she even old enough to date?"

Ginger rolled her eyes. "A month from tomorrow, she will be seventeen, Rex. What were you doing at seventeen? Better question, what was *I* doing at seventeen, Rex?"

When she stared at him with a raised brow, he chuckled and ran a hand over the back of his neck. He knew exactly what Ginger was doing at seventeen, because he was the one she was doing it with. For a few months, they fucked every time they managed to get a few moments alone. Then they went their separate ways for a couple of years, only to end up prospecting their respective clubs at the same time. Not long after that, they fell back in bed together.

Clearing his throat, he replied, "Fair point, but that doesn't make me feel better about her dating."

"Better get over it, Uncle Rex. It's going to happen, eventually." She took another sip. "What did you want with Top? And does it have anything to do with the hickey you're sporting on your neck?"

Rex winked at her. "It has to do with Doc. It's mate stuff."

"Don't do it," Emerson rumbled as he walked behind the bar. His hair was longer than Rex had ever seen it and was in desperate need of a brush. He didn't smell, but Rex suspected that had a lot to do with Top forcing him to do at least the basics of hygiene. Apparently, brushing his hair and eating weren't high priorities on that list. With blank eyes, he grabbed a bottle of what looked to be whiskey and headed down the hall.

Rex felt a sharp pain in his chest as he watched the young wolf shifter walk away. It was one thing to be newly mated and to have your mate die. That was bad enough. But to have your mate die in front of your eyes and to be unable to stop it... No one could make it through that without being irrevocably changed. Rex's wolf let out a low whine at even the thought of something bad happening to their mate.

Emerson used to be a happy, good-hearted, responsible young man who was ready to take life on and give his mate everything that she wanted. He didn't even see a glimpse of that young man in the detached and abrasive shell of a person who had just walked past him. Changed... irrevocably.

As he was staring after Emerson, he felt Ginger's hand on his forearm and then she said, "Top has him."

Rex swung his gaze back to Ginger. Her fire-red hair was braided back away from her perfect face and dark pink lips. She was stunning... a stunning badass female warrior.

"Now, tell me what's on your mind, and I'll see if I can help."

"I think... I might have..."

Ginger rolled her eyes. "It's me, Rex. Just tell me."

He huffed out a sigh. "I think I might have screwed up the mate and Ol' Lady conversation with Doc. She's a thinker... a problem solver... a scientist. She asks questions, and all I can say is *Magic*. It's..."

"The truth," Ginger supplied. "Listen. As long as you're honest with her about what you know and how you know things to work, she'll accept it or she won't. And if I know anything about the mate bond, she'll accept it. The look on your face when you talk about her tells me what I need to know. She makes you happy. And if you didn't make her happy, you wouldn't still be on the longest first date ever." She chuckled. "Besides work, have you spent any time apart since your first dinner?"

Rex thought about it, but she was right. He couldn't stop himself from smiling.

"Exactly." Ginger laughed.

"So basically, I just need to let her work it out."

Ginger nodded. "Yup. Let her work it out."

Rex faced forward, but he looked at Ginger from the corner of his eye. "You gonna hang with me while I drown my sorrows if she rejects me?"

"Yes, but only for an hour, then I'll kick your ass and tell you to go after your woman."

Rex found Axle in the cafeteria room, eating with his family. Sitting at the table with him was Gorgeous, Trip, and Darlin'. Trip was holding his son, Cane, and Axle had a sleeping Nugget tucked in his arm.

Carrying two cans of pop and the to-go containers he had packed in the kitchen, he stopped at Axle's side and quietly asked, "Keys and Skull find anything?"

Axle shook his head. "Church at nine in the morning."

Rex nodded, but before he could say anything else, Darlin' asked, "What's that on your neck, Rex?"

"Yeah, Rex," Gorgeous added with a grin. "What's that on your neck?"

Rex just grinned back and gave them a wink. "Gotta go feed Doc."

"Looks like you might have already done that," Trip commented, and raised a brow.

As the Weber brothers chuckled, Rex walked away and headed for his room.

Jolene

After taking a shower, Jolene decided to slip on a pair of leggings with one of Rex's tees. If she had any say, and she had all the say, they would be staying in his room and would watch mindless television. She had too much rattling around in her brain to be able to deal with people.

The doctor part of her wondered if he was suffering from some kind of chemical imbalance or brain injury. What he said to her was inconceivable. She understood that there were some things in the world that just couldn't be explained, but it was in her nature not to trust them right away. That was where she was at.

Before jumping in with both feet, she wondered how she could rule out a medical condition that caused him to believe such things. Would he be willing to get an MRI on his brain? Blood tests to check his hormone levels?

As she reevaluated their time together, she realized just how much time they spent fucking each other. She knew she was the first woman to take control of him in the bedroom, probably in any part of his life. Was it just lust? Was he just influenced by the off-the-charts chemistry they had?

And if he was telling the truth, did that mean that he only wanted her because his wolf told him he did?

The door swung open, and Rex walked in, carrying two to-go containers in one hand and two cans of pop in the other. He had a pair of jeans, a tee, his cut, and biker boots on, with his hair pulled up in a manbun. Sex on two legs.

Lifting her phone, she swiped to open the camera and snapped a picture. As she sent the photo off, she thought that her mother was just going to have to do without a topless one.

"Did you just take a picture of me?" He set the bounty on the nightstand, hung his cut on the hook by the door, and plopped down next to her on the bed.

"Yes."

"You could have given me a heads-up. I could have let my hair down, took my shirt off… ya know… prepped."

She grinned at him. "It's for my mom."

He shrugged and yanked his shirt off. "Well, if you're going to show me off, do it right." After pulling the elastic band from his hair, he reclined back against the headboard, looking like the temptation he was.

Laughing, Jolene opened her camera app again and adjusted so that she was on her knees facing him. She took several shots of him, some close up and some full shots, but all of them were sexy. He was incapable of being anything else.

She picked the least scandalous one and sent it off to her mother.

"Did you send them?"

She nodded, then his arms wrapped around her waist and pulled her down on top of him. He snatched her phone from her hand, pressed things she couldn't see on the screen, and while pressing his lips to hers, he snapped a picture.

Against her lips, he said, "I don't care if you send her that one, but make sure you send it to me."

She shrugged and straddled his waist. As Jolene took her phone back, she replied, "If you earn it."

Just like that, the blue light was shining from his eyes and his hips lifted to show her exactly what effect she had on him.

Running her hands over his abdomen and chest, she softly said, "Later. Can we just... watch something stupid and *be* for a bit?"

His grin faded and glowing eyes were replaced by furrowed brows and a wrinkled forehead. "Yeah, Doc, if that's what you want." He gave her thighs a squeeze. "Do you want to cuddle with me as wolf or human?"

Remembering how she told him she had barely spent any time with him as a wolf, she appreciated what he was trying to do. Her hesitation lessened as she stared back at him. He was doing his best to give her what she needed.

She still had questions and reservations about the whole thing, but none of them were about his worth as a man. If she knew without a doubt that he wanted her for her, not just because his wolf demanded it, she wouldn't give a damn about the rest. She might not rush into it, but she would be more accepting of the rest.

"Wolf," she answered as she shifted off of him and sat cross-legged.

Between one blink and the next, he shifted, and the large gray and tan wolf laid his head on her lap, ice-blue eyes gazing up at her.

Running her hands through his coarse fur, she let out a sigh and gave him a soft smile. "I suppose you're not so bad, Fido."

The wolf opened his mouth, let his tongue hang off to the side, and began to happily pant. She snorted a laugh and used her phone to snap a photo.

T.S. Tappin

Chapter Twenty-One

Jolene

Jolene wanted to be irritated with Rex, since he insisted on bringing her to work and picking her up, but she was trying to be understanding. Rex and his family were on edge. He had tried to call Nevaeh to get her to come back, but she flatly refused, saying she had classes she couldn't miss. Her man was a bit stressed, and she tried not adding to it more than necessary.

When he picked her up from work in a van with Top and Ginger, Jolene was surprised, since he hadn't given her a heads-up. She didn't mind, though. They were two of his closest friends, so she was actually looking forward to spending time and getting to know them.

"The clubhouse kitchen needs restocked," Ginger told her with a smile as she slid onto the backseat of the van.

With Top driving, Rex turned around to look at her from the front passenger seat. "Hey. How was your day?"

"Busy, but good, besides the usual suspect. I'm used to it, though."

He frowned. "Usual suspect?"

"The owner."

Rex looked over at Top, who glanced at him, both looking like they were silently scheming, before he pulled out of the parking lot.

Jolene could see where that was going and no. "No," she said firmly, pulling Rex's attention back to her. "You will not do anything about the owner. Not a look. Not a word. Not a *talk*. No buying the clinic."

It started with Ginger's snort, but before long, they were all laughing, then Rex gave her a grin and a wink, and replied, "Yes, Ma'am."

In the produce section of the big box grocery store, Jolene felt a little out of place. She didn't know what they needed to get. After a few awkward moments, she pulled up her big girl panties and asked Ginger, "How can I help?"

Ginger looked at the long list in her hand. "Uh… we need a variety of berries — Strawberries, raspberries, blueberries, etc. Grab three to four containers of each."

"You got it." Jolene made a beeline for the berry section. She was stacking plastic containers in her hands when she saw Rex out of the corner of her eye.

"Nice *berries*," he said with a grin.

Her gaze dropped to the two large cantaloupes in his hand. "Nice *melons*."

Top chuckled as he walked by with a bag of cucumbers.

Jolene raised a brow. "I don't know why you're laughing. That's a nice *sack* you got there."

"Don't comment on another man's sack. That's just rude," Rex objected with mock offense.

She shrugged. "If you had a sack, I'd compliment it." She winked and headed back to Ginger and her cart.

Halfway there, she felt Rex behind her before he whispered in her ear, "I'll show you my sack later."

"Promises. Promises."

Ten minutes later, they were out of the produce and on to the main aisles of the store. Top stopped halfway down the aisle and held up a box of macaroni noodles. "Want some *noods*?"

Rex took the box and grabbed two more before dropping them in the cart as he said, "The more *noods*, the better."

Ginger rolled her eyes, but crossed noodles off the list.

When they got to the next aisle, Rex grabbed a jar of relish and held it up. Looking into Jolene's eyes, he expressed, "I *relish* this time with you."

"Then follow my orders or," Jolene reached over, grabbed a jar of pickles, and held it up, "you'll end up in a *pickle*."

Ginger and Top started laughing as Jolene and Rex shared grins.

They chit-chatted about the family and Jolene's favorite animal patients. Ginger asked about Jolene's mom and how her recovery was coming along. Rex chimed in, and Jolene's heart melted a bit when he offered to see if the Ol' Ladies of the retired chapter members could check in on her. She pictured how her mother would react to a handful of biker babes showing up on her doorstep to help her. Truth be told,

T.S. Tappin

her mother would probably like that. It would up her *cool* factor in her community and with her friends.

As she told him that, Rex slipped his arm around her waist and pulled her closer as they walked.

Top grabbed five large boxes of cereal off the shelf and held them up. "Doc's mom will be *raisin* the roof with the Ol' Ladies." Then he dropped the boxes in the cart, topping it off. As the rest of them laughed, Top grinned. "I'm going to grab another cart."

They kept walking as Top jogged away.

After filling two more carts, they headed for the front of the store. Top winked at Ginger. "Time to check you out."

As they unloaded the carts onto two different belts, Jolene examined the trip. Maybe it was for Rex's sake, but Top and Ginger seemed to go out of their way to make her feel like part of them. She appreciated it either way. The more time she spent around members of the Howlers and the Claws, Jolene realized that Rex hadn't been exaggerating when he said they were just a big family. She liked that for him and for his daughter, and she could picture a world where she actually belonged there.

Who knew an emergency house call for a tiger would bring her a family?

Chapter Twenty-Two

Rex

After picking Doc up from work the next day, they hung out in his room for a couple of hours. She took a shower before they cuddled on the bed and talked about their days. It was when he mentioned that he hadn't seen any sign of the Pathfinder, and neither had anyone else, that Doc began asking questions.

"So… I know you said you were being followed, and that you thought you knew who was doing it. I need you to explain that more." Rolling over to face him, she looked into his eyes. "Who are these people?"

Rex ran a hand over his face and along his beard as he tried to figure out where to start. In the end, he decided to start at the beginning. "You know, months ago, when we first met, there were videos released about shifters?" She nodded, and he continued, "Well, the videos had been leaked for days, possibly weeks, before then. Some people saw them and did what humans often do when faced with something *unknown*. For instance, the witch trials. I'm sure there are more than just this academy, but an academy was set up. From what we understand, its purpose is to train people to kill shifters. They think we're monsters. That's actually how they refer to us. We had a member get close to one of them without revealing his connection to the Howlers. He didn't get a lot from her, but he learned that the academy does exist and that they think we are a danger to people around us. They apparently think we could just suddenly shift and hurt innocent people, and that we don't have any control over ourselves. That's just not true."

"Even when Bullet was out of it and shifted while I was stitching his skin together, he didn't lash out at me." She shifted into a sitting position. "So, they're fully prepared to kill people just because of something they haven't *proven* yet? That's not defending people. That's just murder."

Staring at the anger in her blue eyes made Rex smile. She was seriously pissed on the behalf of shifters everywhere. As a person of science, Doc was probably offended that they weren't doing their due diligence before establishing a conclusion and course of action. Fuck, he was so attracted to her for so many reasons other than her body. Her brain and her backbone were hot as hell.

She glared at him. "Stop fucking smiling. This shit isn't funny."

"Yes, Ma'am," he replied and started laughing when she smacked his arm. "Sorry."

"Seriously!"

Rex pulled himself together and covered her hand laying on the bed, giving it a gentle squeeze. "I'm sorry. I just... Seeing you get upset on our behalf made me happy."

The corners of her mouth twitched, before she asked, "And now you think they're following you?"

He nodded. "It's the logical conclusion, at this point, but we're trying to find out more information. Unlike them, we don't condemn things without actually doing research and gathering intel."

"But you haven't been followed in a couple days?"

He shook his head. "Not since the day we locked down. Not sure what to make of that, yet."

She reached over with her other hand and ran it through his hair on the side of his head. "You better keep yourself safe, or I won't be happy."

Rex shifted until he was sitting in front of her. Leaning forward, he pressed his lips to hers before saying against them, "Yes, Ma'am."

Jolene

After everything she learned from Rex about shifters, mates, and biker culture, Jolene was in desperate need of someone to run her thoughts by in an attempt to get some kind of clarification. Or at least, she needed someone from the outside to tell her she wasn't crazy for having questions or for the part of her that wished she could just take his word for it and just jump in with both feet.

She asked Mama Hen to join her at the compound for dinner. Normally, Jolene would have gone to Mama Hen, and she could have if she wanted to. She was at the compound because it was what Rex needed from her to take the edge off of his worry. Because of that, she had Mama Hen come to her.

They were sitting at a table near the far corner of the room, eating steaks and baked potatoes that Rex had made for them.

Mama Hen finished chewing a bit and nodded. "That man can cook a steak," she commented.

Jolene chuckled. "He's a good cook."

"What's the sitch?"

After taking a drink of water, she explained what Rex had told her. She had already known that Mama Hen was aware of shifters. During one of their late night talks, Rex had suggested she speak with her friend, Mama Hen, if she wanted an outside perspective.

For half an hour, Jolene went through everything he said and all the questions she had. When she was done, Mama Hen sat and stared at her with a knowing smirk on her face.

"What?" Jolene asked as she narrowed her eyes at Mama Hen.

"Let me put it like this. We were trained to hear what we're being told, but to also assess the situation, to follow the trail of facts, to find the cause, and to seek out everything that's hidden. With your schooling, that was reinforced."

Jolene nodded. The woman wasn't wrong.

"That's what you are trying to do. I think you need to realize that you were taught the truths of the human world, and this is something outside of that world, so of course it doesn't fall within that truth."

Jolene let her words sink in as she took a bite of steak and chewed. After she swallowed, she asked, "Are you saying I need to just accept what he's telling me?"

Mama Hen chuckled. "I'm telling you to change your lens of critique. Have you witnessed any of them shift?"

She nodded. She had. Between Bullet and Rex, she'd seen shifting up close multiple times.

"And you've witnessed other abilities they possess, correct?"

Jolene thought about Bullet's fast healing and Rex's eyes glowing, and nodded.

"They exist. That is a fact. What he's told you about their abilities is true. Why wouldn't the mating thing be true? I'm not saying just believe it. I'm saying use the skills you've been taught, but look at it from another perspective. See if that clears things up a bit."

"Makes sense," Jolene uttered, right before they heard a ruckus across the room.

Glancing over, they saw a few of the Howlers giving the twin prospects shit. Jolene smiled as she watched and listened to the display. "Reminds me of…" She paused and then shrugged. "Well… that's what happens when you're smokin' and jokin'."

Mama Hen nodded and met her gaze. "BOHICA."

Amused, they finished their meal, while Jolene made a promise to herself to look at the shifter situation with a different perspective.

Ranger

As a human in a group of shifters, Ranger often experienced jealousy regarding their abilities. There were times when he wished he had advanced strength or healing, and it wasn't uncommon that he wished his vision was as strong as theirs. Usually, thinking about the bullshit shifters had to deal with reminded him of the cost they paid. It wasn't worth it, in his opinion.

Eating his dinner at the table next to Mama Hen and Doc's table, Ranger used the skills he was taught in the military to pretend he couldn't hear the women's conversation. He wasn't really trying to eavesdrop, but he wasn't trying *not* to hear them either.

For the most part, they weren't talking about anything too juicy. It wasn't a surprise that someone like Doc would have issues accepting the magic of the shifters.

It wasn't until the phrases *Smokin' and Jokin'* and *BOHICA,* which stood for *Bend over, here it comes again,* were used that his interest increased. They weren't terms that civilians used, but they were commonly used by soldiers. Mama Hen using the phrases was one thing. There were things about her past that lent to her being from some branch of the military or government service. It was Doc's use of one of the phrases that had him mentally standing at attention. Did she just pick up the phrase from hanging with Mama Hen, or was there more there?

Ranger didn't know, but he sure as hell was going to try to find out.

Chapter Twenty-Three

Rex

Standing with Dragon and Top near the bar in the main room of the clubhouse, Rex sipped his beer and watched as Ginger helped Avery, her and Top's oldest, with her makeup. One of her friends was sitting next to her and attempting to do her hair. The frustrated growl that came from the young lady had all three of the men wincing.

"What are you trying to do?" Ginger voiced the question but kept her focus on applying Avery's eyeshadow.

"I was going to French braid the sides, but… UGH!"

Rex looked at Dragon, who was looking in his direction. They both shrugged and stepped forward. Rex approached one side, and Dragon the other. "What's your name, sweetie?"

The young girl looked from him to Dragon and back again before she stuttered out, "S-S-Sandra."

Rex gave her a gentle smile. "Nice to meet you, Sandra. I'm Rex. He's Dragon. If you're okay with it, we can help you."

"Y-You know how to… braid?"

After a nod, Rex replied, "All kinds of braids."

The gazes of the three other young girls sitting around the table shot in their direction, shock on their faces. One of them, a redhead who could have been Ginger's child, asked, "Can you teach us?"

"Sure," Rex answered. "Let us take care of Sandra's braids, then we'll do a quick tutorial."

In a matter of three minutes, they had French braided both sides of Sandra's head. She was astounded by it and very appreciative. Rex told her she was welcome, but Dragon just shrugged off her appreciation. He'd never been good with that sort of thing.

"You gonna be the model or am I?" Rex looked over at Dragon.

Dragon just raised a brow and pointed to an empty chair.

Rex chuckled as he took a seat, and Dragon pulled up another chair behind him as he instructed, "Gather around, girls."

Ginger laughed as all the teenagers surrounded them, even Avery. "Avery, you know how to French braid."

"If you think I'm missing out on watching Uncle Dragon braid Uncle Rex's hair, you've lost it."

Rex rolled his eyes, but grinned.

"Okay... First, you section off a line at the base of where you want your braid, like th... Damn, did you even brush your hair, Rex? Ginger, hand me that brush." Once he had the brush in hand, Dragon dragged it through Rex's hair repeatedly, starting on the bottom and working his way up. "Hand me that conditioner spray." After Ginger handed the yellow bottle over, Dragon spritzed that shit all over Rex's head. "There. See? So much easier to manipulate."

By the time Dragon actually started the braid, Ginger was bent over with laughter, her face a deep pink from lack of oxygen.

"Now, you break it up into three equal sections..." Rex tuned out Dragon as he continued on giving his demonstration. About halfway through, Rex looked across the table and saw Top barely containing himself. His best friend was enjoying it a little too much.

When Dragon was done and the girls returned to their spots, Top walked around the table and put his hands on top of Rex's shoulders. "Good boy," he quietly uttered.

The snorted laugh brought Rex's attention to the hallway, where he saw Doc's amused face right before she turned around and headed back the way she came.

"You're an asshole," Rex told Top through a laugh as he stood. As he went after his woman, he passed Gorgeous who had just entered the room and called out, "Okay. Who still needs makeup?"

Rex caught up to Doc halfway up the stairwell to the second floor of the apartment building. Wrapping his arms around her from behind, he kissed her neck. "Where you going?"

"I was coming to find you, but... you were busy."

Hearing the humor in her voice, he nipped the skin of her neck, making his wolf rumble. "Top thinks he's funny."

Doc turned in his arms and kissed his lips before she lifted her hands and ran them over his braid. "So... Nevaeh got her modeling chops from her dad?"

Rex rolled his eyes and uttered, "Duh."

With amusement and something hotter in those blue eyes, Doc gave his braid a pull. "You look kind of badass with a braid." She bit her bottom lip, then released it. "Very… viking-esque."

Rex lowered his head and sucked on her lower lip. After giving her a thorough kiss, he asked, "Would you like to raid my village, or shall I raid yours?"

"What if I'm in the mood to plunder?"

His wolf howled at the thought. After a shrug, Rex replied, "I could run from you, if you want."

Doc snorted a laugh. "Run, Fido, run."

Rex released her and jogged up to the top of the stairs. After glancing back at her, giving her a wink, he shifted into his wolf and darted down the hall to his room. His intention was to jump onto his bed, but he was thwarted by the shut and locked door.

Well, shit…

Doc casually strolled down the hall, swinging his keys on a ring around her finger. "Looking for these?"

After sitting down, Rex gave her a wolfy grin and waited patiently for her to make her way to him.

When she finally stopped in front of him, she ran her fingers through the scruff behind his ear. "You are a very handsome wolf. You're growing on me."

Shifting back, Rex replied, "I'd like to be doing something else on you."

Jolene

Staring at her man as he took the keys and unlocked the door, Jolene decided she didn't want to plunder. She wanted to let her man have time to do what he wanted. Even though she was giving him the power to make decisions, it didn't mean she wasn't in control. That was something she was coming to learn with Rex. Whether she was giving him orders or not, Rex was always watching and assessing what she needed. Unlike some other partners she'd had in the past, his goal during sex was to please her, not just to find his own pleasure.

When they stepped in the room, she shut and locked the door behind her, before turning and facing him. "What would you like to be doing to me?" When he opened his mouth to speak, she held up a hand to silence him. "Would you rather *tell* me or *show* me?"

His eyes flashed blue light right before she was lifted up and tossed on the bed. Rex came down on top of her and pressed his lips to hers as he began to undress her. He kept kissing her until he was unable to maintain the connection while taking off her clothes. After breaking the kiss, he helped her remove her shirt and bra, tossing them to the floor.

Holding himself up with his fists in the mattress, he bent his head down and sucked one of her nipples into his mouth, keeping his gaze on her face as he did. Pleasure shot through her from her nipple down to her clit with each pull on her breast, and each swirl off his tongue around the nub had her shivering with anticipation.

The look in his eyes had just as much to do with it as his actions. In those ice blue depths, she saw lust, but she also saw determination and consideration. He wanted her to enjoy what he was doing just as much as he liked doing it. *That* was probably the biggest turn-on she had ever encountered.

She cupped the back of his head with one hand while she slid the other down between her thighs. He pulled off of her nipple as his eyes tracked the movement. When her fingers met their destination and circled her clit, he growled with approval and latched on to her other nipple.

Jolene wondered if he would let her continue. She was surprised when he let her play for a little bit, before he released her nipple and kissed his way down her body. When he reached her mound, he pushed away her fingers and took over, using his tongue. Sliding two fingers into her pussy, he maintained eye contact with her. He didn't rush through the motions or get impatient. He just kept up what he was doing, gauging her reactions and making adjustments as necessary, until she began to convulse around his fingers.

Bliss surged through Jolene, making her gasp as she arched off the bed. Rex continued his ministrations as she moaned his name and rolled her hips as she rode out her orgasm. Her muscles began to relax, and she collapsed back to the bed, panting and twitching.

She heard his chuckling right before she felt his lips trail up her body, stopping briefly to nuzzle the inside curves of her breasts, before continuing on. He nibbled along her collarbone, his beard tickling her skin as his left hand curled around the back of her knee and lifted it to his side.

Jolene let out a sigh of contentment as she wrapped her legs around him and traced the lines of his braid with her fingers.

"I love tasting you," he said against her skin. "I love kissing you." He gave her neck a wet, slow kiss. "I love pleasing you." He reached between them with one hand and softly circled her clit with a fingertip, making her gasp and twitch as he lifted his head and gazed into her eyes. After a moment, he pressed his forehead against hers, maintaining eye contact.

Jolene cupped his face in her hands, loving the connection between them.

She felt him line up the head of his cock against her entrance. "I love you, Jolene," he whispered as he slowly slid inside of her.

Both his movements and his words shot heat into her blood, filling her with his emotion and stealing her breath. She didn't speak. She couldn't. She just stared into his eyes as they shared the same breath and made love.

His hand curved around her ass and gripped. Lifting and tilting her so he could go deeper, their bodies rubbing together with every thrust, as he dropped his walls and let her all the way in.

Yet again, the man gave her something she needed without her having to say a word. He didn't tell her he loved her with expectations of her saying the same. He said it because he meant it and wanted her to know. It was a true gift, a blessing she would cherish.

As his rhythm quickened and increased in intensity, Jolene slid her hands to the back of his head and dug her fingers into his braid as she struggled to meet him thrust for thrust. The man was on a mission to make every man or toy in creation pale in comparison to the pleasure he could give her, and she had no doubt he would achieve his goal.

"Rex," she shouted as another orgasm came out of nowhere and carried her away.

"Fuck yes, Doc," he growled as he slammed into her over and over again. "Take me with you."

As she clamped down on him, she felt his body tense in her arms and saw the blue light shine from his eyes. Two strokes later, he thrust into her and stayed while his body twitched with his climax, and he whispered her name against her lips.

Emotion clogged in her throat as their orgasms ebbed. She didn't know what to say, couldn't find the words to tell him how he made her feel or what he meant to her.

Rex just smiled and kissed her lips. "It's okay. I get it. I feel it, too," he said softly as he wrapped his arms around her and rolled to his side. For a while, he just held her, and Jolene allowed herself to just be at peace with her wolf shifter, bedroom sub, biker boyfriend.

Chapter Twenty-Four

Rex

After three days of nothing, Axle had loosened the restrictions a bit on the Ol' Ladies and children. Doc had used that fact against Rex in order to drive herself to work. As he watched her drive away in her little SUV, under strict orders to not follow her on threat of a very vanilla sex life, Rex wished he hadn't told her about the change in restriction status. His wolf growled his agreement.

Knowing there was nothing he could do about it, Rex turned his attention to what he had to do that day. Originally, he was going to be helping install drywall at the new club building, but Axle had sent him a text asking him to go to the apartment building on Elm to replace the bathroom pipes in two of the empty units. They had recently been vacated, and Howlers Properties decided it was time to upgrade them, which meant they were getting new bathrooms. The Howlers weren't known for doing anything halfway.

It smelled like it was about to snow, so there was no way Rex was going to take his bike, but the change in job assignment required him to take his truck, anyway. He had to grab the tools from the shed on the Howlers Properties lot, along with the supplies from the hardware store. Before he did that, though, he needed to head to the units to make sure he knew exactly what to grab.

Work smarter, not harder.

After climbing in and starting his truck, he drove out of the parking lot and headed down the road. He was two blocks from the apartment building when he saw the Pathfinder drive past him on the driver's side. Without hesitation, he made a turn and followed it.

Three miles down the road, they turned into a parking lot that was almost completely hidden by the thick trees that surrounded it. As soon as the Pathfinder stopped, Rex put his truck in park and waited. A few seconds later, a man got out of the driver's seat. He had dark brown, almost black hair that was short but perfectly styled, and a trimmed goatee on his face. He was wearing a black polo and black cargo pants, along with black combat boots, looking like a dutiful soldier of some fucked up army.

After retrieving his gun from the locked compartment in his truck and releasing the safety, Rex slid out of his vehicle and aimed at the man as he approached. "Who the fuck are you, and why are you following us?"

Rex suspected he knew. If he was right, this was a hunter from that fucking academy a few hours away. They were playing at being soldiers, but if they kept their shit up, they were going to find out what war really was.

The man just grinned as the back window lowered a couple inches, then a muzzle was slid out. Before Rex could do much, there was an odd noise, then Rex felt the sting of a needle in his neck. Lifting his hand, he grasped the dart and yanked it from his skin before he collapsed to the ground. White flakes began to fall from the sky, and the last thought he had before everything went black was, *I knew it was going to snow.*

Jolene

When Jolene got to work, she was actually five minutes early, but you wouldn't be able to tell by the way the owner reacted. Dr. Thatcher started her day by asking where in the hell she had been, and before she could reply, he started ranting about there being an emergency and needing another set of hands.

The urge to tell him where to go was strong. If she let that side out, though, she'd be letting out a soldier who was capable of eliminating a man and burying his body in a discreet location without losing a wink of sleep. Jolene hadn't been a typical soldier. No, she had been part of an off-the-record unit that did all the things no one wanted to claim. She had not only been trained to do a myriad of horrendous acts but also how to do them without remorse. That part of herself, she had learned to put in a lockbox and set about starting a new life for herself, but it didn't go away. It was always there, just waiting for her to turn the key.

Shoving the urge down, Doc washed her hands and gloved up before she headed into the small operating room in the back of the clinic.

It was going to be a long day.

T.S. Tappin

Chapter Twenty-Five

Rex

His head was throbbing, and his mouth felt dry. As Rex slowly came back to consciousness, he kept his eyes closed and tried to figure out what was wrong. Something was off. Where was he? Why did his body ache?

Trying to take slow, even breaths, he used his other senses to piece things together. He was laying against something hard, like concrete. Concrete? Why would he be…

The scene in the parking lot came back to him in a rush. The man in the fake soldier get-up, the Pathfinder, the open window, the sting in his neck, and the snow all flashed behind his eyelids, filling in some of the blanks.

Suddenly on alert, he listened more intently and heard voices at a distance, but with his shifter senses, he could still hear them clearly.

"How long do you think it will take for them to wake up?"

"Don't know. It's a new formula. They tweaked the blocker and added a tranquilizer," a male voice replied.

Fuck. They shot up him with a dose of the shifter blocker mixed with tranquilizer? Rex tried to sense his wolf, but where he would normally feel the canine, there was nothing but an emptiness. Panic spiked in his system, and the pain of his missing wolf threatened to cripple him, but he had to push all of that aside. He couldn't lose focus or crumble when his life was on the line. The rest could be addressed when he wasn't wherever the fuck he was being held. He had to assess his situation and figure out how to get out of it.

His head spiked with sharp pain again, causing him to wince, while he wondered why his healing abilities didn't seem to be taking care of it. He tried to remember if the blocker affected healing capabilities, or even if the Howlers had been given any information on that, but he couldn't think clearly through the pain.

After a few moments, he was able to push aside the pain and focus on his senses. The scent of mildew and dirt filled his sinuses as Rex concentrated on the way the voices echoed in the space. It had to be a somewhat large location with concrete floors, possibly concrete walls.

Not sensing the presence of anyone close to him, he slowly opened his eyes a sliver and attempted to look around. He saw mostly darkness, but a few feet to the left, he spotted a woman hanging from a concrete wall. She was short and curvy, and didn't seem to be conscious. He couldn't see much of her face with the way her head was hanging forward, but he kept scanning her body for any bit of recognition. Peeking out from behind the long strands of blond hair, he saw patches on a leather cut. One of them read *Shortcake*.

Fuck!

His arms were up above his head, and it wasn't from his own doing. He glanced up and saw that his wrists were cuffed and connected to chains that were affixed to the wall. He wasn't lying on the ground, like he originally thought. He was leaning against a wall. Wrapping his hands around the chains, he braced his feet shoulder-length apart on the floor and pulled with every ounce of strength he had. It didn't take long for him to realize that his shifter strength was failing him.

They were wholly and truly screwed.

Jolene

Multiple times throughout the day, Jolene sent text messages to Rex in order to let him know she was okay. She saw the worry on his face that morning when she insisted on driving herself to work. She was still working through things and contemplating what he told her days ago, but she was warming to the idea of it all.

The previous night, when he confessed his love for her and promised her that it was him, and not just his wolf, who felt that way, something shifted inside of her. Some part of her hesitancy dissolved as she gazed into those ice-blue eyes and saw the truth of his words there on display. He truly did love her.

During lunch, she sent yet another and began to worry when she saw that he hadn't answered any of her texts.

JOLENE: I'm on lunch. Had food delivered and eating at my desk. Are you busy?

After a few minutes, she received a reply.

REX: That's good. Just busy.

She felt a little better when she got the reply, but it seemed short. Jolene couldn't put her finger on exactly why her gut was yelling at her, but it was. She contemplated contacting Axle to make sure everything was okay, but she decided that would be an overreaction. Rex was probably just busy with the plumbing he was working on that day.

Jolene nibbled on her sub sandwich and fries as she coached herself on not being a clingy woman just because a man professed his love for her. She had never been that kind of woman, and she wouldn't start now.

After a moment, things he said to her floated into her brain. *Humans feel a pull. Don't you feel it?* She wondered if what she thought of as clinginess was really just the pull he told her about.

Hmm... Something else to consider.

Rex

When they had heard Rex trying to break his chains loose, four people rushed over. Two men and two women watched as he struggled, but nothing happened. When it was apparent he wasn't getting anywhere, the two men taunted him as the women grinned. He memorized their faces as he accepted that he wasn't going to be able to just break free.

"Not so big and bad now, are ya, freak," one of the men taunted. It was the same man who had climbed out of the Pathfinder earlier, with his fucking perfectly styled hair and plucked brows.

The other, who looked like he belonged on the cover of *All-American Douchebag* magazine with his light brown curly hair and sharp features, crossed his arms over his chest and chuckled. "I thought it would be tougher to take a couple of you beasts, but it was like taking candy from a baby."

Rex spit at him, the saliva landing on the fucker's pant leg. "If your taunts are anything to go by, taking you out will be like getting your mom to suck my dick… easy as fuck."

"Good luck with that," the woman with long curly hair said as she approached Shortcake, pulled back her arm, and swung, slapping Shortcake across the face.

Shortcake groaned as her head swung from one side to the other as if she was struggling to lift it.

Rex cursed every one of them as Miss Curly shouted, "Wake up, Bitch! The games are about to begin!"

The other woman, who had her dark brown hair pulled back in a stark bun, joined Miss Curly, and they each took hold of Shortcake's legs and began to attach the ankle cuffs that were laying on the floor.

Rex realized his ankles were still free. Why the fuckers hadn't already attached them, he didn't know, but he was about to make them regret it. As soon as Miss Curly was focused enough on her task, Rex kicked out with his closest leg and managed to kick her into Stark Bun, toppling them both.

Deep down inside, it killed him to treat a woman that way, but desperate times and all that.

Chaos erupted as the men attempted to grab his ankles and attach the restraints, but Rex didn't make that easy for them. The females had managed to complete their task with Shortcake, but not without her coming to and spitting blood and saliva on them.

Rex knew they were going to suffer, probably greatly. He could only hope that Keys was paying attention to their tracker apps on their phones and realized something was off.

"Messer!" All-American Douchebag shouted and looked across the space. "Make yourself useful and get them towels! Christ!"

"Get your own fucking towels," a female voice said, echoing through the room.

Rex looked in the direction the voice came from and saw that standing in the shadows of the large basement room was a familiar looking woman. When she stepped forward into a shaft of light from the single bulb that was hanging from the ceiling, it was confirmed. The fucking hunter that had come to town to investigate them.

"I fucking knew it," Rex growled as he glared at the bitch who was the reason they were in the mess to begin with. If she wouldn't have told the others anything about the Howlers or Warden's Pass, he would be replacing pipes and Shortcake would be doing whatever it was that she had planned for the day.

Her expression blank, Messer dropped her gaze to the floor and didn't say a word.

Annoyed with her presence, Rex glanced around again and saw the parking lot guy fucking around on a phone that looked suspiciously like Rex's.

"What in the fuck are you doing on my phone?"

The asshole grinned. "Letting someone named Doc know you're too busy to talk."

Fuck.

Rex wasn't sure how much more he could take, and he wasn't even the one being tortured. Shortcake had slices up and down her shins. Her screams had long since ceased, leaving her only whimpering and moaning as they continued to shout questions at her and cut her when she didn't answer.

Guilt and hatred washed over Rex. His wrists pinched and burned as he struggled repeatedly to break free, but the chains wouldn't budge. He should have been able to save her. It was the mission of the Howlers, after all, to help women in situations where they were mistreated or abused. He should have been able to stop it.

Gritting his teeth as he once again yanked on the chains, desperately attempting to pull forward his wolf, but nothing. Rex growled out his anger and frustration. The fuckers better hope he didn't get a moment of freedom. They better kill him, because if they didn't, he would tear them apart as soon as he was able.

"Who else?! Who?" The shouted questions had been going on for hours, each of their captors taking turns, except for Messer. She was standing off to the side in the darkness with her arms crossed over her chest. The look on her face said she was not happy about how things were going down. At least she wasn't blank faced anymore. Probably was pissed that Shortcake hadn't given them anything, and no matter what they did, Rex wasn't going to, either. If he thought for a moment that telling them something would save Shortcake's life, he might consider it, but he knew it wouldn't. These assholes were determined to kill shifters, and they had two in their clutches.

He hadn't accepted his fate, though. As he watched Shortcake's blood trickle down her legs, catching briefly on each cut in her jeans, and over her boots to pool at her feet on the concrete, Rex promised himself that he would watch for any chance to break free and end them.

Shortcake hadn't been his favorite person. He didn't hate her, but he didn't know much about her. They were from two different worlds — her being the young, vivacious beauty and him being an older, single dad. Regardless, she was family, and he felt a responsibility to avenge her.

Rex refused to take his eyes off of her. Every once in a while, she lifted her head enough to look over at him. He tried his best to give her hope and strength, but he could tell it wasn't working as she began to hang, relying more and more on the cuffs to keep her up.

In a voice that was almost too low for the fuckers to hear, Shortcake mumbled, "Fuck you."

Miss Curly, who had just been shouting the questions, stepped forward and grabbed a handful of Shortcake's hair. Yanking her head up, she asked, "What did you say?"

In a slurred, but louder voice, Shortcake repeated, "Fuck you."

Miss Curly glared as she pulled back her free hand, already balled into a fist, and swung forward, hitting Shortcake in the eye.

Rex knew Shortcake had completely given up when she just quietly laughed. He was almost positive she was to the point where she no longer felt pain, probably due to the amount of blood she had lost.

Whatever they had put in that blocker had affected their healing abilities, causing each and every one of the sixteen slices on her shins and lower thighs to bleed more than they normally would. She was slowly dying, and there was nothing he could do to stop it. He wished they would just end it.

Rage compounded with grief and guilt inside of him until he couldn't contain it any longer. Opening his mouth, he let it out on a roar. Not a roar from an animal. No, a roar from a man that was pushed beyond the point of despair.

His shout was like an on switch. As the echo of his fury faded, Miss Curly and Stiff Bun went to town on Shortcake. After stabbing her several times in the gut, Stiff Bun lifted her knife to Shortcake's throat and sliced, finally ending her.

As Shortcake's body slumped, Parking Lot Guy began his slow walk in Rex's direction, a giddy, evil glint in his dark eyes. "Your turn."

T.S. Tappin

Chapter Twenty-Six

Rex

Staring at Shortcake's prone body hanging from the cuffs and chains attached to the wall above her head, Rex didn't even feel the first several punches. It probably had something to do with despair, but it also had something to do with the fact that the asshole's muscles were obviously for show. There was barely any power behind each blow to Rex's gut.

It wasn't until All-American Douchebag took a turn that Rex's attention was actually pulled from Shortcake. Turning his attention to the fuckers in front of him, Rex snarled, "You say *we're* monsters, but who's beating who?"

A punch to the jaw forced Rex's head to the side, but he just righted it and didn't make a sound. He wouldn't give them that pleasure.

They ignored his comment and asked, "Who else is a shifter?"

Rex shrugged. "The Pope? The president? Mick Jagger?"

The fucker pulled back his arm and swung it forward. The knife stabbed into Rex's thigh. Gritting his teeth, he met All-American Douchebag's stare. He would not scream for them.

"Who *in the clubs* are shifters? Who else?"

"Hey, numbnuts, I never claimed to be a fucking shifter. You're just fucking guessing. *Keep* fucking guessing." Rex grinned. "Go on. Head to the compound. Take your pick. See what happens."

"It wasn't a guess." All-American Douchebag chuckled. "We've been watching you for weeks. We've seen your eyes glow, you freak. That's a sign, right, Messer?"

Messer didn't reply.

"So, along with an obvious problem with delusions, you also have eye trouble? So sad," Rex said in a deadpanned voice. "The healthcare system in this country is certainly something that needs to change."

Rex bit back a groan of pain as AAD pulled that knife from his thigh and stabbed him in the bicep.

"My eyes work just fucking fine, freak."

After breathing through the pain, Rex forced a smile. "If your eyes work fine and you can see yourself in a mirror, what's your excuse for that haircut?"

Parking Lot guy stepped forward and stabbed another knife into Rex's other thigh. Twisting the knife, causing Rex to groan despite himself, the fucker leaned in close and whispered, "That Doc is pretty for an older lady. Bet she's great in bed." He lifted his free hand and showed the screen to Rex. "Is it the fact that she's a veterinarian that makes her like fucking animals?"

Staring at the selfie he had taken and she had texted him, the asshole's words fanned the flame of fury coursing through Rex's veins. The pain faded as his heart began to race and his breathing picked up. Shouting unintelligible things at them, Rex pulled his head back and threw it forward, head-butting the fucker as hard as he could.

"Fuck!" Parking Lot guy stepped back, dropping Rex's phone to the ground as he lifted his hands to his face, blood gushing from his nose.

Rex kept shouting, not giving a damn what they did to him. He would kill them. He would, if he could just get free. If he could just get one of the chains to break, he would take out all of them with their own fucking knives.

"I won't tell you shit! No matter what you do! I won't tell you shit! Fuck you!"

That was when the beating began.

Messer

Messer couldn't take it anymore. Watching the Elites beat the hell out of a man and stab him in places they knew would hurt like hell, but wouldn't kill him, turned her stomach. The absolute glee on Elite Perez's face enraged her as he used his knives on their prisoner's limbs and Elite McCort pummeled the man with his fists. She didn't join the academy to torture people or to physically assault them out of rage and spite. Sure, there was a time and a place for *creative interrogation*, but there was also a line where you were no longer trying to get information and were just inflicting pain for the hell of it.

Unable to justify being there a moment longer, Messer snuck up the stairs and out the back door of the abandoned house they were using. She rushed through the falling snow to the Pathfinder and yanked the driver's door open. Looking around, she tried to find the fob, hoping like hell they left it in the vehicle. When she didn't find it, she sent up a prayer and pushed the start button, but nothing happened. The fob must be in the basement with the others, and the distance was too great for it to work. She thought for sure that they would forget t in a cup holder or something. Apparently, they d d have a brain cell or two between the four of them.

She wouldn't be leaving in the Pathfinder, but there was no way in hell Messer was staying there. She needed to be far away from the fuck-up foursome the academy sent her to Michigan with.

As she headed on foot for the county road the house was on, Messer thought about what had happened to the two prisoners. They knew Rex was a shifter. Besides seeing his eyes glow before, there was a picture in his text string with *Doc* that showed a gray and light brown wolf cuddling up to her side. That sealed the deal in their mind.

Jogging down the shoulder, carefully taking each step in the quickly accumulating snow, Messer tried to figure out a plan. Where could she go? She needed a ride, money, and a place to lie low and plan. *Fuck!*

The only places she knew that were close were connected to the Howlers. The Howlers... When they learned what was done to their members, the world would burn. If they figured out she was involved, they would come for her... unless she came to them and gave them the information they needed first.

Thinking back on what she just witnessed, guilt swirled in her gut. She didn't like the way the situation was handled. There was nothing honorable about what happened in that basement. The woman was gone, but the Howlers might be able to save Rex if she got to them quickly enough.

Shaking off her doubts, Messer made a decision and set about carrying it out. She would flag down a car and hitchhike to the Howlers. Hopefully, she would get to them in time for the Howlers to make a rescue. Fingers crossed, they would let her keep her life in exchange for that information.

The kind elderly man stopped his truck at the mouth of the cul-de-sac that held the biker compound. His bushy white eyebrows pulled together as he eyed the place.

"Are you sure this is the right place, young lady?"

Messer gave him a gentle smile. "Yes, Mr. Clemmings. Thank you for the ride." She took hold of the interior door handle and pulled the lever to open the door. "I really appreciate it."

"You call that number I gave you if they give you any trouble."

Biting back the snort of hilarity at the thought of this man facing off with the dozens of bikers in the compound, Messer gave a nod. "I will. Have a good night." She climbed out of the truck and shut the door, giving him a wave as he slowly pulled away.

Taking a deep breath, she turned and headed for the clubhouse. The snow wasn't falling quite as heavily as it had been earlier, so she could clearly see the whole of the compound. As she took each step, more and more people looked her way. Most of them were customers of the various businesses that lined the street, but she recognized a few people in the diner as members of the Tiger's Claw MC. Glancing the other direction, she saw three members of the Howlers MC standing in a garage bay, staring at her, one of them had a phone to his ear.

She suspected the man was calling Axle, and her suspicions were confirmed when the clubhouse door swung open and Axle stormed out with a blond man, palming a gun.

As she reached the bottom of the steps to the clubhouse, that gun was raised and aimed at her as Axle bit out, "What in the fuck told you that this would be a good idea?"

"I have information you need. It's life and death."

His eyes narrowed on her before he glanced around. She figured he realized that they had quite the audience, because he quietly ordered, "Frisk her and bring her into my office." He turned and yanked open the clubhouse doors. "And then start making calls. I have a feeling we're going to have another shitshow on our hands."

Jolene

After picking up Beast from Mama Hen, Jolene headed for home, going a bit slower since the large snowflakes were making it difficult to see. She had tried contacting Rex again, but the phone just rang. There was an uneasiness in her that she couldn't shake, but she told herself that it was just the new mating stuff that had her off-kilter. The only thing that lifted her mood was that the snow began to lighten up as she pulled into her driveway.

In her kitchen at home, she fed and watered Beast before heading to her room, where she changed out of her scrubs and into a pair of thick black leggings and a red tank top.

It was dinnertime, and her stomach was complaining, so she decided to make dinner. If Rex

Rex's Release

showed up, she'd make him something, but she wasn't going to wait on him to get started.

After examining what was in her freezer, Jolene settled on a frozen lasagna. Once it was in the oven, she poured herself a glass of whiskey and crossed the house to turn on the radio. She needed something to fill the silence. The house was too quiet, and it was making her anxiety worse.

As she passed the front door, she heard odd noises coming from outside. From the kitchen doorway, Beast began flip-flopping between whining and growling.

Alarm bells went off in her head and in her gut. She dove for the bench next to her door and retrieved her pistol from the hidden drawer in the bottom. Quickly checking it over, making sure it was loaded, and releasing the safety, she took a deep breath and approached the front door from the side.

Listening closely, she heard slight moans and the slamming of multiple car doors. Another deep breath, then she swung the door open, lifting her gun to aim, but her eyes dropped down to the large man slumped on her stoop. He was bleeding and looked to be heavily beaten.

There was so much blood in his long hair and swelling and bruising on the face that it took her a moment to realize it was Rex. Her heart dropped as she engaged the safety on the gun and set it aside before figuring out the best way to get him inside.

The squealing tires made her jump and look toward the road. Through the falling snow, she saw a black Pathfinder rounding the corner a block away and speeding off.

Concern for Rex mixed with fury running through her system, but she called on her former training to compartmentalize the situation. First, she needed to get Rex inside. Second, she needed to get Rex stable. Then she would hunt those fuckers down and make them pay for what they did to him.

Standing by his head, she reached down and slipped her hands under his back and hooked them through his armpits. As carefully as she could, she pulled him through the doorway, apologizing profusely when he moaned.

He was mumbling, but she couldn't understand what he was trying to say. Laying him out on the floor of her foyer, she used her foot to close the door. She looked around for her medical bag, but didn't see it anywhere. Then Jolene realized she didn't have it with her when she left for work that morning. *Fuck!* She had left it at the compound.

Reaching down, she put two fingers to his wrist and felt for a pulse. It was steady, but not as strong as she would like it to be.

Think, Jolene! Taking a deep breath, she headed for her bathroom to grab her first aid kit. As she stepped into the hallway, her gaze landed on the door to the basement. Taking another quick left, she yanked the door open and bolted down the stairs. Once at the bottom, she crossed the space and shoved an old, empty bookcase out of the way to get to the locked door behind it. It wasn't any normal door. It was reinforced steel with a combination lock and a fingerprint scanner. She punched in the combination and put the pad of her left thumb to the scanner. There was a beep and then the sound of the metal rods adjusting, signaling it was unlocked.

Yanking the door open, she stepped inside and ignored the weapons for the moment. Her priority was Rex. Once he was stable, she would arm up. Vowing to herself that she wouldn't let his attackers get away, she grabbed the medical supplies she needed from a shelf, along with a stethoscope. She rushed back up the stairs, leaving the door to her hidden room open.

Once she was back in the foyer, she dropped to her knees and got to work on Rex. When she heard a whimpering to her right, she calmly said, "He'll be okay, Beast. Everything's okay."

"Love you," Rex mumbled, his voice low and grainy.

"Stop it," she bit out. "Don't you fucking dare give up. You hear me? Are you going to leave your mate to roam this world without you? *My mate* wouldn't do that. You fucking fight... fight for us, Rex."

"Listen." He tried to move his arm to reach out to her, but the knife wound in his bicep made it difficult. Yanking open a field bandage, she leaned down. Looking into her eyes, he said, "Tell Axle... County Road 452... Abandoned house... five miles outs... outside..." He winced, and his eyes lost focus. "Outside town. East."

Her eyes clocked all the wounds she could see. He had knife wounds in each thigh and in both biceps, and cuts on his forehead and lip. The bleeding and awkward angle of his nose suggested it had been broken. Blood loss was her biggest concern.

Using her stethoscope, she checked his breathing and found his lungs sounded clear. That was good. She carefully lifted his head to check the back of his head. Surprisingly, there weren't any contusions. That was also good.

"Why aren't you healing?" The question was more a mumble to herself than an inquiry to him.

"Blocker," he mumbled. "Stops... wolf... stops... heal."

Fuck! Opening suture kits, she got to work on assessing and closing wounds, then wrapped them in the field dressing bandages that she had grabbed from her stock.

Using her fingers, she assessed his nose and determined she could set it, but it would be painful. Apologizing, she put her fingertips to his nose and manipulated the affected area.

Rex shouted, then his eyes rolled. She double checked his vitals and wiped off the worst of the blood.

Feeling confident that he was stable enough, she washed her hands in the kitchen sink. Then she called Mama Hen as she headed back down to her basement room.

"Jolene, hey, girl."

Jolene didn't bother with pleasantries. "I need you at my house. Now."

"Report." Mama Hen was suddenly all business.

"Rex beat, stabbed, and dropped on my doorstep. He's stable. I have a bill to pay."

"On my way. You call Axle?"

"Wait until you're here. Then you can call him. He's my mate. This is mine," Jolene said firmly as she put the phone on speaker and set it on a shelf. She grabbed her bulletproof vest and put it on, strapping it tight, before she pulled a shoulder holster on and armed up.

"Understood." Then the line went dead.

After pulling a light jacket over it all, she slipped extra ammo into the pockets. Jolene quickly put on a set of combat boots and slid a knife in the inside hidden sheath before grabbing her phone from the shelf.

Rage steadied her heart rate, and she moderated her breathing as she climbed the stairs. The veterinarian wasn't in charge anymore. No, it was the unapologetic, government-trained killer who was handling that mission.

T.S. Tappin

Chapter Twenty-Seven

Messer

Following Axle into what looked to be an office at the back of the clubhouse building, with the blond walking behind her with his gun in hand, Messer gave thanks that they at least spared her life. She had no illusions that she would make it out unscathed, but she'd be happy to just make it out alive.

"Sit," the blond ordered.

Messer sat down in one of the visitor chairs in the room, across the desk from where Axle was now sitting.

"What is this important information?" Axle asked, leaning forward, with his forearms resting on the top of the desk.

After taking another deep breath and sending up another prayer, Messer let it all out. She told them why she was in town, who came with her, and admitted they had been following various members. She explained that she didn't have any authority on the mission, and that she had been demoted when she didn't bring back enough new information after her first trip to Warden's Pass. After she got through all of that, she said, "Yesterday, they put trackers on Rex's truck and a female's car. I think you call her Shortcake. This morning, they shot them up with an altered shifter blocker and kidnapped them."

"What?!" The blond put his gun to her temple.

"Where. Are. They?" Axle's growled question was accompanied by a silver light, announcing the level of his rage.

"She's gone," Messer admitted quietly and sucked in a breath, waiting for the shot, afraid to move too much with the muzzle of the gun against her skin. When it didn't come, she exhaled slowly. "Rex was still alive when I snuck out. I was horrified by what they were doing and couldn't…" She closed her eyes and then reopened them. "It wasn't right. I doubt they're still there, though. They were—"

Axle's phone rang, and he instantly answered it. "Mama Hen, I'm bus—"

Blondie and Messer waited while Axle listened to the hotel owner. His eyes widened.

"He's stable?" More silence. "Where the fuck is Doc?" He winced. "Okay. Sorry. I *said* sorry. Do you know where Doc is?" He listened, then he thanked Mama Hen. "Get everyone in here, right now," Axle ordered to blondie.

"Prez," Blondie began to protest.

"*Now,* Pike. Whoever is on site."

Blondie grumbled, but he turned and left the room. Messer finally breathed normally without the gun pointed at her.

"You know you aren't free, right?" Axle glared at her. "You are our prisoner. And you better hope we're able to find him and that he's alive. I will let Crush decide what your punishment for Shortcake will be."

"I understand, but know I didn't take part in the kidnapping or the... questioning."

Axle let out a humorless laugh. "You are who you hang out with," he told her and nodded to the logo on her polo shirt.

Less than a minute later, six grown men walked into the room, but she only had eyes for one. *Matthew.* They locked gazes for a moment, his chocolate brown eyes showing recognition. Her eyes scanned his body and halted on the leather cut he was wearing. She was stunned.

Pulling her focus from him, she felt her heart begin to pound harder in her chest. Was he playing them or had he been playing her? *Fuck!*

Axle quickly ran through what she told them before he demanded she write down the address of the location she last saw the Elites.

"If they dropped Rex off somewhere, they won't be there anymore. And I don't know where they would go. They didn't exactly trust me."

There were some rumbles in the crowd of bikers, but it was drowned out by Axle's commanding voice. "We need someone to fill Crush in. We also need someone to watch the prisoner and protect her from Crush... for now."

"I got it, Prez," Matthew said in that low, growly voice of his. It both comforted and terrified her.

Axle eyed him for a moment, then he gave a nod. "Brute, stay with him. The rest of you in the vans. Now."

Rex

It would have been easier for Rex to identify where he *didn't* hurt than for him to catalog his injuries. They had made sure to tag all of his limbs, and that was before the beat-down. As he laid on the floor of Doc's foyer, waiting for her to return, he wondered how long the newest variant of the shifter blocker would stay in his system.

Trying yet again, he was unable to sense his wolf. The space where his wolf should be was just empty. That was the most worrying. Sure, Crush got her tiger back, but it was a different variant of the drug than they gave her. On top of that, he worried about how long it would take to heal. With shifter healing he would be right as rain in a few days, but it didn't seem to be working.

He ignored the increased throbbing in his head and face as he turned it to look around for Doc, but he couldn't see her anywhere. *Where did she go?* He didn't remember much after she reset his nose.

Hearing a whimper, Rex shifted his head again to look down along his side. Beast was slowly easing in his direction, sadness and concern in those dark brown eyes. He let out another whimper as he approached Rex's face, then he licked his cheek before Beast laid his little Yorkie body down and cuddled into the crook of Rex's neck.

Rex smiled, even though he was still hurting. It was an extreme measure to go to in order to get a dog to accept him, but he'd do anything for Doc.

"You can't be hurt that bad if you're grinning like that," Mama Hen said as she walked up with a sawed-off shotgun with a hot pink stock in her right hand, Maxie trotting at her side.

"What are you… doing here?" Rex asked as he stared up at her.

"Well… *Someone* had to stand guard. Your mate took off to end the fuckers who attempted to end you."

His head throbbing, Rex narrowed his gaze. "She *what?!*"

Jolene

After leaving Warden's Pass, Jolene took a right on Phillips Road and turned left onto County Road 452 going East. Rex said five miles, so she alternated between watching the odometer, the road, and the properties that were scattered along the distance.

Just over four and a half miles from Phillips Road, she saw an abandoned two-story house. Taking a right into the driveway, she visually scanned the property. Jolene didn't see signs of anyone, and there were no vehicles besides her own small SUV.

Pulling out the small flashlight that she kept in the glove box and a gun from her holster, she got out and kept her head on a swivel as she slowly approached the house. The driveway was dirt, mostly packed, but she could see fresh tire tracks. Someone had been there recently.

Glancing at the front porch, she saw that there were rotted and missing boards. Deciding the back porch and door were the better, safer option, she headed that way.

Doing her best to not make much noise, Jolene creeped up the three steps at the rear of the house and crossed the small porch. The back door was wide open. Remaining vigilant, she entered the dark space and stopped just inside to listen. When she didn't hear anything, she flicked on the flashlight and began searching the place.

Walking through the kitchen, she saw a small yellow notepad on the kitchen counter, but it was empty. Continuing on, she made her way through the dining room and into the living room. Besides left behind furniture, there wasn't anything that caught her eye until she got to the fireplace. There was no fire burning, but there were ashes left behind. In the firebox, lying at the bottom next to the grate, was a piece of paper with scorched edges at one side. It looked as if the piece fell while the rest of the page burned.

Carefully, she picked up the piece of paper and examined it. Jutting out from the scorched end were five digits. Staring at it, she tried to figure out what the number could be.

A phone number?

Pin code?

Social security number?

As she worked through the options, she realized the color of the piece of paper was yellow, like the pad that was on the kitchen counter. Retreating to the kitchen, she snatched the pad off the counter and shined the flashlight on it. There was a visible imprint on the surface of the pad.

Glancing around, Jolene didn't see a pencil, so she took the pad into the living room and used ashes from the fireplace. She rubbed the ashes along the expanse of the pad until the full imprint was revealed.

GPS coordinates.

Pulling her phone from her pocket, she took a picture of the piece of paper and of the pad, before she typed the GPS coordinates into the notepad on her phone and into the reverse geocoding application.

Now having an address, she continued on through the rest of the house. She didn't find anything until she went into the basement. The blood and gore hit her first and rolled her stomach. That was where they tortured her mate. Rage boiled up inside of her and was only egged on when her eyes landed on Shortcake's prone body, still hanging from cuffs and chains attached to the wall.

After giving Shortcake a moment of respect and silence, Jolene let the rage take over, and she stormed out of the house. Before she peeled out of the driveway, she sent Axle a quick text to let him know the address of the abandoned house, the temporary resting place of their family member.

T.S. Tappin

Chapter Twenty-Eight

Messer

Emotions rolled through Messer as she was hustled down to a cell room in the basement of the clubhouse. It was a concrete-walled room with a normal door and also a barred door. She was brought into the room by Matthew and a man Axle referred to as Brute. He looked a lot like Matthew, who was wearing a patch that identified him as Trick.

Trick, like the way he tricked her into thinking he was helping her find out more about the Howlers. Or maybe he really had been. Was he helping her and got sucked into the Howlers' web? Or had he always been a part of them? She had so many questions that did nothing but fuel the tornado of emotions in her chest.

She expected them to lock her in the room and leave, but Matthew didn't leave. When Brute stepped outside the room and shut the barred door, Matthew crossed his arms across his chest and leaned back against the wall on the other side of the room from her.

"So... which is it?" she asked in a calm tone despite the mix of emotion she was feeling.

Matthew lifted his gaze from the concrete floor to her. "What?"

"Were you playing me or them?"

He snorted a humorless laugh. "*Playing you?*" He shook his head. "You came to town with the intention of killing the people I love. You got close to townsfolk with that same intention. You tried to spy to get information on my family. But *I* played *you* by creatively stopping you from being able to *hurt my family?*"

"So, you *were* lying to me!" Her heart began pounding harder in her chest, almost to the point of pain.

"That's fucking rich coming from you!"

When the tears started to gather in her eyes, she hated herself a little for it. She didn't want to show him that weakness. "Were you a member, then?"

The anger was still in his chocolate brown eyes when he replied, "I was a prospect."

"When did you become a member?"

"Not that I owe you a fucking thing, especially not an explanation, but… when you left town."

She nodded as tears fell from her eyes. She angrily wiped them away and turned away from him. "You bought your membership at my expense. Got it."

Messer was swung around by a yank on her shoulder. It didn't hurt. He was careful enough to not hurt her, but when she looked in his eyes, she could see his rage. The odd thing about it was she wasn't scared of him. Something about him made her feel safe with him, but she couldn't pinpoint why. He could and had every right to kill her where she stood. Whether she was safe or not in his presence, Matthew was pissed.

Rex's Release

"I didn't do it for a fucking membership!" He scoffed and glared at her. "What the fuck did you want me to do? Huh? You want my family dead! You expected me to invite the enemy in? Swing the doors wide and let you and your merry band of misfits in to murder my family? No! Fuck that! I'd protect my family from that for free!"

She shook her head, still angry about being bamboozled. Betrayal was a bitter pill to swallow. "You feel safe around them? After everything I told you?"

A gold light shined from his eyes as his face screwed up even further with anger. "Yes. I. Fucking. Do."

She gasped. She couldn't believe what she was seeing. *No!* He couldn't be.

"That's fucking right, Messer. I'm one of those *monsters* you think you know about."

"No," she breathed and shook her head. "No, that can't be. You can't be... No! I would have known."

"Shifters have been living around you your entire life!" He turned away from her and put his hands to his hips. "Fuck!"

She leaned back against the wall and softly asked, "And how many people have they murdered?"

One second, she was staring at the Howlers MC logo on the back of his leather cut, and the next, there was a large black bear roaring in her face with his paws pressed against the wall on either side of her head.

Messer's heart nearly stopped. A fucking *bear* was within inches of her face! Long fangs and angry chocolate brown eyes were all she could see. He breathed into her face for a moment, before she blinked and Matthew was standing there again, his hands now pressed against the wall where the bear's paws had been.

"A lot fucking less than humans have, especially the ones *you* hang out with," he answered.

"You... you're... you're a bear!" Messer was stunned and outraged.

Matthew clapped slowly. "Very good. They take pride in intelligence over at that academy of yours, don't they?"

"You were a shifter when..."

He rolled his eyes. "I've been a shifter my whole life." He stepped away from her and put his hands back to his hips as he shook his head.

She couldn't process everything. Her brain simply refused to process any of it. Survival was all the only thing she had enough brain power to focus on in that moment. "What... what are you going to do to me? Are you going to kill me? Do you even care what happens to me?"

He shook his head, but after a moment, he looked at her. "I wish I fucking didn't."

She wiped away the tears that were once again streaming down her face. "Why do you?"

He let out a humorless laugh and answered, "Because the Gods are apparently comedians."

She didn't bother pushing on that, and he didn't offer further explanation. Instead, she asked, "You expect people to just believe that they are safe living next door to shifters when shifters can turn into animals that they are warned to keep their distance from?"

"They've always been safe living next door to us!" He shook his head again. "You people are all the same. Murder anything different from you."

"You people? *You people?* What the hell is that supposed to mean?"

He glared at her. "It means *full-humans* always route out anything different from them or anything they don't understand, then they *murder them*. Newsflash! Shifters are *not* the monsters. You. Are."

Rage filled her as she surged toward him and shoved his chest. "Fuck you."

He barely moved an inch. "Nah, I'm good."

"I told you where they were!"

He snorted a laugh. "You want a fucking gold star? You stood there and let them murder one of my sisters. You're no better than the ones doing the deed."

Shaking her head and cursing the tears that wouldn't stop leaking from her eyes. "I risked everything to come here and tell you."

He rolled his eyes. "Right."

"Then why didn't you just kill me on sight when I showed up? I was unarmed. You could have."

Matthew gave a fake smile and raised a brow. "And yet, we didn't. But *we're* the monsters."

Feeling like she was in a nightmare she couldn't wake up from, Messer dropped down to sit on the floor against the wall and rested her elbows on her bent knees. Covering her face in her hands, she forced herself to take slow, even breaths.

What in the hell am I going to do?

Ranger

After Skull parked the van in front of Doc's house, Ranger and Siren darted out of the back and bolted for the house. They knew Axle, Dragon, Pike, Rebel, Score, Skull, and Top would catch up. Ranger swung open the front door and immediately halted when he spotted the sawed-off shotgun pointed at him, held by Mama Hen. Siren barreled into his back, almost knocking him over.

"Oh… Good." Mama Hen lowered the gun. "'Bout time you boys showed up."

Ranger let out the shaky breath he'd been holding and turned. He dropped to the floor next to Rex and a little Yorkie. Siren took the other side. The rest of the men filed into the house as they went to work assessing Rex's injuries.

When Mama Hen told Axle that Doc made sure Rex was stable, she wasn't kidding. Most of the injuries were covered, and the ones that weren't, were cleaned. Rex was awake and seemed to be in pain, but his eyes were clear and pissed off.

As they looked him over, Rex tried to get up several times. "Let me up! I have to get to her."

"Who?" Ranger asked but was distracted by the bandage job that Doc had done. They weren't standard bandages that you got at a pharmacy or even from a hospital. Ranger looked across Rex to Siren.

"Doc," Rex bit out.

Ranger's gaze dropped back down to the military field dressing bandages, then he uttered, "I don't think you need to worry about Doc."

In the background, Ranger could hear Rebel giving Axle a play by play of what they were doing and what they were seeing.

"Those are bandages that are standard in the military. You can order them online, but yeah, they are—" He stopped when everyone turned to look at him. "What?"

"Where did you find out about them?" Axle asked.

Rebel shrugged. "In a book."

"Dude, I think you're spending a little too much time at the library," Score commented.

Ranger snorted a laugh, before he brought his attention back to Rex. "How were you injured?"

"Knife wounds. She stitched me up."

Siren nodded. "Well, she's Doc. I trust her abilities more than mine, so we should probably leave them alone."

Axle's phone pinged, and he checked it. "Siren, stay with Rex. We have an address."

"County Road 452?"

At Rex's question, Axle gave a nod. "Doc just sent me an address. Let Siren watch over you, and we'll protect your mate."

Rex didn't like that, but they ignored his protests. He didn't have a choice. They weren't letting him go anywhere with his injuries.

Ranger stood and said, "I don't think she needs our protection. Will probably be the last one standing, and most likely, won't even break a nail." He looked over at Mama Hen, who was sporting a smirk. "You seem close to Doc." Mama Hen didn't reply. "You know more about her than even Rex." Still no reply. "Is that because the two of you have similar backgrounds?"

Mama Hen hiked a brow. "How many times do I have to tell you boys not to ask questions that could result in your death? Because if I answer them, I'll have to kill you."

Ranger was positive that Mama Hen and Doc were in the military or worked for one of the initialed bureaus or agencies, but he wasn't about to push. There were things civilians could know, but there were things civilians could *never* know. He would respect that. Not to mention, he wasn't stupid enough not to take Mama Hen's threats as promises.

He gave a nod before he followed his club brothers out the door and back to the van.

Chapter Twenty-Nine

Jolene

Following the directions from her navigation system, Jolene was going well over the speed limit in her little SUV. If the cops spotted her, she would be screwed, but she wouldn't let the fuckers get away with this. They hurt her mate, and they would pay for that. He was going to be okay, but that wasn't the point. Not to mention, what they did to Shortcake was beyond cruel.

Jolene could feel it in her bones. The *demand* for revenge was hot and coursing through her, bits settling in the very marrow of her bones. She couldn't stop it, not until each of them paid for every slice, punch, and kick they had dared to inflict on her mate. The Howlers and the Claws wouldn't take it lightly. She wouldn't even begin to guess what they would do in retaliation, but she knew exactly what she was going to do... and it was not going to be pretty.

When her phone began to ring, she pressed the answer button on the digital display, and Axle's voice rang out through her speakers. "Doc, where are you? We're at the address, and you're not here."

"Did you find Shortcake?" she asked in a no-nonsense tone.

"Yes," Axle growled the answer. "Where are you?"

"On my way to some coordinates that I found at the house. Hopefully, they'll be there. If they are, I promise they won't be alive when you show up."

She pressed the button to end the call and pressed harder on the accelerator.

Doc wasn't stupid. She was well aware that the club had a habit of putting tracking apps on their phones and tracking devices on the vehicles of anyone they cared about. It was with the intention of being able to find them if the family member was lost or in trouble. They probably put one on her vehicle. She hadn't bothered checking because she knew it would make Rex feel better that it was there. Keys, their resident tech genius, was probably tracking her at that moment. They had better hurry up if they wanted in on the action.

Axle

When the call ended, Axle was pissed. "Fuck!" He turned in the passenger seat of the van and looked back at his IT guy. "Keys, did you put a tracker on Doc's SUV?"

"No, but give me two seconds." He pressed some buttons on the laptop that he almost always had with him, then his eyes lifted to meet Axle's gaze, and he rattled off an address. "Her SUV is stopped there... or at least that's what her NAV system indicates."

Axle punched the address in the GPS system attached to the dash and ordered Skull to drive. He could only hope Doc didn't get hurt. If she did, Rex would burn the world down. Ranger seemed sure that she would be fine, and Mama Hen's words were cryptic, but he wasn't going to push. If Ranger felt he needed to know, he would have filled Axle in. His main concern was the safety of their family. Next on that list was revenge.

It might take some time, but that fucking academy was going to find out just how dangerous shifters could be when their family was harmed. *That* was when they became the monsters they were accused of being.

Jolene

After parking off to the side of the driveway a quarter mile from the coordinates, which satellite maps showed was a cabin, Jolene got out of her SUV and walked the rest of the way, staying in the tree line, attempting to keep herself as hidden as possible. The building was a small shack in the woods that looked like it was probably an old hunting cabin that had long passed its prime, but Jolene didn't give two shits about the fuckers' accommodations.

For being trained hunters, they sure sucked at keeping watch. There wasn't a guard in sight. No one watching from a window. No one patrolling the grounds. No one positioned outside the front door. Nothing.

She walked past the Pathfinder parked in front of the cabin, up the front steps, right to the front door without anyone sounding an alarm. In case they weren't as stupid as she suspected and actually had hidden cameras or something, she went with the assumption that they knew she was there, so she didn't give them time to prepare. She just kicked the front door in, gun in hand and ready.

Expecting to be facing shooters, she was surprised when what she saw was one hunter asleep on the couch and another carrying what looked like a plate of nachos in from the kitchen area. At sight of her, he dropped his nachos and shouted in surprise. She shot him in one kneecap and then the other. He dropped to the floor, screaming in pain.

The hunter on the couch came awake and jumped to her feet. When she reached for the gun lying on the coffee table, Jolene aimed for the hunter's head and fired. She dropped to the ground as Jolene darted for the table and snatched up the gun. After securing the safety and slipping it in the empty slot of her holster, she trained her gun on the one with the bad knees, who was lying on the floor and moaning.

A door opened a crack on the other side of the room, Jolene shifted over so she was hidden from view by the corner of the wall, but she could still keep her gun trained on the idiot on the floor.

"Come out, or I'll end him," she called out.

"Who are you?" A male voice asked from behind the cracked door.

"I'm Doc, and you're about to find out just how bad you fucked up." She glanced around the corner and saw the door open more. A male and a female, both curly headed, stepped out, trying to get dressed. The female had just pulled a shirt over her head when Jolene pulled the trigger, ending the nacho-loving hunter. Shifting around the corner again, she shot the female in the left side of her chest, before aiming at the man. "On your knees, hands up!"

The man tripped over the pants he had been trying to pull on and burst into tears as he followed her orders. "Please, don't kill me! I was just following orders!"

"And what is the name of the person who gave those orders?"

"Commander West. I don't know his full name," he answered through his sobs as the scent of urine filled the air.

"I'll be sure to tell him you send your regards." Then she pulled the trigger again.

She spent the next few moments making sure they were all dead, before she started searching the place.

Axle

They passed Doc's SUV on the side of the driveway but didn't stop. Axle was betting she had already made her way to the location. When they pulled up next to the Pathfinder, he looked at the cabin and saw that the front door was wide open.

"Shit." He pulled his gun from his holster and hopped out of the van, his club brothers following behind him. It didn't surprise him at all when Pike and Dragon jogged ahead and stepped through the door in front of him. As sergeant at arms, it was Pike's job to protect him as the club's president. Dragon, being the club's enforcer, took the security of the club members and their families very personally. Axle had no doubt he was kicking himself for what had happened to Rex and Shortcake.

"Damn," Dragon uttered in a low tone as he stopped just inside the door and looked around.

Pike called out, "No worries! Doc took care of it."

"What?" Axle stepped past them and looked around. He counted four casualties — two male and two female. Then his eyes landed on Doc. She was relaxing in the recliner with a plate of nachos on the arm of the chair and a laptop in her lap, staring at the screen as she was casually munching on a chip.

Doc swallowed and smiled at him. "Hey. I found out who gave the order. I got through most of the encryption. Was able to use their expense card to order a thousand pink dildos to have delivered to the academy to let them know exactly how fucked they are. But I think I need Keys's help to get into the rest of the files."

Keys, who had just come to a stop at his side, looked over at Doc and asked, "Are you taken? Yes. Shit. Yes, you are." He cleared his throat and gave an awkward laugh. "Yeah, sure, I can help."

As Keys crossed the room, Axle asked, "Who *are* you?"

Doc just grinned and answered, "I'm Rex's mate." She gave a wink. "That's all you need to know."

Keys took possession of the laptop and plopped down on the couch, ignoring the body on the floor in front of it. "So... did you send a note with the dildos?" he asked with a grin.

Doc nodded. "It read, Don't bother fucking yourself, because we're about to do it for you. And I signed it, the monsters."

Then the room erupted in laughter.

Axle shook his head. "You'll fit in with us just fine, Doc."

Keys was clicking away on the laptop. "Looks like they put trackers on Shortcake's car and Rex's truck. They were activated yesterday. My guess? They were picked because of a combination of limited info and bad timing. From the notes on here, they only had guesses on the shifter/non-shifter status of most of the members, and they hadn't caught the others alone."

"Shitty fucking reason to be tortured or killed," Dragon growled right before he stormed out of the cabin.

Axle sighed and ran his fingers through his hair as he thought, *Dragon's not fucking wrong*.

Crush

Angry was not a big enough word to describe how Crush, the president of the Tiger's Claw MC, was feeling as she stared down at the tortured and dead body of her club sister, Shortcake. With her sisters around her, Crush took several deep breaths and exhaled slowly, trying her best not to let the rage and grief inside of her take over.

"They're gone," her brother, Bullet, told her from across the bed from where Shortcake had been laid.

Moments before, when Bullet found her in the church room for the Claws, she knew something was wrong. His furrowed brow and the pain in his eyes were all the only indications she needed to know that their world's axis had been rocked yet again. The fact that he stepped foot in that sacred room without an invitation was just another red flag. In MC culture, it was considered disrespectful for a member from another club to enter their church room without expressed permission.

The words he said to her didn't register at first. It took a few moments for them to sink in and process. *They got Shortcake. She's dead.*

The next thing she knew, she was standing in Shortcake's room, looking down at her. The brutality of what they did to her sent chills down her spine. How in the world could they treat someone that way just because they were different? It was unthinkable to Crush.

Her tiger was prowling around inside of her hissing and roaring, urging to be let out. Revenge. She needed revenge.

Bullet continued, "Doc killed the four responsible for this, and Messer, the one Trick was watching, is locked up in the basement."

Her eyes shot to Bullet. "We have one locked up?"

His eyes narrowed as he stared back at her. "Crush, no."

She ignored him as she turned and pushed through her club sisters. As she left the room, Nails and Pinky followed behind her.

After heading down the hall, down the stairs, and through the clubhouse to the basement, Crush spotted Brute standing right outside the cell room. The bulky black man's eyes widened when he saw her and her two club sisters heading his way.

He held up his hands in an attempt to ward them off. "Crush, I'm under orders. You can't go in there."

"You're not my boss and neither is Axle."

He tilted his head to the side a bit and raised a brow. "But this is our clubhouse," he replied. "I can't let you in."

As much as they shared the clubhouse, Brute wasn't wrong. It was the property of the Howlers MC, not the Tiger's Claw MC. He had every right not to let her in, but she didn't have to like it.

Her eyes glowed a greenish gold as she let out a low growl and stepped to the side. Looking past Brute and spotting the hunter sitting on the floor against the wall, she pointed a finger and promised, "I will kill you! I will make it slow and painful! You will regret every fucking thing you shared with that damn academy.

And when I'm done with you, I will burn that fucking place to the damn ground!"

The hunter just stared back at her.

Crush stepped forward, basically up against Brute, as she continued, "You thought we were monsters before?" She gave a laugh she knew sounded evil. "You have no idea how much of a monster I can be."

Taking comfort in the fear shining from the hunter's eyes, Crush let her fangs slide down and hissed at the hunter before she turned and stormed away.

T.S. Tappin

Chapter Thirty

DOC

By the time she returned to town, Siren and a few other Howlers had moved Rex to his room at the compound. At the time the decision had been made, they didn't know she had taken out the hunters. Siren made a judgment call that the compound was the safest place for Rex to be, and in Doc's opinion, that was the right call.

Mama Hen had brought Beast to her house after she convinced the scared pup to come out from under the guest room bed where he took off to after the Howlers had shown up. Doc was grateful for that, so it took that worry off her shoulders for the time being.

Hours later, sitting in the chair next to his bed, she glanced down at her hand holding Rex's. She didn't remember when she sat down or when she grabbed his hand, but that didn't matter. What mattered was how *in* she was with having a relationship with Rex.

Was there a lot about shifters and the mate stuff that still left her with questions? Yes, absolutely, but she was sure there would never come a day where she wasn't asking *how, what,* or *when.* She was a doctor, after all, a scientist with a need to understand the root cause and the inner workings of everything. However, when faced with the very real possibility of his death, Doc realized her questions were not enough to justify denying the truth.

She was his mate.

She was his.

He was hers.

They were meant to be.

Doc felt it in her heart and soul. The chemistry between them was off the charts. He appreciated the quirks in her that often drove others insane. She cherished his charming arrogance and his humor. He was extremely open-minded with her. The least she could do would be to return the favor.

Time after time, he had proven to her that he was mature and ready to be the man she needed him to be. She had laid the challenge down, and he rose to it. Now she needed to step up and give him the same commitment in return.

Truthfully, wasn't that all any woman wanted anyway? To have someone who was made for them? To have a person love them for who they were, without expecting them to change? Rex was that person. He just happened to also be a wolf shifter. As a vet, that wasn't exactly a deterrent. Animals were quite literally her gig.

Did she love him? Yes, she absolutely did. She wanted to spend her life with him. It was quick, but so what? They were in their forties. They were beyond the age of uncertainty when it came to knowing what they wanted.

As soon as he was physically able, she would tell him what she decided, but not before he was moving around on his own. The last thing she wanted was Rex to hurt himself more because he tried to fuck her brains out while injured.

And he would.

With a content smile on her face, she rested her head on the back of the chair and closed her eyes.

Axle

After taking care of the clean-up at both the abandoned farmhouse and the cabin, Axle and the Howlers returned to the compound. He took a moment to check in on Rex and Doc, where he found them both asleep. Rex looked a lot better than he had on the floor of Doc's foyer. His color had returned and most of the blood had been cleaned off. Even the deep wrinkles of pain and worry that had been on his forehead were smoothed out.

Knowing Doc would take good care of Rex, Axle eased out of the room as quietly as possible and let them be.

He made his way to the clubhouse, where he found Crush, Nails, and Pike waiting for him in his office. As soon as he stepped in the room, Crush made her stance known, and Axle couldn't say he was surprised.

"Dead. I want the bitch dead, and I want to be the one to take her life. I *will* be the one to take it," she growled, greenish-gold light flashing from her eyes.

Axle rounded his desk and sat down in his chair with a sigh, before he looked over at her and met her pissed off gaze. "I understand why."

"Good. Then there's no reason to argue."

He glanced over at Pike and Nails, who were standing behind Crush's chair. Both of them looked as if they agreed with Crush. *Shit.* He had his work cut out for him.

"She's responsible for *a lot* of harm to our family," Pike said carefully, and crossed his arms over his chest.

Axle sighed again. "I know. I get it." The problem was he was going to have to fight her on it. He just prayed to the gods she would see his point of view before the discussion got too heated. "I need you to hear me out, first."

Crush shrugged. "Say what you want to say, but I doubt my stance will change. I have a *right* to avenge my sister."

Axle was about to out his club brother, and he was sorry for that, but he didn't see any other way. "Lucifer's home club caused much worse and did horrible things to members of our family."

She scoffed. "He was a prospect."

She wasn't wrong. Lucifer was a member when they raided the clubhouse of the Indiana chapter of the Hell's Dogs MC, but barely. He had been patched in earlier that same day. The members of the Howlers and the Claws that had gone down there had killed the rest of the remaining members, except for Lucifer. Crush had insisted he remain alive, and she basically kidnapped him. She saved his life and brought him back with her because he was her mate. There was a discussion about whether or not to take him out as well, with Crush allowing the clubs to vote, but in the end, the majority of members couldn't justify killing a member's mate without giving them a chance to prove themselves.

The situation was much like what they were dealing with when it came to Messer.

"Yes, he was, but he was a part of the club who committed *horrendous* acts against our family. You left that vote up to us because you knew you couldn't be impartial. If he wasn't your mate, we would have ended him that first day without an ounce of regret. We saved his life for *you*."

She huffed out a breath. "What does my mate have to do with anything? He's proven his worth. He saved Sugar, and he fought beside the clubs in the war. You've given him a prospect cut, for fuck's sake. What does his past have to do with the fucking hunter?"

Axle met her gaze head on and calmly stated, "She's Trick's mate."

The room drained of sound, even the clock on the wall didn't tick as the second hand went around.

After several long, silent moments, Pike threw his hands up and bit out, "Well, shit."

And just to push his point home, Axle told her, "I know you have to put your club first and will need to bring it to the table. I have to bring it to mine, and I will, but I can already tell you what my brothers will say."

Pike uttered, "We won't kill his mate."

"And if my sisters demand her head?" Crush slowly rose to her feet. "Then what?"

Axle did the same. "Then our partnership is about to face its biggest test... because we *will* defend our brother." He watched as a million different emotions filtered across her face before she sighed. He took that moment to soften his tone and say, "You, of all people, should understand how Trick feels."

"We'll see how the clubs vote," she ground out, but Axle could see the empathy in her eyes.

T.S. Tappin

Crush

The rage was still coursing through her as she stomped across the street and around the strip mall, but it was tempered a bit by doubt and empathy. As she headed for the door at the bottom of the stairwell that led to her apartment and the Tiger's Claw MC church room, she saw Lucifer jogging toward her from the other end.

"Need a minute?" Nails asked her as they stopped at the door.

Crush gave a nod. "Call all the girls together. Emergency church. No exceptions."

"You got it, Boss Lady," Nails replied and walked back the way they came, pulling her phone from her pocket.

When Lucifer reached her, wearing jeans, a tee, and his Howlers prospect cut, he cupped her face in his hands and gazed into her eyes. Well attuned to her in the weeks since their mating, his eyes were searching, trying to read where she was at emotionally. "Talk to me," he said, low.

Crush exhaled slowly as she soaked in his strength and support. "Messer is Trick's mate. Axle is refusing to let me have her until we vote, but he said he knows how the Howlers will vote and Pike confirmed it. They won't kill Trick's mate."

Lucifer nodded. "Yeah."

"But she's responsible for Shortcake's death. We deserve to avenge her." Crush's rage rallied and pushed forward again. "He compared her situation to yours, and it's not the fucking same!"

"You're right to feel the way you do." He took a deep breath and let it out. "Can I give you some perspective?"

She didn't like the way he asked that, mostly because it indicated that she wasn't going to like what he had to say, but she nodded anyway.

"I'm alive because I didn't kill or hurt anyone in the clubs, but mostly because I'm your mate."

She nodded.

"Kitten, she didn't either… and she's Trick's mate."

"But—"

"It's your grief talking. Listen. Why did your club vote to keep me alive?"

"Because you're my mate and you didn't actually kill one of us."

Lucifer nodded. "Who's to say I wouldn't have? If you wouldn't have shown up when you did and taken out the rest of my club, how do you know I wouldn't have been put in the position to do that? You don't."

Crush cringed at the rightness of his point.

"And she came to us," he added. "We didn't have to chase her down."

Grudgingly, she nodded, hating that his points were valid.

"All I'm saying is I deserved a chance to prove that I could be trusted, and you all gave me that. Maybe she does, too."

After huffing out a sigh, Crush grumbled, "I don't like the idea of her being around the kids and the mates."

"So… don't let her be." He shrugged, then a soft smile grew on his face. "My pretty kitty should *maybe* retract her claws."

Crush rolled her eyes, but she couldn't help the twitch at the corners of her mouth. "You're an idiot."

"But I'm *your* sexy idiot."

"I didn't say sexy."

"It's okay to be forgetful sometimes." He chuckled and kissed her lips. "You can take your frustrations out on me later."

Snorting a laugh, she pulled out of his hold and headed up the stairs.

Crush wasn't sure how the vote was going to go before her club joined her in the church room, but she probably should have. It went exactly the way Lucifer's vote went. There were two hold-outs — Ginger and Vixen — who were the same two who voted to take Lucifer's life. They were overruled by the majority. It was the mate element that held her club back. Many of the members made comments along the lines of not feeling right about taking a shifter's mate. If Messer had killed Shortcake by her own hand, they would have had a very different conversation.

After ending church, Crush found Lucifer in their apartment and walked into his arms. Holding her tight, he just let her soak him in. She didn't need his snark or his words. She just needed his support, and he seemed to recognize that. Once again, she thanked the gods for him.

Ten minutes later, he was walking hand in hand with her to the clubhouse. He wouldn't go into Axle's office with her, because she needed to do that herself, well, with her sergeant at arms, Nails. Having her mate holding her hand in the meeting would undermine her power, and that was not the leader she wanted to be.

Just inside the doors of the clubhouse, he kissed her lips and promised her he would wait at the bar for her. Crush gave a nod to him, before motioning for Nails, who was waiting at a table, to join her. Together, they made their way down the hallway to Axle's office door.

Axle

The Howlers voted the way he expected. Rex was the only member not in attendance, but his two best friends were there, and the club trusted them to speak on Rex's behalf.

Top said it best. Having just met his mate, Rex wouldn't want to be responsible for taking that from another brother. He'd vote to watch her, but to let her live.

It was basically the view of every member of the Howlers MC. Watch her, but let her live... for now.

Sitting in his office, he waited for Crush to return. Pike was pacing the open space behind the visitors' chairs. As sergeant at arms, his concern would be the club's safety and the blowback from a possible war between them and the Claws. Was the possibility there? Yes. Did Axle really think it would happen? No. He expected the Claws to come to the same conclusion that he had — Messer had responsibility for what happened to Shortcake and Rex, but she also deserved a chance to make it right.

Crush didn't bother knocking. She just opened the door and stepped in, with Nails quickly following. Without taking a seat, she faced Axle and said, "Looks like my club agrees with you... this time." Turning on her heel, she left without giving him a chance to say anything.

T.S. Tappin

Chapter Thirty-One

Rex

The next morning, Rex woke up with the worst of full-body aches. There was sharp pain, burning aches, and throbbing in every limb. He felt like he had been run over by a semi-truck that had backed over him and then ran him over again.

He opened his eyes and waited for the sleep fog to clear from them. Once he was able to clearly see the navy ceiling and walls in his room at the compound, he looked around, moving his head slowly at first to keep from causing more pain.

His gaze landed on Doc sleeping in the chair that had been pulled to the side of his bed. Her legs were folded in front of her, and her left hand was clutching his where it laid on the bed at his side. Even with her head tilted back and to the side and her mouth wide open, she was the most beautiful woman he had ever seen. Her short blond hair was sticking out everywhere and soft snores were coming from her tempting lips. Fuck. She was so damn adorable.

Rex decided he would go through anything just to be able to wake up to her face every day for the rest of his life. Well, he already knew that, but seeing her like that only reaffirmed it. She was his mate, his heart, his soul.

He didn't really want to move. Laying there and staring at her all day sounded like a fantastic plan, but his full bladder had other ideas. Carefully slipping his hand from hers and biting his lip to stifle the groan at the pain he felt from the act, Rex shifted to get to his feet and head for the bathroom.

Doc jolted up and looked over at him sitting on the edge of the bed. He knew the second she clocked the pain he was in because her eyes narrowed and her voice was firm as she ordered, "Lay your ass back down, Fido."

He smiled and winced at the way it pulled at the cut in his lip. As he internally cursed the fucking shifter blocker for affecting his healing abilities, he replied, "I have to use the restroom."

Her glare held him in place as she opened her mouth and called out, "Boys!"

The door opened, and Top and Score entered the room. "Yeah, Doc?" Top asked, then his attention moved to Rex, and he scowled. "What in the hell are you doing?"

"I have to use the fucking restroom," Rex insisted, his irritation mainly coming from the pain that he was feeling.

"Oh." Score rushed over and slid an arm around his waist. Top did the same on his other side. Together, they helped him stand. Slipping their other arms behind his knees, they lifted him and carried him toward the bathroom. It wasn't until they reached the bathroom door that they realized there was no way they would fit through the doorway in their current position.

"Shit." Top shifted, so he was taking more of Rex's weight. "I got him."

Score let go of Rex and reached out, opening the bathroom door.

"This is fucking ridiculous," Rex grumbled, feeling like a toddler.

"It's fucking *necessary*," Doc called out from behind them.

With a sigh, Rex resigned himself to being treated like a child until he healed enough to walk on his own.

After he took care of his business in the bathroom and his brother helped him settle back in bed, Rex made it clear he wanted to be alone with Doc. His brothers, being the smart individuals that they were, left quietly but quickly.

"You better stay put this time," Doc said sternly. "If you don't," she nodded to the Velcro straps attached to the corners of his bed, "I'll use them for a different reason." Her brow shot up in a challenge.

Rex grinned at her. "Yes, Ma'am."

Doc moved from her chair to sit on the bed on his other side. "How are you feeling?"

"Like hell, but it helps to have you here."

When she took his hand in hers, he watched her as memories of the night before came flooding back in. He had panicked when he found out that she had gone after the hunters who had tortured him.

"How did you... What happened when you left your house?"

Her gaze shifted from their clasped hands to something across the room. "I... I killed them."

"You... killed them?" He took a deep breath and let it out slowly, trying not to get upset with her. "Why in the... Why would you put yourself in danger like that, Doc? The Howlers could handle it."

"Because you're mine," she bit out, and her gaze shot to him, stubbornness and determination in those blue depths. "Vengeance was mine to take. I didn't need the Howlers' assistance to do that."

That confused him more. "Why didn't you need the assistance of the Howlers?"

She didn't answer him right away, but when she did, she admitted, "All I can tell you is I was part of a *government-trained* unit that the *government* won't recognize, and we did things for the *government* that they will not claim. That's all I can tell you."

Rex stared at her for a long time, those ice-blue eyes looking contemplative. "So... professional badass? Got it."

"I had the skills to complete the job, so I did." She sighed. "I needed to do it myself."

"Because I'm yours." He watched her give a nod. "Does that mean what I think it means, Doc?"

Her eyes were filled with heat when she answered, "I'll let you know once you're able to walk yourself to the bathroom without assistance."

"I'll do it right now," he said and went to move off the bed.

After grabbing his wrist to stop him, she added, "*Without* injuring yourself more."

Rex chuckled as he settled into the mattress. "Yes, Ma'am."

Doc

Doc was in the middle of giving Rex a much-needed sponge bath when the door flew open and a gorgeous young woman stormed into the room.

"Dad, I—Oh, shit!" She immediately stopped, turned around, and walked right back out the door. The young woman was obviously Nevaeh, Rex's daughter, judging by the use of the word *Dad*.

Rex chuckled as he continued to lie naked on the bed. "She just saw a whole lot more than she wanted to see."

"Trauma," Doc replied, and set the rag in the bowl of warm water on the side table. Deciding he was clean enough, at least all the blood was gone, she set about re-wrapping his wounds. When she was done, she covered him with a sheet from the waist down and headed out to the hallway.

The raven-haired woman was pacing back and forth in front of her father's door. Wearing a black Howlers MC tank that was short enough to show off a good portion of her midriff, an unbuttoned black and green flannel, and a pair of black leather pants, she went back and forth on her sky-high heels, muttering, "I did *not* just see my dad naked. I did *not* just see my dad naked. I did *not* just see my dad naked."

Doc smiled as she crossed her arms over her chest and said, "I'm sorry you just saw your dad naked. He needed to be cleaned up, but he can't take a shower yet."

Ice-blue eyes that were very much like her father's lifted as Nevaeh looked Doc's way. "What... How... Uncle Top said he was hurt."

Nodding, Doc told her, "He was stabbed several times, but he's okay. He just needs to heal."

"When did this happen?"

"Last night."

Nevaeh's brows pulled together. "Why isn't he healing? He should be walking around, at least."

After thinking on it for a moment, Doc decided Nevaeh was old enough to have the truth. If that was the wrong decision, she would argue with Rex about it later. "Do you know about the shifter blocker?"

Nevaeh nodded. "Aunt Crush was injected with it months ago."

"Before all the injuries happened, he had been injected with the drug. Apparently, it disables shifter healing for a couple of days. He's still healing. It's just taking a bit longer."

"Are you… a doctor?"

Doc chuckled. "I'm a vet."

Nevaeh's eyes widened, before she blurted, "You're dad's mate!" Then the young woman was clapping and jumping up and down, which Doc thought was dangerous considering the heels she was wearing. "I'm so happy to meet you!"

"Nice to meet you, too," Doc replied, right before she was yanked into the arms of Nevaeh and squeezed tight, obviously happy for her father.

It was at that moment Doc fell in love with the heart of her future stepdaughter.

When Nevaeh pulled back, Doc told her, "He's covered, by the way, and I know he would love to see you."

Nevaeh nodded and headed in to see her dad. When she noticed Doc wasn't following, she waved her arm. "Come on. He's going to want both of us in there."

"I was going to go grab him some food."

Rolling her eyes, Nevaeh replied, "That's what the prospects are for."

T.S. Tappin

Chapter Thirty-Two

Rex

The second day after his kidnapping, Rex was ready to pull his hair out. He loved his daughter, but he was done. He needed a break from her babying him. She wouldn't even let him feed himself. Yes, it hurt to lift his arms, but he was able to do it without injuring himself more. At first, he was humoring her, because he knew she was upset seeing him hurt. After twenty-four hours, he was more than done.

When Doc came out of the bathroom in her scrubs, Rex cleared his throat and looked over at Nevaeh sitting in the armchair. "Hey. Can you give me and Doc a minute?"

"Sure." On her ridiculous heels, she strolled out of the room and shut the door behind her.

Rex's gaze shot to Doc. "Please, for the love of the gods... *Please*, give her something to do other than being my nursemaid," he begged in a whisper, so Nevaeh's shifter hearing did pick it up.

Doc's face broke out in a grin. "Feeling a little kenneled, Fido?"

"Yes," he answered honestly.

After a chuckle, she said, "I'll see if she wants to go to the clinic with me. Someone left a litter of black Lab puppies. The techs would appreciate having someone help take care of them."

"Hopefully, they respond better to her than Beast does to me."

Doc shrugged. "We'll see." She bent over him and gave him a slow, deep kiss before she pulled back and smiled down at him. "Be good. Don't go injuring yourself more while I'm gone."

He grinned. "Yes, Ma'am."

Doc

"Got some sneakers with you?" Doc asked Nevaeh as she stepped out of Rex's room.

The young woman stopped her pacing and looked over at her. "Uh… yeah."

"You're driving your dad bonkers. I know you love him and want to take care of him, but he needs a break to rest. Change into an outfit you don't mind having animal hair all over and put on your sneakers. You have ten minutes."

"Animal hair?"

"You're going to the clinic. You can help by playing and walking the animals for us."

Just like the day before, Nevaeh began jumping up and down on those high heels and clapping her hands. Doc shook her head, wondering how long before she was going to have to wrap the girl's ankle from rolling it by doing that.

"Puppies and kittens and all the little furries?"

"We might have to ease you in, though. My dog is scared of your dad since he's a wolf shifter like you. So… we'll see how it goes."

"I'm so excited," the young woman replied, ignoring Doc's words. "I'll love on them and play with them and tell them how adorable they are! I always wanted a pet, but Dad always said no."

Doc couldn't help but smile at the girl's enthusiasm as they headed for the room Nevaeh was using while she was there, since the Howlers weren't fond of the idea of Nevaeh staying at Rex's house alone.

"Let's get you changed. We gotta get going."

Doc was a bit surprised when the puppies gravitated to Nevaeh. Maybe it had more to do with the fact that she was smaller than Rex. Rex's size made him intimidating without the wolf shifter aspect. Nevaeh was shorter and a lot smaller, especially sitting on the floor with a lapful of little black, furry blobs.

One puppy hung back, taking a tentative step toward Nevaeh every few seconds. When the young woman noticed, she slowly extended her hand to the puppy, keeping it low and relaxed. The puppy extended its neck and gave her hand a sniff. After a few moments, the puppy trotted forward, allowing Nevaeh to scoop him up and cuddle him close, protecting him from his over-excited brothers and sisters.

"It's okay, little one," Nevaeh said softly. "You are so very precious. Look at your little face. So friggin' adorable."

"You picked a great day to bring her," Julie commented as she came to stand next to Doc. "Dr. Thatcher is out. Said something about a migraine."

"Never before have I wished a migraine on someone," Doc began, as she continued to watch Nevaeh cuddle puppies, "but I hope it lasts a few days."

Julie chuckled and walked away.

"Nevaeh, they need to be fed and taken outside. We have a fenced-in area through that door. How about you take them out individually and let them use the restroom. Then, I'll show you how to feed them." She held out a leash to Nevaeh. "One at a time for now."

The young woman grinned and climbed to her feet, taking the leash from Doc's hand.

Hours later, Nevaeh was still playing with the puppies. She had spent all day taking care of them, making sure they had food and water, playing with them, and taking them on walks around the fenced-in yard. Thankfully, the snow that had fallen days ago had already melted, and the ground had dried out enough, so the area wasn't muddy. She was a very attentive caretaker, and Doc considered asking her if she would like a summer job when she returned to town in May.

It was obvious that Nevaeh had a favorite, though. The puppy that had been hesitant had spent most of the day being loved on by the young woman.

"When can they be adopted out?"

"Well, they were well taken care of before they were dropped off," Doc told her as they took the puppies out in a group to play in the yard. "We guess their ages to be around twelve weeks, and they are pretty well house trained. We will find them foster homes for now, at least while we are finding forever homes for them."

Nevaeh looked over at her with tears lining those ice blue eyes. "They have to go to strangers' homes before they get families? That doesn't seem right."

Doc smiled gently. "The strangers are vetted fosters. The puppies will be treated properly."

"They need love, not just food and water."

"Four of the puppies have forever homes currently being vetted. The other two will be fostered, unless Julie decides to adopt one. She was talking about it."

"Which one is the last one?"

"Your fave." She nodded to the puppy that had taken to playing at Nevaeh's feet, instead of running around with his siblings.

The tears spilled over. "That just breaks my heart," Nevaeh told her. "He's just as adorable as the rest. No, he's *more* adorable."

Doc couldn't dispute that statement. Something about the puppy's cute little pout and distinct puppy grin tugged at her heart as well. "I promise to find him a great forever home. Okay?"

"Can… can we find someone in the family to… foster him? At least then I know he'll be taken care of and loved."

She hated seeing the young woman upset. Internally, she groaned, knowing damn well she was going to end up bringing that puppy home with her. In an effort to change the subject, she asked, "Would you like to give him a name?"

Nevaeh's eyes widened. "Yes! Can I?"

Doc nodded.

"I'll have to think about it." Nevaeh reached down and scooped the puppy up, cuddling him to her chest. "What's your name, little guy?"

Pulling her phone from her pocket, Doc sent Rex a text to let him know she was going to be staying at her house, since Nevaeh just talked her into fostering a puppy while they tried to find it a forever home.

The texted reply had her rolling her eyes.

REX: My girl worked her magic, I see. I should have sent you with the antidote. My bad. And if you're staying at your house, so am I.

DOC: You will do no such thing until I am satisfied that you can walk to the bathroom and back to bed without assistance.

REX: We'll argue about this later

"Why are you scowling?"

Doc glanced over at Nevaeh and sighed. "Your dad is being… stubborn."

Nevaeh giggled. "Yeah. Sounds like Dad."

Chapter Thirty-Three

Rex

Rex was not happy about spending the previous night without Doc in bed with him. He wasn't allowing that to happen again. Sure, she was the one in charge when it came to playtime, but he had a say in their relationship, and he was putting his foot down on that.

"What do you need?" Trip asked as he stepped into Rex's room through the open door.

"I need you to go to my house and install temporary support bars from my bed to my bathroom, so Doc will allow me to go home."

Trip grinned. "Support bars? Aren't you a bit young for that, my man?"

Rex flipped him off. "She's worried about me re-injuring myself when she's at work. Just do it, okay?"

Trip carefully patted Rex on his shoulder as Rex forced himself to his feet. "You got it, Brother."

Rex handed Trip his house keys, even though he knew Trip could get in if he wanted to without them.

"Give me a few hours, and it will be done."

Once Trip was gone, Rex shuffled his way to the bathroom and took care of business. His shifter healing had finally kicked in. The split on his lip quickly healed overnight, and he noticed that the stitched areas were closing a lot faster than they had been.

As soon as he noticed that, he tried to find his wolf inside him. There was a very vague hint of him, as if seeing a shadow through the fog, but it was there. Every once in a while, a phantom growl or whimper sounded inside of him, letting him know his wolf was returning.

Relief coursed through him at the knowledge. His wolf was a part of his soul. He needed the wolf to balance him.

He was able to walk around in small doses, but it still hurt like a bitch. Doc even gave him the go-ahead to shower.

Nevaeh had ditched him for the puppy, but he wasn't mad about it. She had called last night and convinced him to let her and Doc have some girl time. She told him that they were hanging at Doc's with Beast and the new puppy, and it would do him some good to stay at the compound and get some rest. He stayed at the compound, but he sent prospects to keep an eye on Doc's place. *Former Professional Badass* or not, she was his soul, and he wanted her protected.

When Doc had checked in on him that morning, she told him that she and Nevaeh had played with the puppies and watched movies. Apparently, Beast loved the new puppy and Nevaeh. He wouldn't admit that he was a bit jealous Nevaeh got the dog's acceptance so quickly. He was glad they were bonding. It meant the world to him that his two favorite women liked each other.

But they had their girls' night. He wanted Doc back in his bed or hers that night. He wasn't particular, but he was going to have his house prepared, just in case, because sleeping without her was hell. Rex had gotten used to having her up against him, which made sleeping without her hell. Tossing and turning all night caused his wounds to ache. When he had finally woken up, he felt as if he hadn't slept at all.

Hours later, he received a text from Trip.

TRIP: Temp bars from bedroom to bathroom door. Permanent bars installed in shower. Thank me later.

REX: Dragon sent me an interesting picture that involved you and Rope. Don't make me send it to Darlin'

He pulled the picture up and prepared to send it to Darlin'. Then Rex thought about having Doc in his shower and having multiple ways to obtain leverage. Grinning, he deleted the draft and put his phone away.

For the first time that Rex could remember, the Howlers MC was having church in a room that wasn't their actual church room. Axle had insisted they have church in the cafeteria with the doors closed, instead of forcing Rex to climb the stairs to the second floor, especially after he had huffed and puffed his way down a set already.

Rex appreciated the concern for his mobility issues, but it grated on his nerves that he needed the concession. Shoving down the hit to his ego, Rex slowly shuffled into the cafeteria, with Top and Score flanking him. The two of them had watched him, ready to act if he needed them to since the moment he stepped out of his room. He knew they were just trying to help, but fuck, he was a grown man.

In the center of the room, someone had pushed rectangular tables together to create one long table like they had in the church room. Rex took his usual seat between Rebel and Siren.

Once Top and Score took their seats, Axle pounded his fist on the table from where he sat on the end. "Rex asked for a quick meeting, so I'm giving him the floor."

Rex cleared his throat and nodded. "I want to claim Doc at the table."

Many of his brothers grinned, some hooted and hollered, but every single one of them made sure he knew how the vote would go.

Bullet was the one to speak. "She's got my vote. Hell, I think I like her more than I like you, Rex."

Rex grinned down the table at him. "Fair enough."

With a smile on his face, Axle looked over at Skull. "Take it."

"I'll never deny a brother his Ol' Lady," Skull replied and looked to Score.

"You all know my vote." He met Rex's gaze and let the love he had for Rex shine through. "Aye."

Zero nodded. "You got it, Brother."

It jumped to the other side of the table, to Pike, and the other officers gave their votes. All around the table, he was given approval. The last one to vote was Top.

Top grinned at him and asked, "Did Doc give you permission to call this vote?"

Rex chuckled as he lifted his right hand slowly, because it still ached, and flipped him off, as the rest of the Howlers howled with laughter.

Since Dragon was a Dom, it didn't surprise Rex when he leaned forward and stared their Chaplain down until he raised his hands in surrender. Top may be his club brother, but there was a certain level of respect that Dragon would automatically give Doc, and he wasn't about to let anyone cross the line. Top was getting close.

Obviously recognizing he was facing a fight he didn't want to have, Top returned his attention to Rex and continued, "You need her in your life, and I think she'll make a great addition to the Ol' Ladies. She had my vote months ago. Aye, Brother."

Axle slammed his fist to the table again, and through his chuckle, declared, "Looks like our brother, Rex, has found his Ol' Lady. Congrats."

Rex gave a nod. "Thanks."

He noticed Siren slide out of the seat next to him and head for the door, but he didn't think anything of it. When the other members started laughing again, Rex followed their gazes and saw Siren pushing in a wheelchair.

"Doc's orders," Siren said with a chuckle.

"She didn't," he grumbled, praying that Doc did not actually order that they bring him a wheelchair.

Siren shook his head, but kept chuckling. "Just fucking with ya."

Rex slowly rose from his chair and headed for the door in a shuffle. "You're all assholes."

"If this is news to you, we should probably get your memory checked," Score replied as once again, he and Top flanked him.

When they reached the main room, Top suggested they have a seat. Rex glared at him, thinking he was being a smartass, but he dropped the glare when he saw the seriousness in Top's eyes. Whatever reason he had for them to take a seat, it wasn't a joke.

Rex gave a nod and shuffled over to the closest table. After the three of them were seated, he looked over at Top and asked, "What?"

Top took a deep breath and ran his fingers through the curls on the top of his head. "Uh… you know the hunter who Trick was watching?"

Rex nodded. "Messer. Yeah. She was there the day I was kidnapped, but she disappeared at one point."

"She came here with the intention of giving us the information to find you. By the time she got here and talked to Axle, you were dropped off at Doc's."

"She's here?" Rex tried to remember if he had been aware of that. For a bit after he was dropped at Doc's, he had been in and out of it. It was possible he had known that, but he couldn't be sure.

"Yeah, but… Long story short, Crush wanted to kill her, but she's Trick's mate. Axle pushed back. There was a vote. Both clubs voted to let her live, but we decided to keep a watch on her." Top met his gaze. "I proxied your vote, since you weren't in a position to make a decision. I told them you would vote to keep her alive."

As angry as he was with the hunters, he wouldn't want to take Trick's mate's life. If it was unavoidable, then okay, but that wasn't the situation at hand.

"She didn't touch either of us," he told Top.

Top nodded.

"You were right. I would vote to not kill her."

"Either way, we don't like the idea of her being around the children until we're sure she's no longer a threat to them, so Trick is taking her away."

"What?" Rex was confused. *What did that mean?* "Where?"

"That's between Trick and Axle. All I know is Trick is taking a leave for a while, and he is going to take her away while they... work things out."

Rex considered Top's words for a while. As much as he didn't like the idea of his club brother being away from them and on his own, he understood the situation Trick was in. They had limited options. If they were to stay in town, she would be a prisoner. How could Trick build trust with her and a relationship if her choices were taken away? But if they left for a while and put distance between them and the club, Trick could feel comfortable that she wasn't a danger to the kids, but he wouldn't have to be her prison guard. He could just be her man. They could work things out and get to know each other better. As much as he didn't like it, it was the right move.

"He's going to check in, right?"

Top shrugged. "I imagine Brute and Rock aren't going to let him go silent."

That was true. His brothers would make him check-in, if for no other reason than to give their mother, Mama Nia, some peace of mind.

"I think Trick has it under control," Score said, and leaned back in his chair. "It will be a rough go, because I'm not sure they like each other yet, but he can handle it."

"It'll make Trick's sex life interesting, if nothing else," Rex said with a laugh.

"Angry sex is fun," Top commented, making all of them laugh.

T.S. Tappin

Doc

Doc was going to turn Rex down and tell him to stay at the compound for another night, then he mentioned that he had his club brothers prepare his house with stability equipment. She was hesitant, worried about him injuring himself and delaying his healing, but he was insistent. Eventually, she promised to pick up the puppies and Nevaeh, and bring them to his house.

When she arrived and made her way up the stairs to check out the accommodations, she was impressed. As a matter of fact, the boys might have gone a little overboard with the support bars. Rex could walk the entire way to the bathroom without having to go more than a few inches without holding on to a bar.

When she spotted the newly installed permanent support bars in the shower, she smirked as thoughts of how they could be used when he was fully healed drifted through her head. Filing away certain positions and ideas, she left the bathroom and made her way into his bedroom, where he was lying on the bed.

His ice blue gaze shifted from the phone in his hand to her. "Does it pass your standards, Doc?"

"I think your brothers care about you very much."

He snorted. "Sure... but they are also assholes. Overboard assholes."

She sat on the edge of the bed. "Maybe, but they want you to recover... and they aren't above setting things up to make you happy." Rex's brows pulled together. "The shower bars. They gave me ideas."

His confusion slid away, and he chuckled. "Yeah... I already had those ideas, so we're on the same page."

She winked at him. "Then I guess you should follow doctor's orders and heal up, huh?"

"Guess I better." His grin was full of heat and sin.

T.S. Tappin

Chapter Thirty-Four

Doc

Months ago, before her mother's accident, Doc had put in a request to take the week of and the week after Christmas off for vacation, with the intent to spend it in Florida with her mother. When Rex found out about her trip, he asked if he could join her, so she decided to shorten it to only the week after Christmas. She didn't want to be the reason he didn't spend Christmas with Nevaeh and his family.

After their celebration with his family at the clubhouse on Friday, Christmas day, they would catch a flight and head down to see her mother. Nevaeh was going to stay with Beast and the foster puppy while they were gone, but Doc knew Rex was already arranging for various aunts and uncles to drop in and check on them. Adult or not, she was his little girl, and he would always protect her.

With no need to head into work, Doc was sitting on a stool at his kitchen island while she watched him move around the room preparing them lunch. From what she could tell by the ingredients on the counter and the pans he was using, he was making grilled ham and cheese sandwiches with a cream cheese dipping sauce and homemade sweet potato fries. *Yum!* The man was a god.

Doc felt like she had really hit the jackpot with him. He could cook, grocery shop, make a decent cup of coffee, take orders like a champ, and went out of his way to make sure she was happy. He cared about her and Beast, and wanted to enrich her life in any way he could. They were made for each other. Whether that was because of fate or not wasn't important. And Doc was all-in.

Ten minutes later, when he set her plate down in front of her and kissed her lips, she decided it was the perfect time to tell him. He was fully healed from his injuries. *Thank the gods for shifter healing.* And he was fully committed to her. It was time for him to know she felt the same way about him.

As he rounded the island to stand on the other side and eat his food, she said, "I want to do the mating thing, but I want to be married first."

Okay. She probably should have waited for him to finish chewing his first bite. She hopped up and rounded the island to smack him on the back as he sputtered through choking on the bite of sandwich.

Once he had recovered, he looked down at her and asked, "Are you sure?"

She nodded.

"Okay. We can go to the courthouse." He pulled his phone from his pocket. "I could have us in this afternoon. Just need to call the clerk to arrange it. Unless you want a big wedding? I'm cool with that too, but ASAP."

Doc grinned. "I'm good with the courthouse."

"Today?"

"Whenever."

Then she was sitting on the island next to his plate, and he was kissing the hell out of her. When he pulled back, he whispered, "I love you, Doc."

"Love you, too, Fido."

He refused to let her off the island, insisting he wanted her close as he hand-fed her the lunch he prepared.

Rex

A few hours later, after making calls and pulling strings, Rex and Doc went to the courthouse. He fully expected to have a moment where the old him tried to change his mind because of fear. Six months ago, he never would have believed that he'd be marrying anyone ever, but that voice never entered his brain. That old Rex was dead and buried. Doc's Rex was the one running the show, and he was all about committing to his woman.

The smile on Doc's face when he said the words, *I do,* filled his heart with more joy than he had ever felt in his life. He already knew they were meant to be together, but it made him feel complete when he made her happy, as cheesy as that sounded.

Looking down at the marriage license after the ceremony in the courthouse, he saw where Doc had signed *Jolene Penelope Hendrickson* and grinned. Almost giddy, Rex put the pen tip to the paper and signed on the line — *Terrence Lee Piccolo-Henderickson.*

"You're hyphenating?" she asked at his side.

He shrugged. "I know why you want to keep your last name, and I get it. You're Dr. Hendrickson. But I want us to have the same last name, but I also like having the same last name as my daughter, so… hyphenated."

Doc reached up and hooked a hand on the back of his neck. After pulling him down to her, she pressed a kiss to his lips.

When she pulled back a bit, Rex asked, "Are we getting mushy? I feel like we're getting mushy."

Doc chuckled and rolled her eyes. "*You're* getting mushy. I'm just being a girl."

After finishing their business with the county clerk, Rex slid his arm around Doc's shoulder and led her out of the courthouse with a grin on his face. Once they were in his truck, he pulled his phone out and sent Nevaeh a text.

REX: Staying at Doc's tonight. Need you to take care of the dogs at our place. Keep it quiet for now, but you have a stepmom now.

NEVAEH: Duh. You just have to mate her.

REX: About to go do that, but I married her first.

He swore he heard her scream of joy from across town.

Chapter Thirty-Five

Doc

Rex had insisted on carrying her over the threshold, and while she rolled her eyes and gave him shit for it, she really thought it was sweet. He was like a kid in a candy store. As he carried her down the hall to her bedroom, he talked about taking her to get rings, because he wanted her ring on his finger, and if she was okay with it, he wanted her to have his on hers. It was adorable the way he rambled on.

For the entirety of her adult life, she couldn't picture herself married to anyone. She always found something about a man that kept her from ever even coming close to taking that step. With Rex, everything she learned about him pushed her in that direction. Every piece of information about him brought more confirmation that she wanted him as her future.

And now he was. Terrence "Rex" Piccolo-Hendrickson was her husband, her future, her everything.

Deep, strong emotion for him flooded her body — Pride, appreciation, joy, and love took over. She wanted to repay him for everything he had brought to her life, give him a reward, or a present.

After he set her on her feet at the foot of her bed, she cleared her throat and looked up at him. "In honor of our wedding, I... I'm going to let you be in charge tonight."

His face softened, and he lifted a hand to run the back of his knuckles down her cheek. "Doc, that's very sweet. I appreciate what you're doing here, but... I want our wedding night to reflect our marriage, and I married my Domme."

Tears welled in her eyes as she swallowed around the lump in her throat and replied, "Strip."

The grin he gave her lit up the room along with the blue light that shone from his eyes as he slid his cut off his shoulders and said, "Yes, Ma'am."

Rex

Rex's heart was racing in the best possible way as he quickly stripped down to nothing. His woman was about to order him around until they both reached ecstasy, and he was down for that. It was sexy as hell when she took charge and drove him crazy.

Standing in front of her, he waited for her next order.

As she pulled off the jacket she was wearing, a fleece-lined flannel, her gaze scanned him from head to toe and back again. When she reached for the buttons on her blouse, she ordered, "On the bed. On your back. Arms up and out."

He didn't waste a second as he followed her orders. After yanking the covers down to the end of the bed, he got into position and watched as she continued to strip down to her bra and panties. Today, they were a pretty blue that made the color of her eyes pop. The red lipstick she was wearing made him want to nibble on those fleshy bits, but it was the love oozing off of her that had him hard as a lead pipe.

A large part of him was having trouble wrapping his head around the fact that he was able to make a dynamic woman like her feel that way about him. He didn't know what it was, but he hoped it was more than their mating bond. Either way, he was grateful to be on the receiving end of it.

Reaching over, she pulled open the top drawer of her dresser and pulled out a loofah mesh like the one they used their first time together. It was even navy in color. She held it up and hiked a brow in question. He barked out a laugh and nodded. He remembered. *Oh lord*, how he remembered.

"This time, I want your eyes on me, though. Don't take them off of me. Got it?"

Rex nodded again. "Yes, Ma'am."

With the loofah in her hand, she took the few steps to the bed and climbed on. After straddling his waist, she set the loofah next to his side and reached up to secure his wrists. As she leaned forward to do so, it put her breasts in his face.

Breathing in her sweet scent, he lifted his head and gently ran the tip of his nose along the curve of each mound. "I could die right here and be happy."

Doc chuckled and sat up, having completed her task. Rex let his gaze travel over her body. She was a sexy woman, with her curves and bright eyes, along with that blond bob. The sexiest thing about her was that inquisitive brain of hers, in Rex's opinion.

"You're so beautiful," he expressed, his gaze lifting to eyes.

T.S. Tappin

She gave a soft smile as she ran her hands up his abdomen and chest. She traced the tattoos on his pecs before she slid her fingers into his beard and fisted, pulling his chin down. The tug sent pleasure coursing through him, from the bite of pain and the anticipation of what *his wife* had planned for them.

Leaning forward again, she ran her tongue softly along his bottom lip. Rex groaned and shifted his hips, rubbing his hard cock against her ass.

Her gaze never left his as she used her other hand to grab the loofah and run it slowly up his side. She released his beard and took the loofah in her other hand, giving his opposite side the same treatment. The tickle it caused made him twitch and chuckle. He loved everything she did to him.

Sitting up again, she reached back to do the same to each of his thighs, causing shivers and making him curse through his laughter. Never before had lovemaking been so damn fun and sensual. He had needed his Doc to show him what he had been missing.

"Thank you," she said softly, bringing his focus back.

"For what, Doc?"

Her eyes twinkled with unshed tears. "For loving me for me. For being you. For being everything I ever wanted in a life partner."

As she spoke, she slid back and rubbed her panty-covered core along his length, making him suck in a breath.

"You don't have to thank me for that," he replied when he was able to process her words. "Do you know how easy it is to love you? Doc, you're… *everything*."

Her chest heaved a little as she sniffed and tossed the loofah to the side before she grabbed a pillow and shoved it behind his head. After giving him a slow, deep kiss that sent his pulse racing and stole his breath, she slid down his legs and wrapped her hand around his length. Rex watched as her pretty lips opened and wrapped around the head of his cock.

When she sucked him in, he groaned and lifted his hips. The smack to his thigh was unexpected, but he liked the sting. He knew she was trying to tell him to still, but he kind of wanted her to do it again. As he thought about it, she slid her lips up his cock, swirling her tongue around the head, before she sucked him down again. He lifted his hips again and was rewarded with a smack to his other thigh.

Doc pulled off his cock and ordered, "Stay still, or you'll lose my mouth."

He grinned and stilled. "Yes, Ma'am."

She gave him a wink, then went back to work, attempting to suck his life out through his dick. Her lips and tongue were hot and wet, sending jolts of pleasure up his spine. When he hit the back of her throat and she kept going, he groaned out her name. Everything she did to him was perfect, but when she cupped his balls in her hand and gave them a squeeze, Rex almost shot down her throat.

"Gonna," he grunted. He didn't want that, though. He wanted to be deep inside of her pussy and gazing into her eyes when he finally let go.

Doc pulled off of him and smirked at him as she reached up and ran the side of her thumb along the outside of her lip.

"Fuck," he said with a grin. "Everything you do is hot."

"You should see what you look like tied up in my bed," she replied and climbed off of him. He watched as she approached her dresser again. With her back to him, she messed around in her drawer.

Rex didn't pay attention to what she was doing. His gaze was glued to her ass and how it filled out her sexy lace panties. Still facing away from him, she tucked her fingers into the sides and slid her panties down. As she stepped out of them, she reached behind her and unclasped her bra, also letting it fall to the floor.

Fuck. He liked her in the panties, but her bare ass was a glorious sight, and begged for his fingers to press into it as he held on while she rode his hard cock. The mental visual had his cock weeping and twitching, aching for attention.

When she turned around, it took a monumental amount of effort to pull his gaze from her beautiful bare slit in order to travel over the rest of her, but he managed it. She was messing with tips on the ends of her fingers. They were black and had pointed ends, almost like nails that had been filed on both sides. He'd seen them before, but he'd never had the opportunity to use them in play. Although, why would he? He had his own claws to use. The thought of Doc using them on his skin had him moaning.

"Fuck, Doc."

His eyes glowed blue light as she crawled onto the bed and returned to straddling his waist.

"It's not fair that you get claws and I don't," she said as she gently followed the curves of his abdominal muscles with the metal tip on one of her fingers.

"I agree," he replied, his chest heaving with anticipation.

"I suppose I do have claws, though, since you're mine."

"You need my claws, Doc, they're yours." Staring at her beautiful face, he saw the small smile that graced her lips. "Anything you need, if I can give it to you, I will."

Her gaze met his as she shifted her hips and slid back until he was deep inside of her. As he cursed at the pleasure of being surrounded by her tight, wet heat, she bit her bottom lip. His stunning wife was just as affected by it as he was. He could tell by the catch in her breath and the way her eyes widened a bit. The chemistry between them, emotionally and physically, was deeper than anything he'd ever felt with another woman.

"I wonder..." He waited for her to finish her sentence, but she didn't. Instead, she dragged one hand of those tips down the center of his abdomen.

Rex groaned as he rolled his hips, unable to keep them still, his eyes slamming shut.

Doc let out a moan. "Keep your eyes on me."

Forcing his eyes open, Rex met her gaze with his own. "Yes, Ma'am." He smiled when her pussy tightened around him at his words. His wife *really* liked it when he called her that.

"You are so responsive," she commented, right before she dragged those tips down each of his sides, starting at his ribs.

It hurt, but the pain warred with pleasure in his lower abdomen before rolling out to each of his limbs and to his cock. He rolled his hips again as he panted, but he kept his gaze locked with hers, soaking in the lust blazing out at him.

Using only one hand of tips, she traced his tattoos on his chest, but she lightened the pressure so it was more of a scratching than actual pain. "Tell me about what's going to happen... with the mating."

Rex swallowed hard, trying to focus, despite the desire to just keep rolling his hips until they were both shouting with pleasure. "Uh... While we're making love, I let my fangs out, and I bite you on your shoulder where it meets your neck. The bond solidifies. From what I hear, you can feel it inside. Then I lick the wound clean, which will help it heal. There will be howling." He knew he sounded like an idiot with the explanation, but she was circling his nipples with those tips, and it was distracting, but it also felt fucking amazing.

"But it will scar, right?"

He swallowed hard. "Yeah. It's not large or anything, though."

"And with that, we'll be shifter-married?"

Rex grinned. "Yes," he said in almost a growl.

"Do you need to be untied for this?"

"Not necessarily. It would be easier to give the bite, but I could do it like this. You would just have to bring that sexy neck close. Your choice, Doc."

She pressed her hands to his chest and lifted her hips. "I'll think about it," she replied and began rolling her hips, fucking herself on his hard length, making them both moan.

"Can I move?" His voice was mostly a growl, but he didn't worry about that. He was using all of his concentration and control to keep from slamming up into her.

"Hmm... Nah." She grinned down at him as she continued to bounce and grind on his dick. "You'll get your turn."

Rex grinned back at her, but laughed. "I love you."

"Love you, too," she replied as she pulled the tip from the forefinger of her right hand and held the fingertip to his lips. "Suck. Make it wet."

Fuck. She was *everything*. He opened his mouth and sucked her finger inside, running his tongue around it.

"Open."

Rex opened his mouth and let her remove her finger, then he watched as she slid it between her legs and circled her clit.

"Eyes up here," she said on a moan as the rhythm of her hips changed and her pussy twitched around his cock.

Rex brought his gaze back to hers as he struggled to keep still. His muscles ached from the effort, but the display before him was so exquisite that he would have stayed just like that for the rest of his life if he could continue to watch emotions wash over her.

"Fucking beautiful," he panted.

Her core clamped down and released on his erection, over and over, as she sucked in a breath and threw her head back. The moan that came from her mouth had him riding the edge of climax, making him bite his cheek to keep it from happening.

After she rode out her climax, she smiled and climbed off of him. Panic shot through his system, but he fought it back, knowing his woman wouldn't leave him with blue balls on their wedding night. He watched as she returned to her dresser and removed the tips, setting them on top.

With an extra swing in her full hips, she approached the bed again and untied one of his hands. Then she walked around and unfastened the other hand, before she got back in bed with him and cuddled up to his side.

"You have a choice to make."

Gazing into her eyes as she rested her cheek on his bicep, he asked, "What are the options?"

"I can use my mouth again," she paused while she reached down and wrapped her hand around his still throbbing cock, "or you can use yours."

In response, Rex slid his arms down and gripped her hips. He pulled her onto him and slid her up his body. His wife was smart and reached up to grip the top of the headboard as she spread her knees. He lowered her onto his face and feasted.

Chapter Thirty-Six

DOC

After using his tongue, teeth, beard, and fingers to bring her to orgasm again, Rex slid her limp, sated body back down. Once she was lying on his chest, he wrapped his arms around her and held her tight, he sat up with her straddling his lap. Doc felt sated and happy, but she wouldn't say she was done with him. The more she had of him, the more she wanted.

Looking into his eyes, she smiled lazily. "You're really good at that."

He chuckled and pressed his lips to hers. His wet beard rubbed against her chin, but she didn't fucking care. It was just proof that he was able to please her.

As he kissed the hell out of her, he rolled them and laid her out on the bed, holding himself up on his bent elbows. She wrapped her legs around his waist and clutched at his back, wanting him close.

He slid inside of her and set a hard, steady rhythm. She could feel the tension in his back and the urgency in his kiss. Her man was on the edge.

She twisted her head to the side to break the kiss, then put her lips to his ear. "Mate me, Rex. Make me yours." She bit his earlobe.

He growled as his thrusts got harder and quicker. With every thrust, he curled his hips, making sure the head of his cock rubbed where she needed it to inside of her and his pelvis stroked her clit. The combination built her pleasure again, and it wasn't long until she was riding the edge of orgasm and aching to come on his cock.

"I love the way you feel, the way you sound," he said against the skin of her neck. "I need it... need *you*."

She dug her fingers deeper into the muscles of his back as her climax approached. "You have me... for the rest of our lives."

It washed over her as she heard him growl, "Mine." Then there was a sharp pain that quickly turned to an overwhelming pleasure that swirled with the orgasm coursing through her system, multiplying it.

Deep inside of her, she felt something adjust. It was a give, the release of resistance, like when a piece of a puzzle finally slides into its proper place.

She was still shaken by that when her husband's head flew back, his wolf fangs flashing as he howled to the ceiling. His hips slammed home and looked down at her, his glowing blue eyes staring into her own as his climax hit him.

Tears of happiness welled in her eyes as they just stared at each other for a long moment. Scientific proof wasn't needed. Doc was sure that he was meant for her, and she was meant for him.

Looking fully satisfied, Rex panted as he rolled onto his back, taking her with him. Doc just settled in, happy to cuddle her man.

Rex

Rex was still catching his breath when he heard the roars and howls from his club brothers. He grinned. "That's the Howlers. They're going to be expecting us to show up at the clubhouse."

Doc lifted her head and looked down at him. "And they can keep waiting until tomorrow, because we are not leaving this house on our wedding night."

Rex chuckled. "I'll send out a text and tell them we'll see them tomorrow."

After rolling off of him, Doc replied, "You do that. And while you're up, get us snacks and drinks. We need to recharge."

After letting out a growl of approval, Rex climbed out of bed and replied, "Yes, Ma'am."

He crossed the room to where his cut was hanging from the doorknob, retrieved his phone from the pocket, and sent out a group text to all of his brothers.

REX: I appreciate tradition and your happiness for me and Doc, you'll have to wait until tomorrow morning to celebrate with us, because we're not interrupting our wedding night for you fools.

Almost immediately, his phone started blowing up with return text messages, but he ignored them, turned off his phone, and returned it to his pocket. Then he set about getting his *wife* some sustenance.

He was almost done cutting up the apples and cheese to add to the plate of crackers and meat slices when he heard an insistent knocking on the front door. His brows pulled together in annoyance. He had an idea of who that was, and he'd kick the asses of

Ranger and Trip if they were truly standing on her doorstep.

Fully naked, he stormed for the door and yanked it open. Standing on the stoop was Sugar, Kisy, and Butterfly, with Top on the walk behind them.

"Well, hello to you, too," Kisy said with a wide-eyed stare as she looked at his crotch.

Rolling his eyes at the women he'd grown to love as sisters, he slammed the door in their faces.

As he walked away, he heard Sugar shout, "But it's tradition!"

Top immediately chimed in with, "I told you he wasn't coming to the clubhouse, and he wasn't letting you in. Now, let's go. We'll see them tomorrow."

After some grumbling, he heard Top give them gentle orders as he corralled them back to the car.

Shaking his head and chuckling, he returned to the kitchen and finished preparing Doc's snacks.

Chapter Thirty-Seven

Rex

Climbing out of his truck, Rex was happy the weather cooperated. It was a bit chilly, but it wasn't too bad. The sky was cloudy, but there wasn't a snowflake in sight. It allowed them to wear jackets, instead of having to bundle up just to walk from the vehicle to the door.

Inside the clubhouse, he knew his family was waiting for them. After their visit the evening before, he received a text from Axle saying they would see him at two in the afternoon and to let Doc know he was happy for them. It was almost two, and if he was being honest with himself, he was excited to introduce her as his woman.

Over the twenty years that he had been in the Howlers, Rex had witnessed a couple dozen property patch ceremonies. The men always walked into the room with a giant grin on his face and spent most of the time touching their Ol' Lady in one way or another. He had often rolled his eyes at it, thinking they were a bit over the top.

As he stepped through the doors of the clubhouse, holding Doc's hand, Rex got it. Pride filled him, and the love and acceptance his family showed overwhelmed him. As corny as it sounded, it was one of the happiest moments of his life. He would cherish it until his dying day.

"Don't go getting soft on me now," Doc softly teased as she gave his hand a tug.

He gazed down at her through the tears that were gathering in his eyes. "I didn't realize it, but I was always waiting for you. If realizing that makes me soft, I'm okay with that."

"Fuck," she bit out and began to blink rapidly. "Don't say shit like that to me in public. I have a badass reputation to uphold."

As he leaned toward her and pressed his lips to her temple, his gaze scanned the room. His cheering family was lined up in front of them, all wearing smiles, clapping.

The crowd parted, and Top stepped through with Score at his side. Score gave Rex a nod and patted Top on the back before he stepped aside and let Top have the floor.

Top gave him a grin, then turned his attention to Doc. "Normally, Pres does this, or… at least, once upon a time, he did." The crowd laughed, and Rex joined them. It had become a joke because Axle had performed the speech maybe once since he took over as president. "Since I'm Rex's closest friend, I get the honor. And it *is* an honor, Doc." He grinned again. "By tying yourself to Rex, you tied yourself to us. By having his back, you have ours. By protecting him, you protect us. By loving him, you love us. We're a package deal. And we understand we're getting more out of the deal than you are." He winked at her, then he continued, "You will never need for anything for long. You will never want for anything for long. You will never suffer. And if for some reason you do," his eyes flashed a greenish light as the men around him growled and hissed, "the one who caused it will suffer far more for their efforts, not that you need our assistance to make that happen, but it's offered to you all the same. I'm honored to call you *my sister*." He held out his hand. Clenched in it was a leather cut.

"Thank you, Top." Doc reached out and took the cut from his hand. She held it up in front of her and looked it over. On the left side, there were two patches. One said *Rex's OL*, and. The other said *Doc*. After staring at it for a moment, she looked up at Rex. "Do you get one of these patches?"

Rex chuckled. "Yes. I will have a patch that says *Doc's OM* or *Property of Doc*, whichever you would prefer." He bent his head down and kissed her lips. Then he took the cut from her hands and helped her put it on over her lightweight jacket. After sliding it onto her shoulders, he put his mouth by her ear. "And your name will be in my skin, right where it belongs."

She turned her head and opened her mouth to say something, but she was interrupted by Sugar shouting, "Shots!"

As Doc was swept away from him by the Ol' Ladies, Ginger approached with a smile on her face. "Ready for your ink? As all-in as you've been with her, I imagine you want it done right away."

Rex nodded. "Yup. Let's go."

Doc

Doc could say that she had never been accepted into a group of females as quickly as the Ol' Ladies did. They gave her shots, and immediately, they talked to her as if she had always been a part of them. And they were fun.

It amused Doc to watch the group of rough men attempt to keep their women off of tables or limit the number of drinks they had. They failed spectacularly, but each of them gave a good shot.

When Dragon stepped up next to Kisy's chair and set a full glass of water in front of her, she shot him a glare. All it took was an eyebrow lift for Kisy to pick up the glass and drink it brattily. Yes, you can drink something with an attitude, and that woman proved it. The look Dragon gave her proved that he was going to enjoy spanking the brat out of her later. Game recognized game.

When Ruby and Gorgeous climbed onto the table to show them a pole dancing move, without a pole in sight, Doc was surprised a fire didn't appear along the carpet by the quickness with which Axle and Rebel crossed the room. The other women booed them as they convinced their women to get down off the table.

Doc was enjoying her time with the women, but she missed her man. As if thinking about him called him forth, Rex stepped through the front door with Ginger. His ice-blue eyes scanned the room until they landed on her. He smiled and headed in her direction.

As Rex got closer to her, she saw a new tattoo peeking out from the neckline of his Henley on the left side. She stood when he reached her and lifted her hand. Pulling aside the Henley, she saw *Doc* in a thick script covering his neck from shoulder to jawline, front to back. Under it was the hint of another tattoo, a black and gray line. She followed it forward, shoving aside his long beard, and saw that he also had a stethoscope tattooed as if it was hanging around his neck, except the two sides were tied together at the base of his throat. Instead of a chestpiece, there was a heart that looked like a locket with a keyhole.

Doc's breath caught. He collared himself… for her. Her gaze lifted to meet his.

"I probably should have asked you first, but—"

She didn't let him finish. She used the grip she had on his shirt to yank his head down, and then she kissed the hell out of him.

As the room erupted in catcalls and cheers, Rex gripped her hips and lifted. She wrapped her legs around his waist and let him carry her wherever he planned to take her. Celebration or not, she needed to show her man exactly what she thought of the precious gift he had just given her.

T.S. Tappin

Chapter Thirty-Eight

Doc

Doc decided she was going to have to give Nevaeh a hell of a Christmas present. She had been watching the dogs for days, it seemed, while Doc had been wrapped up in Rex. The young woman hadn't complained a bit, except for the fact that her aunts and uncles had made repeated stop-bys. Rex had to field calls about them *obviously not trusting her as an adult to take care of her damn self.*

As she listened to Rex try to calm his daughter down, Doc couldn't help but grin. They had never planned to stay at the compound the night before, but after he showed up with a collar tattoo, Doc had tied him to his bed and hadn't untied him until they were about to crash for the night.

Once he finally got off the phone, they made their way down to the cafeteria in the clubhouse and got breakfast. Halfway through their breakfast burritos, Gorgeous plopped down next to Rex and handed him a beautiful blond baby girl.

Rex immediately dropped his fork on his plate and grinned at the bundle. "Well, if it isn't my little lady." He gave her a raspberry on her cheek, which had the baby bubbling with laughter, her little pudgy fingers fisting in his beard. "Sorry, Doc, but Nugget here is the prettiest breakfast date I ever had."

"No offense taken," Doc replied through a quiet laugh. The man was adorable with the baby.

"She loves Uncle Rex," Gorgeous said with a smile as she blew out a breath. "If it's not Daddy or Uncle Trip, she wants Uncle Rex. I think it's a beard thing. They don't mind if she yanks and tugs."

"Could also be the deep voices," Doc told her.

Gorgeous nodded. "Yeah, that makes sense."

"You need me to watch her while you eat, Mama?" Rex tickled the baby's side as he glanced over at Gorgeous.

She shook her head. "No, Axle made me pancakes hours ago. I tried to convince him to play Santa this year at the Christmas party, but he refused. Said something about Nugget getting confused."

"Bullsh—" Rex smiled at Nugget. "Hogwash." The baby giggled and cooed.

"Rex will do it, won't ya, Rex?" Doc gave him a look that said he wouldn't like what would happen if he refused.

Rex looked at her around the baby and just stared for a long moment. "Me?"

Two of the prospects sat down in chairs next to Doc. She met them the day before and had been informed they were Rebel's cousins by Ruby.

"Yeah, Rex," Ryker said.

"You'd be a great Santa," Ross commented with a shit-eating grin on his face.

Doc saw Lucifer, another prospect and mate to the president of the Tiger's Claw MC, head their way, stop, and walk away.

Rex's gaze shifted over to the twins, and his eyes narrowed. "If I'm being Santa, I guess you boys better find some tights, since you *will* be the elves." The twins started to object, but Rex shook his head. "And they better be green and white striped. Oh… and don't forget those shoes with the bells."

Doc and Gorgeous locked eyes a second before they both busted out with laughter.

Rex

Rex had a hard time not laughing at the way the twin prospects' shoes jingled with every step they took as the two of them followed him into the clubhouse on Christmas day. Ross and Ryker thought they were funny egging Doc on about ordering him to do this. Sure, he could have refused, and Doc probably wouldn't have done much, but he didn't really want to find out if that was true.

Since the two wanted to be involved with the talk, they could be involved with the event. They were adorable elves in their green and white striped tights, green smocks, and hats, but Rex's favorite were the shoes.

When they stepped into the cafeteria room of the clubhouse, Rex saw that the Ol' Ladies and his brothers went overboard. It didn't even look like the same room. Instead, Rex could have sworn they'd stepped into Santa's actual house. It was awesome.

The kids were sitting on the floor in a semi-circle around a large rocking chair, but they all started bouncing with excitement when they saw him. Well, at least the little ones were.

He knew Gorgeous was expecting him to sit in that chair and hand out presents from the large bag he was carrying, and he would, but first, they needed Uncle Rex's Christmas gifts.

"Ho! Ho! Ho! Merry Christmas!" He tried to sound completely different than he normally did for the sake of the young kids, but he wasn't sure he pulled it off.

"Merry Christmas," the kids and some of the adults who were on the other side of the room called back.

"We will get to Santa's presents in a few minutes." He set the bag down next to the rocking chair. "But first, your Uncle Rex had to run an errand. He asked me to make sure you all received your presents from him. So, grab the hand of one of your parents and head out to the parking lot."

The kids jumped up, except for the two babies, Nugget and Cane, who were being carried by Avery and Levi, Top and Ginger's oldest children. He ignored the curious and accusatory looks from their parents as the children dragged them from the room.

Axle followed them, glaring at him, asking, "What did you do?"

He shrugged. "It wasn't me. It was Rex." Then he grinned.

Rex trailed along at the back of the group as everyone made their way outside. He was halfway across the main room of the clubhouse when he started hearing the screams of joy from his nieces and nephews.

When he stepped outside, he was circled and confronted by their parents.

"You bought them dirt bikes?" Rock growled. "They have two at the house."

"But they had to share." He leaned in and lowered his voice. "And I didn't do it, remember? I'm Santa."

"What in the hell is Nugget going to do with a dirt bike?" Axle asked, pissed off.

Rex rolled his eyes. "Cane and Nugget's are walkers, Prez. Go look."

Ignoring the rest of the parents, Rex's eyes locked on Doc's SUV as it pulled up to the curb and she climbed out. He maneuvered his way through the crowd and over to her. He stopped a few feet away and smiled at her. "I would kiss you, but it might scar the children if they saw Santa lay one on their Aunt Doc."

"That sounds so weird," she said with a laugh. "Where's Nevaeh? I have a present for her."

"Right here," his daughter said brightly as she jogged over, having already been heading in their direction.

Doc pulled an envelope out of the bag she had strapped over her shoulder. "Merry Christmas."

Nevaeh took it and smiled, but looked confused. She opened the envelope and pulled out a stack of papers. After reading them for a moment, her eyes went wide. "You… You're keeping him?!"

Doc grinned and nodded. "He's yours, though. We'll just keep him at my place while you're in school. I gave him the name you picked, though."

Tears filled his daughter's eyes, and she looked up at him. "I get to keep the puppy. I named him Raptor, because he has a little growl that I imagine sounds like a dinosaur noise and… well… you're Rex like a T-Rex… and yeah."

Fuck. He loved his kid. She was such a great person with an amazingly deep heart. And his woman just gave her the best gift ever. He sent up a prayer to the gods for both of the women near him.

"So, we have Beast and Raptor, now," Doc confirmed.

Rex's gaze shifted over to Doc as Neveah wrapped her arms around his mate's shoulders and hugged her tight. He let his eyes say all the things he wanted to say but couldn't without causing Nevaeh mental damage.

As soon as we're alone, and that better be ASAP, I am going to be the goodest of good boys to show my appreciation.

Doc's lifted brow and smirk let him know that his message was received loud and clear. *She* was the best Christmas present he ever received and the only present he wanted for the rest of his life.

Glimpse of What's to Come

Trick

AFTER THE CLUB VOTED

Leaning back against the concrete wall across the room from Messer, Trick crossed his arms and stared at her. She was sitting on the floor with her forearms folded and resting on her knees bent up in front of her. The look on her face was almost as if she had given up, and Trick didn't like that.

As angry as he was at her and her mission, she was his mate, and it rankled his bear that she wasn't happy. He had to come up with a way to both satisfy his bear and also keep his family safe. He was stuck between having his mate and having his family, but there had to be a solution. There *had* to be. He wouldn't give up the people who had always supported him, but could he walk away from his mate forever to keep them? No, he didn't think he could.

The problem was that keeping her around the compound or even in Warden's Pass would mean he would need to practically make her his prisoner. What a way to start a relationship. The whole situation was a shit show.

"Why in the hell are you staring at me?"

The defeated tone to her voice was like a stab to his heart. Yes, she did it to herself. If it wasn't for her choices, she wouldn't be in that situation. But if it wasn't for her choices, he wouldn't have met her either.

"You're my mate."

"What the hell does that even mean?"

He sighed. "It means we were meant to be. It's like soulmates for shifters."

She rolled her eyes. "Yeah. Okay. Whatever you say."

He chuckled low, but there was no humor in it. "I wish I knew what in the hell I did for the gods to give me a mate that wants me dead."

Her words were so low that had he been human, he wouldn't have heard them. "I don't want you dead."

"Why?"

Her light blue gaze lifted to meet his. "Before I left, I thought..." She shook her head and looked away. "Never mind."

His bear gave a little whimper at that. He *needed* to know the rest of that sentence. "No. Tell me."

"I thought... we had something," she admitted in that same defeated tone.

Trick's smile was slight, but it was there. "Yeah, we did... because you're my mate."

A possible solution to their troubles began to form in his head as he watched her react to his words. If he could get her to agree, he was positive he could win Axle over to it.

Her attention returned to him. "How does it feel to know that your mate is going to be killed by the people you love?"

"Better question." He took a few steps toward her and uncrossed his arms. "What would you do to save your life?"

Top

Top ran his fingers through his curly hair and decided it was time for a trim. It wasn't what he would consider too long yet, but it was getting pretty damn close. At his age, he should probably just cut it off.

It was a couple months past his forty-second birthday, and the curls probably made him look like an older man trying to look younger. Making a mental note to ask one of the UP chapter members of the Howlers MC where he could get a cut the next day, Top followed his club brothers into the local club.

He and the five brothers and one prospect with him were members of the original Howlers MC, out of Warden's Pass, Michigan. They were in the upper peninsula to patch over the former UpRiders MC and to help them grow their numbers while also teaching them the ways of the Howlers. There would be no drug running or arms deals. They didn't deal in flesh, not the nonconsensual kind. The mission of the Howlers was to help those who were not in a position to help themselves, and they took that shit seriously. If this club wanted to wear the Howlers colors, they needed to as well.

From what he had seen from the last month of being in the UP, the new president and vice president were good people and had things under control. He and his chapter would still keep their eyes on the new chapter, though.

The night wasn't about that, though. No, the night was about Arbor's upcoming nuptials. It wasn't really a bachelor party, but you could call it that. Fun was the matter at hand.

The small town they were in didn't have a strip club, but the UP chapter owned a bar that had burlesque performers. In Top's mind, that shit was sexier. He liked the mystique of burlesque. The mystery of what they were teasing you with got your mind working, bringing your imagination into the game. To turn him on now that he'd matured, he needed more than a hot body. He needed to be stimulated mentally long before his cock was really in it.

Sure, he could occasionally just hook up, but it never left him satisfied. In those moments, his ex-wife, who was also one of his closest friends, was always down to help each other scratch an itch. Even then, they had a bond and understood each other, so he still got the mental stimulation.

Top wasn't going into the club with the intention of getting laid, but he wouldn't turn it down, either. He was a single man, and he was long past due for a night of fun.

As they entered the club, Top leaned close to Emerson, their prospect, and said, "Are you sure this won't be too much temptation for you?"

Emerson scoffed and rolled his eyes. "I'm not out of control."

"No, not now, but you were. And I don't want to see you head back down that fucking road. I can order you to watch the damn bikes if you can't promise me that this won't be too much for you."

Glaring, Emerson replied, "Don't worry, Top. Your promise to my dead wife won't be broken. You've done your duty. I won't fucking drink." Then, the widower stomped to the VIP section on the side of the dance floor and plopped down on the end of one of the couches.

Taking a deep breath and reminding himself that beating sense into Emerson was not the way to go, Top went to the VIP section and sat on the couch opposite the prospect who was asking for an attitude adjustment.

Top tried to be understanding. Emerson had watched his new wife get blown up right in front of his eyes and was unable to stop it from happening. Witnessing something like that was bound to change a person. He deserved some time to be an asshole if that was how he got through each day, but it wasn't the easiest of things to deal with. Having made a promise to watch out for him, Top felt a responsibility for the young wolf shifter and wouldn't cut him loose, no matter how hard Emerson was pushing for it.

When the waitress came by in her sequin-covered outfit and feathered and pearled headdress, Top ordered a tall whiskey and gave her a large tip to keep them coming. He'd walk back to the compound if he had to, but he needed to get loose.

She returned a few minutes later with his drink. Thanking her, he took the glass and downed half of it, ignoring the way that Skull was looking at him. Their vice president was picking up on his mood, and Top was sure he was going to get a talking to soon.

As the lights dimmed in the general area of the club and the stage lights came on, the music began to play, and a voluptuous woman sashayed onto the stage from the side. In the middle of the stage, she turned her back to the crowd and Top almost swallowed his tongue. From the red-bottomed black stilettos on her feet, his gaze followed the line up the back of her black stockings to the lace garters around her thighs. He wanted to nibble on the supple flesh just above the garters on the inside of her thighs, before he worked his way up to those silk panties.

The woman was fucking gorgeous in her black leather and lace bustier, with that red feather boa wrapped around her, covering the cleavage he suspected was behind it. *Fuck*, he wanted to storm onto that stage and—

She turned around and gave the crowd a saucy smile. Her lips were a dark red to match the boa, and her hair was silver and pulled back into a tight bun that he desperately wanted to undo. The choker around her neck was black velvet, and it brought to mind all of the things he would like to do to that column of soft skin while he made her feel better than she ever had before.

Yes, Top was attracted to her, but when she scanned the crowd with her gaze and it landed on him, his wolf stood up and took notice.

Mine.

When her blue-gray eyes locked with his, the breath whooshed out him, and every muscle in his body tightened. The beauty on the stage was his mate.

Find her on the Web:

TikTok: Booksbytt
Instagram: Booksbytt
Goodreads: T.S. Tappin
YouTube: Books by TT
BookBub: T.S. Tappin
Website:
www.tstappin.com
Merch Store:
Books-by-tt.creator-spring.com

Any emails can be sent to
Booksbytt@gmail.com

About the Author

T.S. Tappin is a storyteller who spends most of her days playing chauffeur to her children (Tyler, Gabby, & Hailee, not to mention all of Hailee's friends who also call Tara "Mom"), strong (probably stronger than he wanted) partner to her significant other (Mark), cuddler to her American Bulldog/Pitbull (Champ), or cleaner of other people's messes (for work and at home). Reading and Writing are her favorite ways to spend her spare time, but she doesn't have much of that with three busy teenagers in the house. She loves every moment of it. She's that mom in the stands yelling and cheering and generally making an embarrassment of herself. She's a very proud Wrestling-Baseball-Softball-Dance-Cheer-Theater-Robotics-QuizBowl-DECA-Esports-Choir-NHS-Rockstar-Crew Mom!

For More Information

On the Howlers MC or Tiger's Claw MC, go to www.tstappin.com or find T.S. Tappin on TikTok or Instagram using the handle BooksByTT.

Your honest review would be appreciated. This book is on Amazon, GoodReads, and BookBub.

If you have any questions, T.S. Tappin can be reached at BooksByTT@gmail.com

Thank you for Reading!
Dream Big. Dream Often. Dream Always.

Printed in Great Britain
by Amazon